RELUCTANTLY EXPOSED

GL SMIT

Lost Lake Folk Art
SHIPWRECKT BOOKS PUBLISHING COMPANY

IN®
DIE

Minnesota

Cover painting, *Moonlight Bather*, Acrylic on Hardboard by
James David Smit
Cover art and interior design by
Shipwreckt Books

For Sally and Dean Harrington, and for my friends at the Rural America Writer's Center. They listened, they smiled, they clapped, and they kept me writing.

RELUCTANTLY EXPOSED

Contents

A Particular Shade of Green

Yesterday the sky turned an eerie green and I hustled to finish the last few lines of my lecture and shut down the computer. I don't mess around when clouds are blowing every which way wondering how bad it's going to get. Two tornados in a lifetime is experience plenty for my attention to pique and for me to scoot into action when the sky becomes a color it's not supposed to be.

The first time I witnessed a sky like the one I checked on anxiously yesterday afternoon, we—my husband, Jim, our four year old daughter, Rachel, and our two month old son, Noah, lived on the southern edge of Chicago's sprawl where corn and soy beans mingle with the dwindling concrete of the city. We lived temporarily in what Jim's family called "The Cottage." On the back twenty acres of his hobby farm, Jim's dad had dug a pond for swimming and built the cottage for weekend visitors.

The evening was uncomfortable. Warm kitten breaths of air licked the sweat from Rachel's forehead as she sat on the living room floor whining, struggling to remove her Barbie doll's bridal gown. The west wall of the cottage was solid glass. The crank out windows along the bottom were opened, but little air was moving through them. Adding to the heat, the deep fryer was plugged into the only outlet that could handle the amps without blowing a fuse. In the living room against the wall shared by the kitchen, the deep fryer was set on a table next to the sewing machine. With a new baby, and a chattering four-year-old, time to sew was minimal. For several weeks, pieces of a dress attached to their flimsy paper patterns had been folded neatly and draped over the open machine.

The cottage was an expanded house-trailer, a makeshift double-wide. The metal trailer, dented and scraped from years of disregard, was hidden by a new exterior. The entire length of the trailer was connected to a new wood-frame building, the whole of which was covered by a mansard type overhanging roof. The wall of windows was below the overhang and through them we looked across the rather too perfectly circular pond fringed by algae and cattails.

On the far side of the pond, the knee-high corn faded from chartreuse to emerald to cobalt and finally to ebony in the torpid haze. To the south, beyond the high-tension towers that stretched like beads to the horizon, a grove of ancestral oaks had singularly escaped the plow. A euphony of frogs and birds soothed Noah to sleep in the massive ark of the plywood cradle Jim had made for Rachel when she was born. The cradle, a heavy oak desk and several bookshelves were placed in the less traveled end of the long narrow living room. Noah would later be carried up to the sleeping loft.

Jim's brother, Don, and his fiancée, Chris, were guests for supper. The vibes were less than pleasant. Chris, while tearing lettuce in the miniature kitchen of the house-trailer, confessed to me that she was having an affair but still planned to marry Don because all the wedding arrangements had been made. Don and Jim, in the other room, argued about the language Charlemagne spoke as a boy. French of course, Don insisted—he was a history major which made him right. Or, did Charlemagne, also called Karl Der Grosse, born in Aix-la-Chapelle, now Aachen, West Germany have a German tongue as Jim postulated based on logic and his doubt in the exactness of written history? Was French even a language at the time? Did Charlemagne speak some pigeon Latin, a precursor of French? Pushing harder, Jim challenged Don's absolutism with the question, "When does a dialect become a language proper?" Brothers—of course each held doggedly to his own position.

I dropped gooey pieces of breaded Alaskan Pollock into the sputtering oil. "Look at the sky. What a weird color green. What is that color?" I asked. No one answered. Clouds were building, so in case of rain, I shut the windows.

Chris came into the living room. "Doesn't that color mean a tornado's coming?" she asked. The word "tornado" hung in the air long enough to infiltrate the language argument.

"Just a weird sunset," Don said. We all walked to the windows to study the sky. Rachel handed me her Barbie doll and a blouse which I unthinkingly began to stretch onto the doll's disproportioned body.

"Look at those layers of clouds," Jim pointed across the pond. "They're going in different directions."

"We'll be able to see a funnel coming. What is it, maybe ten miles to the horizon?" Don asked.

"We might be able to see it coming unless it's forming around us," Jim said. A sudden gust of wind shook the glass. We stepped back reflexively. A silver maple sapling allowed to grow through the deck was a good measure of the increasing strength of the wind.

"That little tree's going to break. Look at it, it's almost touching the ground!" I said, my voice rising with anxiety.

"Where are we supposed to go?" Chris asked. "You don't have a cellar under this house, do you?"

"No cellar," Jim said, as he kneeled along the row of crank-out windows unable to re-open them against the pressure of the wind. "There it is!" he yelled. "Get down!"

Like the tail of a dragon, the funnel whipped around from the southwest bending the electric towers and twisting off the tops of the century old oak trees. As the black vacuum sucked the air into its center, the windows bowed outward. Water from the pond lifted and parted like the Red Sea. The roar and rumble of a freight train barreling over the ridge of the roof, deafened us. Rachel screamed. I grabbed her around the belly; I knew the windows wouldn't hold. I ran into the kitchen and dove onto the floor holding Rachel tightly beneath me. Chris stood rigid, hands over her ears. "Get away from the windows!" Don demanded, pushing Chris in front of him onto the kitchen floor.

The next minutes were chaos. Jim, still on hands and knees, took a dive and covered his head. The entire set of windows and walls of the new addition were pulled into the air by the overhanging roof. The whole structure went right over Jim's head and left him stunned but untouched.

The house-trailer, now exposed to the full force of the wind, rolled on its side leaving a gaping hole underneath. The furniture was either lifted into the air or pushed into the pit between the new foundation and the trailer. The books fell into the rift just as the sewer line ruptured. Water pipes burst. Electrical wiring stretched and snapped. Hot oil and crispy fish whirled into the sky.

In the kitchen, the refrigerator tipped over pinning Don to the floor. Pots, pans, cans of kidney beans and sauerkraut, jars of peanut butter and jelly, boxes and bags of Cheerios and Oreos tumbled off the shelves and out of the cabinets pummeling my head and back. Then, the entire cabinet unit crashed over me, the edge just missing Chris. Windows exploded. Glass flew like handfuls of sand.

I squeezed Rachel against me covering her with my body. As if I believed the mere repetition of words could affect fate, I chanted, "We'll be okay. Keep your head down. We'll be okay. We won't be hurt. We'll be okay." And then, as quickly as the roar began there was silence—absolute silence. I saw the blue-green kitchen carpet hanging above me. I was disoriented—which way was up? The force of gravity pushing the cabinets deeper into my rib cage and spine renewed my sense of direction. I heaved the cabinets high enough to let Rachel squirm free and then I rolled out from under them. Don pushed away the refrigerator. Chris was shaking, but unscathed.

An awareness crept over me, at first below my threshold of consciousness. In slow motion this awareness consumed me. Noah. I had forgotten about Noah. I spun in circles screaming. "The Baby. The Baby!"

Jim was calling from behind the floor, now the wall of the kitchen. "Are you all right?" he asked.

"Yes. Find the baby!" I screamed, "Find Noah." I felt like I was split in two. Simultaneously, while panic devoured me, a calm voice inside my heart gave instructions. "Climb out of here and search for your baby. Go find Noah." The house trailer had collapsed in a wedge. The south end was held square by our car and the cab of the pickup truck. The vehicles, although smashed, had saved us from being pinned between sheets of tangled metal. Although no glass remained in the south window, a potted plant swung diagonally from its macramé cord.

I hoisted myself onto the window's side—which was now the window's bottom—slid onto the truck's cab, down the windshield and over the hood. I hit the glass strewn ground with bare feet but gave my splitting soles no thought. A straight down rain began to fall. I went around the deck. The maple sapling had cracked in half. I climbed onto the floor of the living room. Jim wasn't there. Nothing, in fact, was left in the room except the desk and Noah's cradle. I stopped in disbelief. I wanted to run to it, but I was afraid. I heard a whimper, then a cry. Shards of glass and pottery were driven into the plywood cradle—into the name, "Noah" and the date of his birth, "April 30, 1974," letters and numbers Jim had carefully painted in ivory and gold.

Half shutting my eyes for fear he had been injured, I looked inside. Noah was wiggling, irritated by the rain pattering his cheeks. One chubby little arm was flung from beneath a light flannel blanket. A flowerpot had broken against the inside wall of the cradle. Pieces of ceramic, dirt and strands of ivy anchored the blanket to the mattress. I carefully pulled Noah from his bed. He nuzzled my chest. Except for a small nick on his elbow, he was fine.

Jim in the meantime, had been searching desperately for Noah through the debris spread hundreds of yards to the east. He tried to lift what was left of the sleeping loft—thinking Noah was underneath. "I found him!" I yelled. "Jim, come here. Noah. I found him. He's okay." Jim came around the north corner of the flattened house-trailer and sprang onto the living room floor. We stood huddled together kissing and hugging each other and our little son. Rachel, Don and Chris soon joined us and together we walked the gravel road to the main house, which was curiously untouched by the storm.

At the hospital, I held tightly to my little boy. I wouldn't let the nurses take him away from me as my feet were stitched. Jim, promised to keep Noah safe while my fractured ribs were x-rayed.

We are so dominated by our highly evolved brains, and yet, when we must depend on our memories, they can fail us. We had forgotten to save our baby. Perhaps Noah's existence had not yet made an impression on our waking minds, but our primitive brains didn't forget. Noah had been in the safest possible place. And maybe his survival had nothing to do with us at all. I'm not one to attribute unexplainable phenomena to higher powers, but I'm glad for the unexplainable.

The sewing machine was found a half a mile away—bent beyond repair. The unfinished dress was never recovered. Our books were covered with sewage. Noah's baby book was hanging in an apple tree, speared completely through by the tip of a branch.

I stood calmly aside the next day and watched as friends, neighbors and family searched the wreckage and the land to the east for salvageable belongings. I didn't really care what was saved or what was not: I had my family. But then, when that silly Barbie doll, naked but for the still unbuttoned blouse, was tossed up and over the kitchen floor, I broke down and sobbed.

So, that's why, whenever the sky turns that particular shade of green—like it did yesterday afternoon—I don't just sit there wondering.

On Being Naked

I haven't had much luck being naked. I am pathologically modest. My ancestors were Quakers and Calvinists. Cleanliness is only *next* to godliness, modesty *is* godliness.

My first mishap with exposure was in high school. I loved to sew and made my own clothes. And why not a bathing suit? A two-piece out of some left-over floral print cotton. Beautiful.

My creation made its debut at the local swimming pool. The boys stood around nonchalantly leaning against the pool's perimeter fence with arms crossed on tanned chests. They glutted themselves on eyefuls of swimsuit beauties. At fifteen, my hormones modified my modesty. I walked supermodel style along the edge of the shallow end and rounded the deep end. I stood for a while with the other girls acting as gorgeous as I could before I climbed the ladder of the diving board. I made my way to the end of the board and took the dive. The second I hit the water my new cotton two-piece expanded—a lot. The bottom was at my knees and the top floated up to my neck. The boys instantly lost their cool, and as I broke the surface, I heard their whistling and heckling and had to endure the ogling of a lifetime. Polyester would have been a better choice.

A few years later, now with a husband and a one year old, I found myself disgustingly grubby after several days of camping in the Smokey Mountains. It was early in the spring and we had the campground to ourselves. My husband bathed in the creek, no problem. I was hesitant; my hormones and modesty had returned to their natural state. But finally, tired of chasing a one year old over rocky uneven ground, I took a break and went down to the creek. A lovely day, and although the water was cold, the rocks had soaked up the warmth of the sun. I stripped down, laid my clothes neatly over the branch of a young pine and stone-stepped to the middle of the creek. Wouldn't you know it? We hadn't seen a soul in three days, but, oh yeah, just my luck, along comes a convertible overfilled with boys. Why weren't they in school? I could do nothing but wave with one hand and cover my privates with the other.

Seven years had passed. It was a languid summer night in a tiny farm town on the cash crop flats of Illinois. I was a tired new mom much in need of a shower. The children were tucked in bed. I opened the bathroom window wide, smelled the scent of new mown grass on the breeze and caught the site of a silky half-moon. I sudsed up. Scrubbed up. Rinsed off. Turned to close the window. A face was smashed grotesquely against the screen. I screamed and then emitted every superlative I knew, but had never used. Fucking bastard! Asshole! Get the hell out of here you peeping Tom pervert!

A couple more years went by and three children had matured me into a Renoir beauty. By now my modesty was fully intact. Again, a choice confronted me. I could bathe in a fast-flowing ice cold mountain stream or go down the mountain into Missoula, Montana for a job interview looking, well, dirty. We had bought a cabin in the mountains that had no running water. Not yet anyway. We needed to buy a metal wash tub, soon.

A wilderness, that's what it was, no one anywhere. Pure heaven. I chose to scrub myself in the snow melt of the creek. I stood for a minute watching the little grey birds scoot over the water worn stones. I took a deep breath of mountain air. "Hey, lady." I heard out of nowhere, "We see your titties!" Shit. I grabbed my towel and sat down. The giggling of the hidden little boys continued as I got dressed. Where were those shameless monsters? And where did they come from?

I'm old now. At least thirty-five years have passed since my last fateful exposure. One morning during the first week of this past July, I ran a bath. I sank into the comforting water. I sipped on a cup of coffee. I heard the click of my old dog's claws on the hard-wood floor. I heard her come down the steps. I saw her nose come around the bathroom cabinet. She came to the edge of the tub and started shaking violently. I laughed. "It's not that bad, is it? You don't look that great anymore either." I wasn't really embarrassed, but still. The dog kept shaking and then started whimpering. "Well, leave already. It was your idea to watch me take a bath." I settled back into the water and just smiled at my silly dog.

An hour later I went out into the early July heat to water the sheep and watch the garden grow. The dog stayed at my heels, still shaking. Just as I said, "Get over it," the neighbor boys set off a string of firecrackers. The dog's shaking wasn't about me.

I think I've outlived my fear of exposure. My modesty is useless now. (Although, cleanliness has kept its rank.) I mean who would ogle, heckle and whistle at me now? It's time to be brave. Maybe it's time to share a little more of my skin with the world. Maybe show a bit more cleavage before it becomes just a wrinkle. Maybe show a little more thigh before the skin sags over my knees—or, maybe not.

The Upper Crust

I am sure you've tried all your life to be classy, to be elegant, and to be sophisticated. You've worked hard at it. You tuck in your shirt. Your take your hat off five minutes before you arrive at work so your hair has a chance to fluff back to its just-washed blow-dried look. You make sure you don't have any runs in your nylons—at least none that show once your shoes are on and your skirt is pulled down.

It takes forethought and conscientiousness to look upper crust. Some people come by their upper crustiness without interference from a real life—like your sister-in-law, Cynthia. She doesn't have to work being married to your husband's brother, an orthopedic surgeon. Cynthia looks simply marvelous all the time and has an ample supply of run-less nylons.

Sometimes, you work against all odds to hold onto the last crumb of the upper crust you've managed to gain. Especially if the odds are that you left your hometown—Chicago—to buy a dairy farm in Wisconsin. Your plan was to live the "good life," raise your kids TV-less and feed 'em on peaches. Cynthia once said she was sure glad it was you, and not her, marrying your husband.

Both you and your spouse need to work off the farm to do more than break even, which means you do the afternoon chores and evening milking by yourself until the kids get home from track practice. They're supposed to take turns helping, but they may or may not help, depending on whether they have homework—they usually say they're swamped. Mostly, assistance in the barn depends on whether your spouse gets home from his day job early enough to kick the kids in the pants.

So, you put on clean white painter overalls and a turtleneck just beginning to fray along the edge of the collar and cuffs. You drink the last sip of your afternoon Earl Grey, slip-on knee-high rubber barn boots that forever feel damp inside and go out to the barn.

You feed the chickens, collect the eggs, throw hay down from the loft, measure the grain, mix milk replacement and feed the calves. You stick your head out of the barn door and yell, "Boss. Bossy. Come home, ya fool cows!" You wait a few minutes. You watch the fluff of dandelions swooping around in the breeze and you notice the green in the tress that was just a ghost of chartreuse last week quickly changing to the substantial green of summer.

The cows don't come home, so you shortcut through the yard past the old snow-apple tree loaded like every year with blossoms already falling. You climb over the wood rail fence and walk out to the back forty. The cows are huddled together well within reach of your continued calling, which probably means they're preoccupied by the birth of a calf. You get to the herd, slap rumps and make a ruckus. The cows finally get the hint; the circle breaks up and they head for the barn in single file.

Sure enough, old Addie has delivered an enormous bull calf. You stand there for a minute looking at the slimy critter and decide to carry it home now instead of later. You get down on your knees—the ground is muddy from amniotic fluid—and you squeeze your forearms between the calf and the grass. Your sleeves get slimed with mud, mucous and blood. Oh, well. You get as low to the ground as possible, tuck your chin against your chest, and roll the calf up and over your head. Before the calf starts kicking you slide your arms down around its legs. Leaning back to get your balance, you bring one knee forward, rise up groaning and muscle the calf off the ground.

The only problem at the moment is the umbilical cord—left a bit too long by mom and still attached to the calf. It's hanging over your head, down the middle of your forehead, along your nose, over the corner of your lips, over your chin and down your chest. Try as you might to flip the cord to the side, its sliminess sticks to your hair. You can't let go of the calf's legs; it's kicking like crazy. It's hopeless. So, you trudge back to the barn with the umbilical cord swooshing back and forth across your face like the tail of a wet cow swishing flies.

The barnyard is soupy from spring rains and manure. There is no choice but to walk on through. One step into the soup and you're in trouble. The rubber boots are sucked off, first from your left foot, then from the right. Giggling leads to worse trouble. All you can think about is your glamorous nemesis of a sister-on-law who wouldn't be caught dead—certainly not alive—in or out of barn boots. Finally, you fall forward, dropping the calf. At least you're free from the umbilical cord.

Still no sign of the kids. You holler toward the house, "Hey, you guys! I need some help out here!" No response. After mucking your way out of the cow yard, you dig a purple plastic sled out of the machine shed, all the while hoping the calf isn't drowning. Your brilliant rescue plan works. You slide the baby onto the sled and drag him safely into the barn. Momma follows bellowing. You finish chores and head into the house.

"What happened to you?" your husband asks, dishing lukewarm mashed potatoes onto a plate. You roll your eyes and try to conceal a smile that escapes anyway. In the bathroom you strip off your barn clothes, wash your arms, hands and face, and then apply just a touch of blush and mascara. You force a comb through the dried crusty stuff in your hair and slip into a long flowing skirt and a matching sweater.

Having regained your poise and serenity, you walk into the dining room, toss your hair with a Cynthia flare, slide gracefully into your chair at the table and smooth a linen napkin perfectly on your lap.

The New Day

noticed white streaks across his suntanned skin. I was curious, and finally asked, "Noah, what are these white lines across your back?"

"I had to jump out of a freight-train because it was turning south to Memphis," he said.

"I don't get it."

"I didn't want to go south," he explained. "The boat was in Hannibal, hidden in a swamp."

"Yes, and . . ."

"I had to jump off. The embankment was rocky, and I scraped my back. It would have been worse without my backpack."

Noah is not loquacious, so I left it at that.

My husband and I joined our son, Noah, at Sycamore Landing on the Tennessee River just below Interstate 40. He was tired, exhausted really. His nose had burned and peeled, burned and peeled. He had one hand on the rudder and one hand on the sail for at least 500 miles. Mile after mile there had been only a nightly reprieve from sun and sail, none from the mosquitoes.

Noah, in mid-trip, had hitch-hiked down to Memphis from Hannibal to play bass guitar with his band which was on tour for the first time. He arrived early in Memphis and slept on a park bench. He was concerned about being mugged and robbed but awakened safely in the morning. With the band, Noah went on to Texas, then circled back to Springfield, Missouri and finally—a few scrapes later—home to his boat, "The New Day."

Three days we sailed with Noah—motored mostly. I read him a mystery for diversion. His Dad took a turn at rudder and sail and encouraged Noah to rest. We tried to coax him to come home, back to Wisconsin where he had launched his boat five weeks earlier. No way was that going to happen. After all, hadn't he spent six months dreaming of and building the New Day while on leave from school? The Gulf Coast was the goal. He was nineteen. Determination was an understatement.

We left Noah at Saltillo, Tennessee, and hitchhiked back to our car. He continued his quiet journey down the Tombigbee Water Way and out to the sea at Mobile Bay.

The sun wasn't shining on the sea when he arrived, and shortly, the outer arms of Hurricane Opal were clutching at the New Day.

Our answering machine took Noah's call at 8 p.m. "I'm okay. There's a hurricane going on. I don't know if you saw the news. I motored out of the Bay and into a creek. I rolled under some people's garage door and am in their house, using their phone. They must have evacuated. I almost lost the sail. The rain is phenomenal. I'll call you tomorrow."

We awoke early in anticipation. The call came. "I'm all right. The sun is out. The birds are singing. My boat's okay. I'm sailing down to the Dauphin Islands. See you soon."

With the New Day finally in open water, Noah had room to tack, he had waves to skip, and he had a smile to share with the dolphins as they swam merrily along the starboard bow.

All Fired Up

My husband flew into the house excited. "An Army recruiter left a stack of brochures and a pile of business cards at the Dairy Queen. Right on the counter! I picked up the whole mess and threw it in the garbage. The hell with that!"

My husband is a pacifist, although he admits getting tangled up in the Hitler argument from time to time. In high school, even before he was eligible for the draft during the Vietnam War, he tried to live the kind of life he thought Jesus would live. Exemplifying Jesus was eventually replaced with a personal conviction based on a variety of philosophies and admirable leaders like Mahatma Gandhi, Martin Luther King, Eugene McCarthy and Nelson Mandela.

In college my husband applied for Conscientious Objector status, but when he received a high draft lottery number he took a chance to avoid the war. When he was freed by the lottery, he could also stop worrying that his C.O. application might be rejected by the draft board.

For the thirty years since the Vietnam War, he's led a quiet life following his pacifist ideals. Because of the circumstances, there wasn't much in the way of war going on, he had little need to discuss his philosophy with anyone but like-minded friends, the kids and the cows—not until the war started in Iraq. Then, my husband became fired up again. He joined a peace group and protested every Friday. He went to draft resistance classes sponsored by The Society of Friends and took every opportunity to speak out for peace.

So, it was a surprise when my husband asked my son if he could borrow a shotgun. It didn't, however, seem much of a surprise to my son who said seriously, but with a hint of sarcasm. "I thought it would come to this."

Every day for the last three years—autumn, winter, spring and summer—an aggressive, territorial, mentally unstable cardinal has flutter-banged against our bedroom window in pursuit of his reflective nemesis. Not only does the red baron start his daily bombings at sunrise, he continues randomly until sunset, smearing his slime in explosive patterns on every square inch of glass. We've tried numerous tricks to dissuade him. The grandchildren have drawn scary monsters to hang on the windows inside the house. I've hung shiny spinning objects, bird netting and red flags outside. Our passive resistance usually works temporarily, for a day or two if we're lucky, until the cardinal finds a snatch of unprotected glass or becomes desensitized to the bright colors, the shine, the spin or the horror of our attempts to scare him away.

The shotgun didn't get stashed as I thought it would. I really couldn't imagine my husband shooting a gun. He had at most used a BB or pellet gun as a kid before he had his pacifistic revelation. But I was mistaken. After arriving home, he loaded the gun immediately. My grandson, who had come to visit for the weekend, looked at me with questioning eyes. I looked back in disbelief.

My husband sat against the trunk of a paper birch, safety off and ready. But our cardinal didn't come. After all, would you show up to sing in a tree under which a man was sitting with a cocked gun waiting to blow you to kingdom come?

After a while, he realized the problem and came into the house gun in tow. My grandson and I, building a toothpick house on the kitchen table, looked at each other again as Grandpa opened the living room window, took out the screen and pulled a chair as close as possible to the opening. He sat in silence for a few minutes and then, becoming impatient, began singing the cardinal's tune, "Doodle doot, doo-doot, doo-doooo." My grandson and I started giggling. We made circles with our fingers around our ears and pointed at Grandpa.

"Are you nuts?" I asked. But then, we heard from outside, a "Doodle doot, doo-doot, doo-doooo" in reply. My husband gradually lifted the shot gun and aimed. We covered our ears. Kaboom!!

That was the violent end of our beautiful, albeit, pain-in-the-ass red bird, as well as the end of the branch upon which he sang his last good-bye. My husband, however, is still very much alive and remains a pacifist *almost* all the time.

For Peter

It's hard when your daughter calls with a catch in her voice
And you know she has been crying.
You ask, "What's wrong, Honey?"
And she replies, "Peter fell off a ladder."
And you quiet your breath and you wait with an armored heart.

It's hard when your might-as-well be a son is put on a respirator
And needs a piece of his skull cut away to relieve the pressure growing around his brain.
To know his long blond ponytail is lying in a garbage can.
To drive for hours in blowing snow to helplessly wait at your daughter's side.
To study brain scans that show dark shadows and white spots that don't belong where they are.

It's hard to wait day after day,
While sedation keeps your seems-like-a-son artificially asleep
Trapped under a plastic net of tubes that pierce his body
While machines without souls murmur nothing in his ears.

And it's hard to be a nurse, an old nurse, who knows too much.
To be a mother, who's not a mother.
To not interfere, but still need to ask why
After five days, your almost-a-son-in-law is not being fed.
To wonder why his stomach is still being suctioned,
To wonder why he's on a respirator when he can breathe on his own.
To wonder why his hands are restrained while his family and his love are by his side.
To wonder why his potassium is dropping and his heart is beating too fast.
To wonder if the cure is going to kill him.
You wish he were your son.

And it's hard, when in the middle of the night,
The doctor calls to say, your not-quite-a-son's heart is in an irregular rhythm.
And you watch your daughter, drugged by anxiety and sadness,
Lying on the floor by the phone, dozing into tortured sleep
Until the doctor calls back to say that her partner of two and a half years is still alive.

It's hard when you learn the heart of your daughter's love had *stopped*
But you didn't go to the hospital because the message of immediacy wasn't clear.
And every organ was in shock
And his kidneys were failing
And his liver and pancreas were inflamed
And his blood cells were being destroyed by the very drugs used to save his life.
And he was burning up with fever
And his muscles were wasting
And he needed to be dialyzed and transfused.

And still he squeezed the hands that held his.
And incrementally his sedative was lowered.
His brain stopped swelling,
And your common-law son struggled to open his eyes.
It was hard to watch him thrash in his confusion,
To fight the restraints,
To move and stretch in agony.
To watch your daughter's vigil of love.

After ten days, it was hard to go home.
To feel of little use.
Your husband said, "Let it go, it's out of your control."

You can't agree.
You spend hours in silence
You crochet a Christmas afghan for the man who loves your daughter.
Each stitch a rosary bead filled with love returned.

And you wonder to whom or to what to pray.
To a higher power who now you wish you believed in.
Who you wish you didn't think was an archetype of the human race,
A figment of the imagination of your more primitive self.
But you pray and you pray and you pray none-the-less.
You hold a vision in your soul of a whole and healthy man standing by your daughter's side.

And then you get the news.
He gave a "thumbs up" to the doctor.
He's breathing on his own.
He said, "Thank you" to the nurses
And he knows your daughter's name.
He said, "This sucks,"
And you cry happy tears.

But it's hard when you get a call at two in the morning
And your daughter says with a catch in her voice,
(You know that she's been crying)
Peter is sad and confused and frustrated.
That he's moaning and begging to be freed.
You don't know how to comfort her.

And you wonder why after eighteen days
Her darling boy
Hasn't been given a simple chip of ice
Or been helped to stand up.
You get angry at western medicine,
Its astounding capabilities

And its miserable failures.
You wonder if the cure will break his will to live.

So you numbly drag yourself through each day.
You go Christmas shopping,
You clean,
You sleep,
You cross-country ski.
You force yourself to feel hope
To see the beauty in the world—crisp and bright.
And your tears freeze on your chest
With your cell phone in your pocket.

And it's hard. It's very, very hard.

One Toe Over the Line

gave the finger to a camera mounted on a gate and got a warning from the Buffalo County sheriff for trespassing. I've been in trouble a few times before for crossing the line.

I can't go anywhere anymore, and it makes me sad. I miss the three acre stand of paper birch where I used to catch my breath at the end of a run. I miss the secret patches of Dutchman's breeches, lady slippers, sarsaparilla, May apples and black cohosh. I miss the wild turkeys, the twelve-point buck and the red-tailed hawk I used to greet on most mornings as I jogged out to this point and then to another.

The triangular bluff that lies between Deer Creek and the Chippewa and the Mississippi Rivers—the Wisconsin bluff I call home—is no longer free. My children were raised going here and there wherever their fancy took them. They would pack a picnic lunch and go exploring. They would come home with stories of skunks, opossums and rattle snakes. But times have changed. Hunters from big cities, investors and wealthy land grabbers have divvied up the land and have hidden their cameras to catch wandering women and their ancient dogs who skip happily through the forest.

One day about ten years ago, I was jogging out to see if an old abandoned apple orchard was in bloom, my sweet dog, Lucy, at my heels. I heard a rumbling and looked behind me. A huge double-cabbed pickup barreled up behind me. The driver jumped out yelling. "What are you doing on my property? You're going to scare the deer away."

"Really? And you're not scarring them in your disgusting gas guzzling truck? You, who I've seen abusing your dog, by running him the entire mile up the bluff road for exercise. You jerk." Of course, I didn't say any such thing. I just got nervous. All I said was, "But it's not even hunting season. Is it?"

Later, I was running through dense woods and brush along a trail that was newly blazed. I thought, "How nice. I wonder who cleaned this up?" The trail ended at a point overlooking By Golly Creek above County Road D. Lucy and I sat on an outcrop for a while and listened to the wind in the oaks and hickories. We back- tracked our way along the trail and were surprised to see a movement camera attached to a tree. I waved and continued on my way.

About one half hour after I returned home, the neighbor called. "My clients in Minneapolis saw you trespassing on their camera.

"Your Clients? In the Cities? Seriously?"

"Yes. They're paying $2000.00 to rent that land for hunting."

"But, it's not your land."

"No, I'm managing it for the owner."

"But doesn't so and so own it anymore? He gave me permission to run out there."

"Sorry, not anymore."

"But it's not even hunting season, is it?"

The farm adjacent to ours was signed into Nature Conservancy and planted with prairie grass and flowers, even though it never was a prairie, oh well. We used to own that back forty and running out to the Twin Bluffs was a usual jaunt. A two-page letter arrived in the mail one day. It read: "You are invading our privacy by running on our land. We do not want you to trespass on our property anymore."

Your privacy? Is it hunting season? Where are you?

There are two tree farms on the bluff. One day I met the owner driving in while I was running out. I said, "I hope it's okay that I run on your land. I've been running here for thirty years."

"Oh, certainly," he said. "It's nice to have someone who lives nearby keep an eye on the place."

"Wow," I thought, "Isn't that nice."

But the next spring I got a phone call. "Did you steal the chip out of our movement camera? You were the last one seen on the video."

"Why would I steal your chip? You gave me permission to run here."

"Just put the chip in the mailbox. We don't want you to run on the property anymore."

"You gave me permission. I didn't steal your chip, why would I?"

"Whatever, just put the chip in our mailbox."

"But … I didn't steal your damn chip. It's June. You shouldn't be hunting."

So now, mostly, I hike up and down the front bluff road or drive somewhere to take a walk. The entire bluff is across the line. Even the back-bluff road, though public, is dangerous, because five hunting dogs have free range to bark and growl and attack a woman and her ancient dog. Ironically, a sign along the road says, "Caution, drive carefully. Hunting dogs."

Oh, yes, the Gate. Some rich guy—I call him "The Ogre," because his name is something like that, has bought up a few farms in Buffalo County including the one across the coulee from ours. He spent millions building a road, digging a well and sewer system, logging hundreds of trees to improve the view and trenching ½ mile to get electricity to his hunting castle.

One day, out of curiosity, I followed the line of the electric trench that ran for a short distance over state land to see what was happening. The fresh dirt was muddy, so I cut across a field and landed 100 feet on the wrong side of The Ogre's newly installed, fancy gate. I snuck around it and looked back. Lights and cameras were flashing. I waved, but then, by gum, I gave the gate, and The Ogre, the finger. And I guess that was one toe over the line.

Yucky Hugging

"Now I've got you cornered," my friend, Roy, said as he and his wife prepared to depart.

I bristled. "No, you do not have me cornered and from now on I would appreciate not being yucky-hugged every time you come down from the Cities for a visit."

I love a good bear hug from a friend, but I hate yucky hugging. Since the late 1960s platonic hugging among family and friends has caught on as an appropriate greeting. It's sweet. Better than before, when men would stiffly shake hands and women would barely nod, and no one touched each other except in bed—heaven forbid. But some people have taken advantage of the new social norm. In my experience, yucky hugging is mostly committed by men, but I suppose some women yucky hug as well. Actually, my husband used to accuse me of it in my more flirtatious days.

Roy has a bad case of yucky hugging. He does it to all the women he greets. He's a big guy and likes to stick his gut into us and squeeze our breasts into his chest and then nibble our cheeks a couple of times and whisper variations of, "I love you, honey." Why I've put up with it for the last ten years is beyond me. I hate to be nasty and confront someone in front of other friends, but Yikes. I finally had it. Now, poor Roy doesn't know quite how to act when he greets me. I quickly put out my hand.

Quite some time ago, Merlin the tractor mechanic hid among the aisles of the Cenex co-op waiting to take a grab at me unaware. The first time this happened, I was surprised and fled. I wouldn't have gone to the co-op the second time if I could have sent my husband after the lawn mower belt that I needed. I was on the lookout. Here came those groping hands. I was furious and said, "Merlin, keep your hands to yourself!" I found out later the whole town knew about Merlin's hands.

Skinny Larry was another one. A wimpy hug was always followed by a few butterfly kisses on the cheek or in the ear that left just a wee bit of spit behind. "Keep your lips to yourself," I should have said. I never had to confront Skinny Larry. His touchy feeliness grossed me out, but it was his temper that finally decided his fate as an ex-friend. After greeting me with a limp hug and a warm breath in my ear, he cussed me out because we had a party when the driveway was muddy, and his low-lying Prius got dirty.

Political Pete. Now there's a gem. Even though he was drunk at the time, I've hung onto my grudge. The musicians were jamming at a Day of the Dead party. Pete took the mic. He ranted and raved about this war and that neo-con. Every other word started with an *F*. A would-be rapper at the age of 65, really sad. Later that night, I was standing at the sink when I felt a hand gently rubbing my back, then felt an arm slide around my shoulder. An alcoholic breath whispered, "Why are you wearing a bra? Women don't need to wear bras. Why don't you take it off so we can see what you've got?" Whose we?? Needless to say, that friend didn't get invited again. He called a few times, "Is something wrong?" Black out or not . . . You're outta here.

Over the holidays I was complaining to my daughter about yucky hugging—especially about, Political Pete, whose name came up because he lives in her town. She said, "You should have told him to Keep His Politics Out of Your Sweater!"

Darn right.

Herbal Peel: A Three Star Remedy for Aging Skin

I decided during menopause that I would age gracefully, naturally. I would not dye my hair, get a face lift or a chemical peel. Come what may, I would let my aging be a part of the beautiful cycle of life.

I recently discovered, however, that smearing poison ivy all over my face was an inexpensive and extremely effective way of peeling off a few layers of old skin. And, it was natural!

I found out about this amazing wrinkle remedy when my husband and I took an off-the-road hike in the back hills of the Mississippi River valley on an unusually warm November afternoon—Wisconsin side.

I'm in the process of making a U-tube video about how to make the remedy. I'll share with you the instructions I've put together so far.

Drive East on County Road D. Turn right on McDonough Road and park a quarter of a mile in on the edge of the road. Let your dog out of the car, walk along the ridge and enjoy the amazing view of the river valley and the coulee country around you. Listen to the wind, the birds, and the farmer disking his recently harvested field.

Notice a four-wheeler trail, newly mowed in preparation for hunting season, and take a little jaunt into the woods. When the trail takes a steep decline, cut back through the undergrowth, and scramble up the road embankment grabbing onto young saplings and pushing away leafless brush and vines to emerge back onto the road.

Let your dog muddy himself in an erosion pond, chase a squirrel or two, and return to your car refreshed and relaxed.

Have supper, watch a movie, and smear your face with cold cream to remove your make-up, sleep well.

Wake up. Wash your face with your favorite goat milk soap, smear your face with your home-made concoction of Crisco and coconut oil, put on your make up and have breakfast with your husband.

Spend your day worrying about the upcoming election.

That's all I've accomplished on the u-tube instructions, but I'll tell you the rest of the story. At seven a.m., I notice a red blotchy area on my forehead, under my right eye and under my nose. Probably chigger bites, I think. I again use my Crisco and coconut oil. My husband and I go out for breakfast before we vote, as is our ritual on Election Day.

We have supper with friends. I'm slightly embarrassed and apologize for the ugly rash on my face. Finally, after an agonizing evening, we drive home. I'm more miserable about the results of the election than my wildly itchy skin.

When I wake up, my right eye is swollen shut, my entire forehead is bubbling, my jaw and neck are itching, and the tip of my nose is blistered. Not good.

I take an antihistamine but notice afterward it has expired.

I check my face in the mirror a hundred times and go to bed with a towel on my pillow to catch the weeping from the now global mess.

I wake up and can't open either of my eyes. At breakfast my husband says, "Maybe I should take you to the doctor."

"You think so?" I ask. "This is probably poison ivy, or a rash from that moldy squash I threw into the wind. It will go through its stages and heal. But, on the other hand, it's really bad, isn't it?"

He nods. I call the clinic. "Come right in," says the receptionist, and off we go.

Almost unperceptively, the doctor startles when he enters the exam room. He dons gloves, takes out a big wad of gauze and proceeds to dab while asking numerous questions. "This is no doubt poison ivy. The forty-eight-hour window is exact. And, I'll have to tell you, this is the worst case I've ever seen."

I feel somehow honored, "Really?" I ask.

"Yes," he says. "And, I'd like to admit you to the hospital."

"Really?" I ask again.

"Yes," he says, "because it's still spreading and if the drainage gets into your nostrils—which it already has started to do—or into your throat, you may be in a lot of trouble."

I look at my husband; he gives the doctor an affirmative glance.

"But, I don't have insurance at the moment. The Market Place has flipped me back and forth and I have to reapply."

"Hmm," says the doctor, who is from Canada, "The health care system in this country has its problems."

"Do I have any other options?" I ask.

A long pause. "Well, I guess this is what we could do. I'll give you an injection and prescribe a hefty dose of oral cortisone to calm down your immune system. You'll need to take Benadryl regularly for the itching, and Zantac so you don't get an ulcer. And you must keep my cell phone number with you. I'll meet you at the emergency room if you have any trouble swallowing or breathing."

My husband stays near me the rest of the day. The dog is worried because he doesn't know for sure who I am. But there is no emergency.

My daughter and her six year old son come over for my birthday on Saturday. I had given her a warning of my appearance. My grandson sits on the couch with a pillow over his eyes for at least five minutes after they arrive and I need to play monster and talk about what a great Halloween mask my face would make. Eventually, the sound of my voice reassures him that I really am his Grandma.

I miss a poetry workshop I was looking forward to on Sunday. I miss my yoga class on Monday, but tonight, I think I look really good.

Even with the doctor bill and the cost of the medicine, this poison ivy peel is a much cheaper and a more natural way to get some new skin than a chemical peel would be. Not that it was a part of my graceful aging plan. Would I rate it a five-star remedy? Probably, not quite.

Summer Construction

"Hold on Honey!" I swerved hard onto the shoulder as a semi-truck crossed in front of me to catch the exit ramp. I held the wheel and steered the car quickly back into the right lane. The distance I had left between my car and the next was gone. I slammed down the brake pedal to avoid tail-ending the car in front of me. To my left was a herd of Hell's Angels, skidding and barreling down on one another as their view, which had been blinded by the semi, opened. In an instant, there was no more room on the road. A Harley sideswiped my little Subaru. The left side mirror flew in a million pieces to the sky. The impact was a slight jolt, no more. The biker, amazingly, kept his Harley erect. Traffic was now at a crawl. Summer construction.

I motioned to the closest biker to pull to the shoulder. The injured man was clearly struggling to keep from falling over. Gradually, we came to a stop between an exit and entrance ramp somewhere east of Indianapolis on Interstate 70.

I looked at my grand-daughter, Meira, in the passenger seat, still holding tightly to the dash and the door. "Are you okay?" I asked.

"Yeah, I'm okay." She replied, calmly.

"I'm going to check on the guy who hit us, to see if he's hurt. You good?" She nodded, recovering her phone from the floor.

I pushed my way through the blur of black leather and bikes. "I'm a nurse," I said. "Is the guy who hit me all right?"

"Don't know," they pointed. "He's up there."

Pale and clammy, the injured man was supported by another biker. I scanned the man from his head downwards. His right forearm was laid wide open as if a surgeon's scalpel had purposefully cut down to the bone. I leaned into his face. "You have a long cut on your arm. It's very deep. I'm going to do what I can." He looked me in the eyes and said, "Okay, Lady." I pried back the bloodied torn long-sleeved black shirt, mentally noticing the clean edge of the wound and the limited bleeding. The biker was lucky, not much flesh involved, but the white of the bone was glistening. A biker brought a first aid kit and together we closed and wrapped the gaping wound.

The injured man, still sitting on his bike, was in shock—his head falling backwards, eyes dazed. "Get him some water," I said, "And lean him forward." I offered to drive him off the interstate and to a hospital. The Subaru was packed with camping gear. My granddaughter and I were returning from a hiking vacation in Shenandoah National Park. We shoved the mess aside to make room.

The twenty or so remaining Hell's Angels stopped the traffic coming down the entrance ramp which was just in front of us. I was escorted, against the traffic and up the ramp, three bikes in front and three behind. We parked at a Love's truck stop. The injured man got out of the car. "I'll take you to the hospital," I said.

"It's okay, Lady. Thanks. The guys will help me now."

"You really need to get that arm sewed up," I said. "The sooner the better."

"Yeah, yeah. I will." He was whisked away.

A couple of the in-charge sort of Angels came up to me. "We should exchange information. We'll get Mike's wallet. You got a camera?"

"Yes, I'll get it," I said. "But don't you think we should call the cops to report the accident?"

"Exchanging information should be enough. It doesn't look like your car is damaged too badly."

"No," I said, "But we need a police report for insurance."

"Oh, no, it should be fine."

"I'm not blaming Mike," I said. "It clearly was not his fault, but in Wisconsin we need a police report for the insurance company. I know this because I didn't contact the police a while back when I got sideswiped during the night and my insurance company wouldn't pay."

"We really don't want the police involved." I walked to my car to get the camera and sat for a minute thinking. Then I called 911. A thirty something biker brought Mike's wallet to me and we took pictures of driver's licenses, vehicle registrations and insurance cards.

I saw the wounded man sitting on the sidewalk in the of the Arby's restaurant. I approached him. "How are you doing?" I asked.

He still looked pale but was alert. "You really need some stitches in that arm," I said.

"Yeah, I know. We'll stop later."

"Please do." I hesitated, "I called the police for an accident report. I know it wasn't anyone's fault."

Mike was visibly agitated. He tried to get up, "Oh no, Lady, no police. I can't. I don't want the police involved. Please, Lady, call them off."

"Sorry man, I really think . . . "

Mike rose with the help of a comrade and hurried away. In the meantime, a rented "Enterprise" van showed up. Apparently, biker groups crossing the country, in this case, all the way across from Stanton, New York to California, have a van follow the group in case of an emergency just like this one.

Five minutes later a very young-looking county policeman drove into the parking lot. I waited in the restaurant until he had finished talking to the bikers. I couldn't see Mike among them. I left the restaurant and greeted the cop. "Let's go inside," he said. But, as he opened the door for me, four state police cars drove up. "I called for backup," he said. "We don't have a great history with the Hell's Angels."

"I'll wait inside," I said. Bikers were coming in and out. I just smiled, and they smiled back.

"Thanks again, Ma'am," the man who had brought the first aid kit said. There seemed no animosity toward me about calling the cops. My granddaughter was patiently waiting, playing with her phone.

The state police left and the county cop sat down across from us in a booth. "They 'disappeared' the injured man," the policeman said. "I called the local hospital. He wasn't there. I suspect he's hiding in the van. You have pictures, I'm told, of the guy's license?"

"Yes," I said and pulled up the pictures on my camera.

"Invalid license," the young cop said, after checking in with the station. "I suspected as much, but no warrants. I wouldn't have arrested him anyway—that's New York's business. And everyone's story is the same. No Fault." He handed me his card. It read, Ryan

Riggs, Wayne County, IN, Patrolman/Investigator. "The number of the accident report is on the back."

"Great," I said, "just in case I get pulled over for not having a side view mirror."

The cop took a call and stood up. "I've gotta run," he said. "Another accident in the same spot."

"I don't think the construction zone wasn't marked very well," I said. "I don't recall seeing any signs."

"The backup is ten miles long," the policeman said as he opened the door. "Ma'am, if I were you, I'd take the back roads around Indianapolis."

"Thanks for the tip, Sir, I will."

Corn and beans, corn and beans mile after mile. My grand-daughter and I calmed down while listening to a compelling audio book love story. In the first town we entered, we slowed down at a four way stop and heard the car make an eggbeater, thump-thump, thump, thump-thump. "What the hell?" I sighed, "Oh, sorry, Meira."

"That's okay, Grandma." Irresponsibly, I drove on, but in the next town, the thumping continued. I pulled into a gas station and looked at the tires. They seemed okay, but I checked the air just the same. The tires were fine, and I didn't see anything else wrong. We drove on to my sister's house, thirty miles south of Gary, Indiana. As we rolled into her driveway, thump-thump, thump. Louder than before. "Shit! Sorry, Meira."

"That's okay, Grandma."

I told my sister the Hell's Angels story in excruciating detail. Meira brought out her phone and showed her great aunt pictures of the bikers on the side of the interstate and the policeman sitting across the table from us in Arby's. I was so wrapped up in my own adrenaline, I was relieved Meira was working it through. She said simply, "It will be a great story," and then asked, "Aunt Elaine, do you have wi-fi?"

The next day I asked my sister's sons and sons-in-law to check the Subaru's thumping. Four of Elaine's five children and their families were over for Sunday dinner. After a test drive, the boys came into the house. "Auntie Glor, the lug-nuts were all loose on the left wheel."

"Really? That sounds bad."

"Yeah, the wheel could have fallen off. We tightened them and the noise is gone."

"What caused it? The accident? I just had new tires put on before we left?"

"Hmm. It's probably from the accident."

"Will it be safe to drive home?"

A shrug all around. The seven-hour drive home was uneventful. I checked the lug nuts twice. They were tight.

On Monday, our mechanic said. "The ball joint on the left wheel is smashed. That's why the lug nuts came loose. The car's not safe to drive."

My insurance company thought they could split the cost of the repairs with Geico, the injured man's insurance company. There was more damage to the Subaru than a side view mirror. There was a broken ball joint. There was a dent that traveled along the door, the front fender and the wheel.

All's well that ends well … for my granddaughter and me. But there is a Hell's Angel out there somewhere . . . Are you okay, Michael Raimo?

For Margaret

"Never play in this old schoolhouse, Nicolai." My husband, Jim, said to our six-year-old grandson. "See how the roof has detached from the wall? It could fall down any minute." Nothing was left in the old school aside from the rusty tin ceiling, a few white globe lamps—still hanging—and a rotting pile of maple flooring. The bell tower—minus the bell—stood sentinel as a yard ornament under enormous spruces and pines. The neighborhood one room school was moved by Clinton Jenson to the eighty acre farm we bought from his wife, Margaret, near Colfax, Wisconsin. Our son lives across the road and needed more acreage for his expanding herd of Icelandic sheep. The outbuildings and barn were caving in and falling over, but the farmhouse was salvageable, and we would use it for a family getaway.

On the night Jim warned our grandson of the danger of collapsing buildings, we had our first family bonfire. As we sat under the stars, rearranged our chairs to avoid the smoke and soaked in the feel of the landscape and spirit of the place, the dogs jolted from their naps and began barking in the direction of the schoolhouse. Crack! "What the heck!" My son yelled. Then, CRASH. Through the thigh high grass and a few rows of corn we pushed our way to see what had happened. The schoolhouse was now a ruin. Our grandson thought his grandfather was the wisest man alive.

Jim and I met Margaret at the farm to negotiate the terms of the sale on a spring afternoon in 2015. We sat with her family in the shade of a spruce tree she had planted in 1948. "I probably planted too many trees, she said. It's too shady in the yard to grow much of anything." We were surrounded by the songs of red wing black birds and frogs in the wetlands down the hill and the smell of lilac and pine in the yard. While the others talked and walked through the house which smelled of mildew and mothballs, Margaret and I walked arm in arm around the yard. "The peonies should be around here someplace," she said. "They must be buried now under all this brush. There is a bridal wreath . . . oh, here it is. The rhubarb was over there by the garage." She shook her head and sighed as we approached a caved in shed. "We just didn't have enough money to keep things up and then we got too old."

Over the next few months Jim restored the house. He put on a new roof and gutters, put in new beams to support the sagging floors and moved around windows and doors to let in more light. I ripped out the stinky sixties' shag carpeting and cleared out sixty-five years of clutter.

One day, after pulling the last layer of shelving paper from an upstairs bedroom closet, I stood on tiptoe to make sure there was nothing left on the shelf, I saw a large piece of paper turned upside-down. In faded pencil was written: To Margaret Jenson, Elkmound, Wisconsin, From: Clinton Jenson, U.S. Army, France.

I turned the heavy paper over to find a charcoal sketch of Clinton, drawn by a USO artist, dated 1944. I quickly went to show Jim the find. "Why would this sketch be hidden in the closet?" I wondered, "It's from World War II."

Our daughter framed the sketch and we brought it to Margaret for her ninety-seventh birthday. She looked at the picture and sighed, "Oh, my," and then oohed and ahh-ed over the box of vegetables we brought her from the farm. "We always had good vegetables, and the strawberries were huge. Come see." Margaret took us into the living room and pointed to a picture of herself and Clinton standing beside the tailgate of a pickup truck loaded with quarts of luscious strawberries. She poured us a cup of coffee and brought out cookies and ice cream. She sat down in her reclining chair and said quietly, "My life didn't turn out exactly as I expected."

Although Margaret and I had corresponded by letter since we first met, she had never mentioned any particular troubles other than she was getting too old and tired to visit the farm.

For her ninety-eighth birthday, Jim and I brought Margaret a few jars of currant/blackberry jam which she said was her favorite. The sketch of Clinton was hanging in the center of the living room wall.

A few weeks later, at Margaret's funeral, we learned that Clinton had survived the World War II invasion at Normandy. He came home a sad and troubled man. He wouldn't allow the curtains to be opened or let his children have friends in the house. Margaret slept in a different room because she was afraid Clinton might hurt her during one of his nightmares. The bell from the schoolhouse was hidden away in a shed in Chippewa Falls. Clinton thought someone would steal it after he and Margaret moved into an assisted living apartment.

During the week she lay dying, Margaret told her son, "I want Gloria and Jim to have the bell after I'm gone. I want the bell to go back to the farm."

Just last week, Jim reinforced the bell tower and used a wench to swing the three-hundred-pound bell into its cradle. Our son drove his tractor into the yard with a wagon full of hay and three laughing teenagers riding high on the load. Jim flagged them to stop. We rang the bell for the first time in honor of Margaret and Clinton. The ring echoed brightly across the land they had loved, exactly as expected.

We Were Just Playing

O ur pet turtles raced across the dining room floor and fell through the wooden grate that covered the heat duct. All three of us with faces against the slats searched in vain for a glimpse of the turtles.

"Gloria," My Aunt Johanna said, "There is no way to open the duct work."

"Let's try, Auntie Jo, please? We have to save our turtles!"

"Okay, let's go look." Aunt Johanna picked up my sister Elaine. I followed her and my brother, Chuck, into the basement.

The basement was warm, unlike in the summer when it was cool and damp. The coal furnace stood like Goliath in the center of the room. Ductwork arms, wrapped in asbestos, reached out to every room, as if holding up the house. I went to the arm that held up the dining room.

"They're in this one, Auntie Jo. Can we take it apart? Please?"

"No, I'm sorry, Gloria. It's riveted together. We can't take it apart." I started to panic. We had to save our turtles. We were just playing and suddenly our turtles disappeared.

"Auntie Jo, let's look in the furnace. Maybe the fire is out." But I knew it wasn't out. I could see the bright orange flickering through the cracks around the cast iron door. But to appease me, Aunt Johanna lifted the handle. The heavy door swung open. I stood on tip toes and studied the flames, staring through them in hopes that the turtles were saved just like Shadrack, Meshack and Abednego were saved from the fiery furnace. I didn't see anything but fire.

"The turtles are dead, children," Aunt Johanna said, hugging us into a comforting huddle.

"Do turtles go to heaven?" I asked.

"I don't think so."

"Then what happened to them?"

"We don't know the answers to everything, but God knows."

Why couldn't Auntie Jo say, "They burned up. They just burned up." Why couldn't God save our turtles like he saved Daniel's friends? And why couldn't he save you, Mother Ruth?

Maybe in the spring, when the furnace gets cleaned out, I'll find a little piece of charcoal that looks like my turtle, and I'll save it and put it on the dresser next to the middle-sized ceramic beagle that Daddy bought me for Christmas.

Sometimes, Mother Ruth, I open your hope chest. I stick my head in and smell the cedar. I touch your doilies and your music books and your glasses and your wedding ring and try to remember you.

We were just playing, and then you were gone.

Dear Mother Ruth

I sit in the long warm grass
The sun is winking through the tree
I strum your mahogany guitar.

Your Gene Autrey chord book helped me learn to play.
Prairie Ramblers,
Patsy Montana,
Skyland Scotty and Lulu Bell,
The Psalter Hymnal.
Music books with your name,
Your notes in the margins,
The songs you sang,
I'm touching them now.

I used to sing,
"I Want to Be a Cowboy's Sweetheart,"
But you didn't harmonize with me.
You didn't leave your voice or your touch
Behind for me in your guitar.
I wish you could sing with me now.

The piano was Dad's gift to you.
I took lessons, but did you play?
Could you play?
Were you too sick to play?
You loved music,
But I can't remember you playing,
Or singing.
Not one note.

Why can't I hear you playing the guitar or yodeling to me?
I strain into my memories.

I tug and pull and tweeze.
Nothing.
Artifacts and remnants,
Photographs.

The corroboration of a multitude of eyes and ears
That with sweet fondness
Can see and hear you still.

Your nieces and nephews
How they loved you
How they love you.
I found them all, everyone still alive.
And I asked them,
"Please. Do you have any memories of my mother?"
"Oh, yes!
She played the guitar for us,
Sang cowboy songs to us,
Told us silly stories and made things out of paper."
Did you make things out of paper with me?

Cousin Marion said,
"How sad I was when your mother died.
It makes me sad still to think of it.
How blessed your childhood would have been if she had lived."

I'll never know,
I can only dream of it.

But I was loved so much.
When I found my cousins,
I lay down in that love again.
I felt comfort in the long warm grass of it.
Saw the delight of it winking through the leaves,
I felt the safety of it in roots anchored to the earth.

The Ultimate Frontier: An Unlikely Anchor

On vacation, at a party in Lyons, Colorado, and exuberant, teepee dwelling, poncho clad, red-braided, red-bearded skinny guy named Knox—or maybe Nash—waved a thin brown-covered paperback in my husband Jim's face. The year was 1972.

"Take it, Man. Seriously. This book will change your life!" The book, *The Ultimate Frontier*, by Eklal Kueshana, *did* change our lives. The cover illustration, entitled "Three men, one mind," depicted, in an overlapping configuration, the author—whose real name was Richard Kieninger—and two other men, supposedly King David and Pharaoh Akhnaton. Richard Kieninger claimed to be the reincarnation of the two ancients. Under the illustration were the words, "an account of the ancient Brotherhoods and their profound, worldwide influence during the past 6,000 years." Sounded a little fishy. Jim passed on the offer, thanks anyway.

By 1973, after finishing college, after Nixon, after Watergate, after Vietnam, we were tired of being skeptical. We had dumped the religion of our youth, had dumped capitalism, had dumped the establishment, had dumped the government, and had dumped anyone over thirty. We were floating without an anchor into the era of streakers and disco. When just about to drown in cause-less-ness, astonishingly, another searching soul riding with Jim on a commuter train through the south side of Chicago offered him a book. *The Ultimate Frontier.*

Now, that had to be a sign. After we both read the book, we excitedly attended an informational meeting about a community being built around the philosophy in the Ultimate Frontier. The community was called the Stelle Group. RICHARD, as he became known with awe, singled Jim from the audience and said, "Looks like you caught your hand in a table saw." Jim's hand was bandaged and yes, he had "caught" it in a table saw. The man must be clairvoyant.

In July of 1974, our house had just been sucked up in a tornado anyway, we moved to Stelle, Illinois. My fingers stutter, but I force them to type. For two years we lived in a . . . a . . . CULT. The weight of negative connotations paralyzes me, but I continue:

Cult (kult) n. 1. A system or community of religious worship and ritual. **2.a.** A religion or religious sect generally considered to be extremist or bogus. **b.** Followers of such a religion or sect. **3.a.** Obsessive devotion or veneration for a person, principle, or ideal, esp. when regarded as a fad. **b.** The object of such devotion. **4.** An exclusive group of persons sharing an esoteric interest. —- **modifier:** *a cult figure* [Fr. *Culte* , Lat. *Cultus,* worship < p. part of *colere,* to cultivate]—-cultic, cultish, *adj.*, cultism, cultist *n.*

Was the Stelle Group a cult? By definition **1?** Yes—as is every religion there ever was. By definition **2a?** Well, most of it was probably bogus. **2b?** Yeah, we were followers. **3a?** Hmm, obsessive devotion? Not us, of course, but some. Veneration for a person? At first, but Richard turned out to be a drip. Veneration for a principle or ideal? Absolutely. But Stelle was hardly a fad. **3b?** Like I said, Richard was a scoundrel. By definition **4?** Yes, The Stelle Group was esoteric and exclusive.

How did we get hoodwinked into moving with our two little kids onto the flats of Illinois to live with an eclectic group of weirdos— although mostly disillusioned hippies—into this . . . a . . . cult? Because Richard Kieninger did his homework, that's why. *The Ultimate Frontier* is a book that weaves into an almost seamless matrix everything theosophical, occult, metaphysical and prophetical. It even captures the essence of most east and western religions. I mean, it has enough hooks to lure folks of all persuasions. The Great White Brotherhood, from whom Richard claimed to have received his information, is a group of highly evolved souls who guide the rest of us lower-lifes through a few more physical reincarnations before we can enter the "Kingdom of God."

The Stelle Group was a gathering of souls already quite advanced (hence the exclusivity.) The gathering of these top-notch souls was important because around the end of the millennium all sorts of havoc was supposed to be wreaked on the earth making it necessary to save civilization from the mayhem of both war and natural catastrophe. I recall that May of 2005 would be the beginning of an especially bad time—coastal cities being inundated by rising seas and such. All of this was prophesied by Nostradamus, Edgar Cayce, and Saint John the Divine. (There were actually plans to build a spaceship to escape during the worst of it, but we lowerlings were kept out of that loop.)

Anyway, during our two years in the Stelle Group, we tried to raise our awareness, our vibrations. We meditated. We practiced telepathy, clairvoyance, astral travel, prosperity consciousness and precipitation, i.e., attracting positive energy, necessities, and luxuries into our lives—Jim and I never got very good at the latter. The men were clean shaven and cut off their hippie hairdos. The women wore skirts and stayed home with the children. Women had babies at home "the natural way" and I, as the only RN among us, became the midwife. We learned how to keep the EVIL ONEs from interfering in our lives. Those naughty, disincarnate souls called the Black Mentalists—BMs for short—were constantly trying to trip us up.

The Stelle Group had its own school for children based in part on the philosophy of Rudolf Steiner, (the Waldorf Schools) and Marie Montessori. Children started school between two and three years old and were taught both at school and at home. The adults were not precluded from reading and sharing esoteric material. We weren't limited to *The Ultimate Frontier* as the infallible word. We studied the history of lost civilizations like Lemuria and Atlantis. We knew about Jesus traveling to India and Egypt. We knew about the Rosicrucians and the Masons. The idea was to advance scientifically, psychologically and spiritually.

Brand new earthquake resistant houses were built on gracefully curved streets in the middle of an ocean of corn and soybeans—an ideal community. Jim and I lived in a five-bedroom rented farmhouse ten or so miles away from Stelle. We raised chickens and rabbits. We had a Holstein heifer calf named Mary who lived in the basement. Jim was supposed to tithe ten percent of his work to Stelle. He bucked the system—sort of—by spending the ten percent at home and raising food for the community.

City girl that I was, the farm was a great education. I learned to use a ringer washing machine, to hang clothes on the line, to butcher chickens and grow vegetables. I learned not to go crazy when left alone for days with little children while Daddy was off building pole barns. I learned what to do when lightening hits a house or giant snapping turtles stray into the yard while kids play in the sandbox. I also learned—and this should be a lesson for everyone—-not to transplant houseplants into any Illinois dirt that's been sprayed with herbicides even though it appears lusciously black.

Women in the Stelle Group weren't supposed to "work away," but I did anyway. I was a nurse and needed time away from the kids and we needed the money. I sneaked away to Kankakee's Riverside Hospital and worked the night shift every other weekend. My rebellion was never discovered.

But in the end, Jim and I were disillusioned. The oligarchy kept secrets. The Core Group, who were the founding members, including Richard and his wife, Gail, failed to accept the associate members, like us, as full members even after two years of faithful study and participation. Only a few knew why Gail and Richard weren't speaking to each other, why Richard was banned from the community, or why Gail took off to northern Wisconsin with a band of her groupies.

The truth was, Richard had lured a few of the group's gullible single women, married women as well, into his bed with the line, "My Sweet. Don't you remember when you were Bathsheba and I was King David? How about when I was George Washington and you were Martha? Etc., etc." Richard was always a bigshot in his past lives. Who would fall for that? Unfortunately, infidelity is catchy and relationships at Stelle became a free-for-all.

We lowerlings ended up overthrowing the oligarchy and replacing it with, yes, a good old-fashioned democracy, just as the White Brotherhood intended for the Kingdom of God.

I often joke about the time Jim and I were members of a cult just to raise hackles and eyebrows, but I have never considered being a part of the Stelle Group a waste of two years. The experience is a large part of who I am and what I believe in. We took from Stelle ideals that have anchored us in a world bereft.

There are two dog-eared pages in our old yellowed copy of *The Ultimate Frontier*. The first ideal is that people can actually become better by conscious effort—-a quote form page 190, "The rigorous qualities of the Great Virtues were held up to him (to Richard by Dr. White from the White Brotherhood) as difficult but attainable goals demanded of all persons aspiring to Citizenship in the Kingdom of God. The Great Virtues are: Charity, Courage, Devotion, Discernment, Efficiency, Forbearance, Humility,

Kindliness, Patience, Precision, Sincerity and Tolerance." We methodically practiced these Great Virtues at Stelle. Each week everyone in the group chose a virtue to work on. We would study our behavior related to the virtue. Were we doing well or not? Could we improve in our actions toward each other?

The second ideal is "The Constitution of the Kingdom of God" starting on page 133. I think you'll find these "Universal or Natural Laws" pretty darn good even though their name and source might be bogus.

One: No one may profit at the expense of another.

Two: No one, nor any government, may take anything from a person or another nation by force.

Three: All natural resources shall belong to the commonwealth of all Citizens and shall not be owned by any person or corporation of persons.

Four: Every Citizen is due equal education and the freedom to choose a vocation, and has equal rights before the law.

Five: All promotions shall be based only upon personal merit and proficiency.

Six: Everyone must compensate fully for every personal possession they receive and hope to retain.

Seven: No person nor the government may operate in the environment of another unless specifically requested to do so by that person. The government, however, may enforce the law in treasonable, criminal and civil suits.

Eight: No one may kill or injure another except in the defense of life or state.

Nine: The sanctity of the home is inviolate.

Ten: If no violation of natural law is involved, the majority rule will apply and will be subject to approval of the Brotherhood's direct representatives whose decisions will be final.

I scribbled a question mark by the last one, and also by the words "treasonable" and "State." I'm not sure if the Brotherhood's direct representatives exist, but otherwise the laws aren't too bad as an anchor to live by.

So, is Stelle a "cult?" Yes and no. Does it matter? I don't think so. Were Jim and I brainwashed? No. Did our two years in the Stelle

Group give us any good stories to tell? You bet. Did we make any life-long friends? Absolutely. Are we glad for the experience and did it change our lives? The answer is a definite, YES!

La Curandera Seizes the Day

would rather be a shaman, a witchdoctor, a medicine woman, la curandera, a sangoma, a plain old witch even. I missed my calling. In 1960, ten miles west of Gary, Indiana, I couldn't find a medicine woman who would mentor me, so at the age of eight I decided instead to follow in the perfectly polished white oxfords of my Aunt Anne, a nurse, who told fascinating but gory stories of her adventures in the field.

Since I became a nurse thirty-three years ago, I've done good work, but now more than ever, I'd rather be a witch. The healing arts in this country are now the healing sciences, and I think that's a shame because the whole Self has been fragmented, frayed, and forgotten. Where is the incense? Where are the drums? Where is the chanting? The praying? Where are the mushrooms? The crystal ball? Where are the spells? Where is the magic?

Only in the last few years, after half a lifetime studying psychology, philosophy, religion, the occult and the natural sciences have I begun to understand what it is that Western medicine lacks. I don't mean to minimize the astounding discoveries and technologies which have saved many lives which couldn't have been saved before, but there is something conspicuously missing. The concepts of the Soul, the Spirit, the Mind and the Body seem archaic, mystical, and religious. The ideas are still with us, we've just replaced the terms with the more modern "subconscious," "the will," "the ego," "the emotions," "the psyche." Renaming the terms has limited them, changed them. The Soul, the Spirit, the Mind the Body need to be reclaimed and re-explained.

The Soul, the Spirit, the Mind and Body are all parts of the Self. To be truly healed, all the "selves' of the Self must have their say, must be acknowledged, must be comfortable. The Western approach to healing fragments the Self. Physicians attempt to heal the Body, religious gurus attempt to heal the Soul, psychologists attempt to heal the Spirit, and teachers attempt to heal the Mind. But if any one of the selves of the Self are locked in the closet, are ignored, indulged or abused, each will—in time—bang on the door, yell and scream, wreak the havoc we call, "dis-ease."

The Body is like a sponge, it absorbs not only the crap we feed it literally, but also the crap we feed it emotionally, mentally, and spiritually. The Body rebels when we deny the Self good food and exercise, connectedness, challenge, or magic. The Body is the hard copy of the Self. If you pay attention to its symbols, its language, you may learn to heal your Self.

What does the Mind need to stay healthy? The mind needs to experience the unknown. It needs stimulation and mental challenge. It needs to be curious and inventive. It needs to learn.

What does the Soul need to stay healthy? The soul needs to play, to be melancholy, to be loony, to watch Hallmark movies, and to weep at parades. The Soul needs art and music. The Soul loves solitude and rainy days. The soul speaks in archetypes, in symbolism, and thrives on mysticism, ritual and all things spooky. The Soul is dramatic. The Soul loves magic.

What does the Spirit need to stay healthy? The Spirit needs action, adventure, excitement, politics, Wall Street. The Spirit needs to work, to be recognized and to feel important. The Spirit needs to make decisions and get things done. The Spirit likes the energy of the crowd. The Spirit likes to bustle.

What does the Body need to stay healthy? The body needs water, fresh air, whole pure foods, exercise, protection from the cold and the heat. The body needs the other Selves to be happy.

As a lover of science, I acknowledge the influence genetic heritage has on our health. We have to die from something—eventually. And even if we are vigilant in maintaining a healthy balance in our Selves, our weakest genes will eventually be our demise. But until that day, we should learn about our family's health history, know what is most likely to go wrong, and practice a bit of preventive health. How hard can it be? My mother's family has cardiac/circulatory problems. Two of her sisters and three of her brothers died young and quickly because of their hearts. Would it not be wise for me to take heed? Should I not exercise, eat right, keep tabs on my blood pressure and cholesterol? But of course. There is diabetes on both sides of my husband's family. Would it not be wise for him to take heed and keep his sugar intake at a minimum and not abuse his pancreas? But of course. If your father, your grandfather, your uncles and aunts have problems with alcoholism, would it not be wise to take heed?

What about accidents? Certainly, there is little that can be done to avoid accidents. Really? Accidents *usually* happen when we're not paying attention or take foolish risks. Why do we do such things? For many reasons. If the Mind is in overdrive chattering away, it can't effectively assimilate the stimuli in the environment. If the Spirit is in overdrive, it feels immortal, powerful, it takes risks. If the Soul is in overdrive it is melancholy and self-absorbed. If the Body is in overdrive, it is hungry or hurting or sleepy. Sometimes, one of the Selves you have been ignoring creates the accident to get your attention. Take care of your Selves and you won't need to have an accident to regain your balance.

Cancer is the great nemesis of our time. I could suggest that the Spirit has been denied and wants to see some action, wants me to get off my duff and follow my dreams, but clearly there is much more to it than that. I think cancer is a disease of our culture. Our Bodies are more than the hard copy of our own "dis-ease." Our Bodies absorb physical contaminants, as well as the ethereal contaminants such as the negativity, unhappiness and the bad energy that surround us. We live in a not-so-nice world, in a not-so-nice time. So as with our genetic heritage, we need to be vigilant, surrounding ourselves with kindness, truth, beauty and purity.

Remedies in the West are so invasive. We cut, we probe, we pierce. We treat cancer with poisons, either in the form of radiation or in the form of chemicals that should, hypothetically, kill the cancer cells. The membranes of cancer cells are just a tad more permeable to the poison than the rest of the cells in the body. Hopefully, just in the nick of time, before the good cells die too, the poison is withdrawn. The poison compromises the body so dramatically that in most cases, death will occur anyway—maybe not as quickly, and maybe not from the original cancer. The immune system will be so weakened it will no longer be able to protect the Body. If I get cancer, I will not be poisoned. I hope I have the strength of spirit. I will diligently try to balance my Selves, purify my body and surround myself with goodness until the day I die or live. And, I may eat some medicinal plants, or if it's skin cancer, smear myself with a tincture of may-apple, bloodroot and a few other ingredients like comfrey, plantain and aloe.

Plant remedies have gotten a bad rap in this country. You can't patent a plant that grows along your driveway or in the woods along your running path, so better to make the masses believe that plant remedies are hocus pocus and synthetically produce something chemically similar. That way, you can charge hundreds of times the actual cost of making the "medicine." May-apple, by the way, contains the compounds podophyllin and lignans which are antimitotics. They keep the DNA of the cancerous cells from reproducing. (Don't go eating the stuff, it will make you puke your guts out.) For hundreds of dollars you might be able to get your doctor to prescribe a synthetic podophyllin based topical to treat your basal cell lesions. Homemade tincture of may-apple root works just as well; ask my family and friends.

We evolved with plants all around us. It's called, "symbiosis." Of course, plants can help us heal. Too bad we don't have more curanderos around to teach us the lost art of herbal medicine. But I'm not an extremist. In my twenties and thirties, I let my ambitious Spirit have the upper hand and because of the imbalance, and because of my genes, I developed high blood pressure—serves me right. I've had to back out of the fast lane, and yes, take something stronger than hawthorn berries—which worked for a while—to keep my heart from blowing a gasket. I've cut my chemicals in half and hope to go back to the hawthorn, which I prefer.

Drug companies and insurance companies must be in cahoots. Both would go out of business if people healed themselves. Fear works great to keep folks buying products they don't need. A little advertising, a little lying and the whole country is duped into thinking they must have health insurance and use drugs. And too bad we don't have a health care system that encourages healthy living and gives back a little of our hard earned money to take care of us when we need it instead of subsidizing the drug companies and building weapons to shoot holes in people in places we don't belong.

Wouldn't it be fun to be a true Healer? To use magic as well as science? That's what I want to do when I "grow up." I want to learn to sense the dis-ease in the Soul, the Spirit, the Mind and the Body and to assist the Self in finding its own remedy. I want to help the Soul be dramatic, to help the Spirit act on its dreams, to help the Mind to learn, and to help the Body be the perfectly functioning vehicle it was meant to be.

Seize your Self. Seize the Day.

No Anger, No Blame

kicked my sleeping bag a little farther under my seat in the Gate C26 waiting area of the Dallas/Fort Worth airport. I clicked loose my fanny pack, bent over to untie my new boots, heeled them off and rubbed my blistered toes. From my lowered vantage point, my eyes were drawn to other new boots and sleeping bags, belonging to other people with fanny packs or security pouches hanging from their necks, Everyone had dutifully studied and complied with the dress and gear recommendations issued to Katrina Relief Volunteers by the Center for Disease Control.

"New boots?" I looked for the person accompanying the question. A woman about my age with short cut wavy gray hair, reading glasses strung around her neck, leaned over a stack of carry-ons a couple of seats to my right.

"Yeah, afraid so." I replied.

"You a nurse?"

"You can tell?"

"Look around," she pointed. "There must be twenty-five of us here. Are you with the Red Cross?"

"No," I said, "I was referred by the Red Cross to the Public Health Service. My local chapter said they had so many volunteers they were referring all medical people to the Public Health Service—under The Office of Force and Readiness Deployment—under The Office of the Surgeon General—under FEMA—under The Office of Homeland Security. It was complicated.

"Do you know where you are going?" the woman asked.

"Baton Rouge for now. My assignment has changed twice already, though. They told me I'd be assigned when I get to what they call 'Tent City.'"

"How about you?" I asked. "Do you have an assignment?"

"I'm with the Red Cross. I'll be doing first-aid in a general shelter at an old Walmart in Baton Rouge. Here come the group from Illinois. I've been guarding their stuff."

During the hour and a half that followed—the flight was delayed because of mechanical problems—I met other nurses, lab technicians, biologists, therapists, physicians, forensic scientists, fire fighters, linemen, and a large search and rescue team from Germany. People mingled more than in the average airport. Jittery with anticipation—no one knew what they were in for.

After gathering my belongings from the luggage carousel at the Baton Rouge airport, I called the contact number given me by the Department of Health in Washington D.C. "You just missed the Public Health Shuttle," an in-charge kind of voice said. "The next shuttle will arrive at 4 p.m., I'll let the driver know you're waiting. Look for the white van that says PHS. My name is Lieutenant McNeil, I'll see you when you arrive."

Well, so far, so good. At least I hadn't been abandoned by FEMA—yet. I sat along the curb on my suitcase, adjusting to the heat, and talked with a grubby group of college girls who were ending their two-week stint at an animal rescue center. Just when the last of the volunteers were transported away—and I was starting to feel nervous—the PHS van arrived. I was driven into Baton Rouge and over the Mississippi River by a driver from San Antonio, Texas. Now in the middle of his tenth sixteen-hour day, his company had been contracted by FEMA to shuttle volunteers. I shared the van with one other person, a pharmacist in her civilian life—a reservist in the Medical Emergency Corps of the Public Health Service. She had been activated yesterday and didn't know her assignment either.

After presenting identification at two federal security checkpoints, I arrived on September 30, 2005, 4:45 p.m., at Tent City, the base camp, my home for the next two weeks. Tucked alongside a levee of the main Mississippi River channel, the camp was being machined back into place after partial dismantling during the threat of Hurricane Rita. Tent City was impressive.

In the center of a circular road, fourteen white and red striped circus-sized tents were set up. Each held over one hundred cots. I would sleep literally elbow to elbow with strangers. On the east side of the camp road, one hundred twenty porta-potties lined the concrete wall of the levee.

Aluminum bridges straddled a drainage ditch approximately every twenty potties, connecting them with the camp road. A portable washstand was set up at each crossing. On the west side of the camp road was the recreation tent—complete with a wide screen TV and cushy leather couches. A double-wide trailer served as the command center. On the entry/front end of the circle was a laundry tent, rows of showers and sinks in steel shipping containers, and the mess hall tent. On the far end of the circle, were the RVs of the camp maintenance staff.

The main annoyance of the camp, initially overwhelming and chronically deafening, was the noise. Dump trucks and front loaders, skid steers and four wheelers roared. At least twenty enormous generators ran day and night. Miscellaneous motors ran industrial fans, opened the creaking gates of the locks downstream, moved vehicles across the overhead bridge and pushed the honking tugboats. Why weren't ear plugs on the CDC's list of needed gear?

Having arrived too late to get oriented, assigned and "federalized," I unpacked my belongings, stuffed them under my cot and rolled out my sleeping bag. I went to the dining hall for a cafeteria style, all-you-can-eat supper of the best Cajun food on the planet. I charged my cell phone with at least fifty others at the charging station, brushed my teeth, climbed into my sleeping bag, wrapped an issued sheet around my head to ward off the noise and the draft, and fell asleep. I was awakened frequently by group after group of medical volunteers that arrived until around two a.m. when the tent was finally full.

The next morning, being one of the first of this wave of volunteers, I showed my cot-mates around. We ate a fat-filled breakfast and were taken to downtown Baton Rouge to a place called the JFO, the Joint Field Office, afterwards known as the "Mini Pentagon." There we waited for an hour, not allowed to pass through security because Commander McNeil failed to give us the name of a contact person inside. She said, "But I don't know anyone inside! I just got here!"

We couldn't get clearance. Each one of my group called someone. I called my contact in Washington D.C., McNeil called her commanding officer. Eventually, an official looking person in khakis with an array of brass and ribbons on his shirt came by. "What's the problem?" he asked. "Oh, I'll see if I can find someone to come out for you." *And why was it we couldn't go in with him?*

Another thirty minutes passed, no water left among us on this 95-degree Louisiana morning, when a pert little, straight as an arrow, lieutenant accompanied us to the "Federalization" area. No one knew what we were about to become or changed into. The JFO was also impressive. An abandoned shopping mall in the heart of the city was converted overnight (almost) into a makeshift federal headquarters. Setting up this communication metropolis was an enormous task and I tried to set aside some of my anger at FEMA for its poorly managed rescue. (When I went to New Orleans the last day of my stay, I understood even more clearly—the devastation was beyond the imagination. No excuses mind you, just understanding.) It seemed to me every government office had to be represented in the JFO. Cubicles on the ground, and communication wires overhead went on and on. This was the place the big wigs came for debriefing, including President Bush and Mr. Cheney. What an honor to walk on the same concrete ...

All that "federalization" amounted to was to sign all the same forms we had signed and faxed to the Department of Health and Human Service before we left home. And yes, I stood with my right hand raised after signing an affidavit, and swore—So help me, God—that, 1) I would support and defend the Constitution of the United States against all enemies etc., etc. 2) I would not participate in any strike against the Government of the United States, etc., etc., and that 3) I hadn't bribed anyone to secure this appointment. It was so ludicrous; I didn't even bother to cross my fingers—I'm not much for swearing to anything. But Jesus, how archaic, to think a terrorist wouldn't terrorize because they raised their right hand and said, "So help me, God."

I had my mug shot taken, received my very official looking FEMA badge—which was NOT to be worn in public because the public wasn't crazy about FEMA at the moment—and was crated back to Tent City. The tension among the volunteers rose along with the afternoon heat. Our "here-to-do-good" attitude was being undermined by the noise and the heat and the frustration at not being able to get an assignment until the following morning. We walked around the camp road dodging dump trucks, but as the frustration was building, so was the camaraderie among the volunteers.

The second day after arriving in Baton Rouge, a convoy of white vans left Tent City for Camp Phoenix—a clever name given to some of the buildings of the Louisiana School for the Blind—now used to house full-time workers and reservists of the Public Health Service. (Phoenix—the city of New Orleans rising again from the devastation—hopefully.) After pep talks and warnings about talking to the press—heaven forbid we would let the press know we were expected to drop what we were doing and be ready in twelve hours, to ride on a paid-in-full by the American public one-thousand dollar flight, to sit for two days with nothing to do—we got our assignments

I had been classified as a "mental health specialist," an RN with a master's in psychology. I was assigned to the Louisiana State University Special Needs Shelter. The vans were full after dismissal from Camp Phoenix, so I stayed behind with a family practice physician from Pennsylvania who asked me to call him "Joe." The commander at Camp Phoenix escorted us personally to the LSU shelter, introduced us to the commanding officer of the shelter, Dr. Libutti, who in turn showed us around and introduced us to the staff and some of the patients. Dr. Libutti asked if Joe and I could work that evening so the staff ending their rotation could get some sleep before early flights the next morning. We were happy to oblige.

The LSU Special Needs Shelter was incredible. Set up in the indoor track and field stadium jointly by FEMA and the State of Louisiana *before* Hurricane Katrina hit, it was used as an emergency center and hospital for evacuees and rescuees—capacity one thousand patients. At its max it housed seven hundred fifty patients in the "inner village' and accompanying family members of the patients in the "outer village."

The medical staff and supplies were brought in by FEMA. The auxiliary supplies—bedding, toiletries, food, social services, etc. were brought in by the State of Louisiana. Since it was no longer functioning as an acute care hospital, the patients who remained in the center were those who needed special care and who were not easily placed among the population at large—paraplegics, amputees, diabetics, oxygen dependent or the frail elderly, people with wounds, infections, mental disability or illness, etc.

M.A.S.H. is what comes to mind. Makeshift everything. The nurse's station was set up in the middle of the track. It had the thrown together look of assorted folding tables and chairs, goose neck lamps, and carts of all kinds packed with supplies—some ancient. The only water for washing hands was far away—in the shower rooms and public bathrooms on the periphery of the arena. We carried hand disinfectant in our pockets.

Patients were inventive in the way they guarded their privacy. They made "homes" by stringing bed sheets and blankets on abandoned IV poles around their beds and around the few belongings they had left in the world. Joe and I returned for our first partial shift at eleven p.m. A few smoking night owls greeted us at the front door. The National Guard and the two ambulance squads stood guard at the other exits. The lights in the field house were off except for two buzzing fluorescents high in the trusses. A few shelter residents were using the phones several of which were set up on fold out tables. A few teenagers were watching a video in the corner recreation area. Anthony was zooming around in his wheelchair.

At each Louisiana supply station around the periphery—the bedding guardian, the toiletries guardian, the social worker, the admission and triage persons were already sleepy and restless. No longer needed really, the State had not released them from duty and, heaven forbid, the Feds—us—might grab a bed sheet or a little sample bottle of shampoo for a U.S. citizen without observation. The guardians were probably necessary three weeks before when the shelter was full and chaos reigned, but now it seemed ridiculous.

After a brief patient report, a PHS nurse, Eunice, showed me around. Dressed in camouflage and army boots, she was intimidating. I quickly learned she was stern but kind and wished to take half the patients home with her. Eunice introduced me to those few still awake, showed me the pharmacy—stocked with samples mostly, and the central supply—compliments of FEMA.

Eunice showed me the charting system. The streamlined paperwork was a nurse's dream—although it was a bit haphazard and confusing. After my orientation, I was assigned a few patients. I made rounds. I did whatever treatments and procedures were needed. I read charts, and I chatted with shelter residents who were still awake.

Having been assigned to the shelter as the mental health specialist, I wondered what type of psychological support services and/or religious/spiritual activities had been provided. I wandered outside to visit with those breathing the damp night air and looking for stars through the glare of the city's lights. I asked the group, "Have there been any religious services since you came? Or support groups?"

Miss Neena shook her head. "Darlin,' what's your name? . . . Miss Gloria, we're going to forget all the songs we ever knew if someone don't start singin' pretty soon."

Hmmm. The next morning, I questioned Commander Labutti about the absence of religious services and support groups at the shelter. "Well," he said, "It *is* a government shelter."

"Yes, and . . .?

"Separation of Church and State."

"Jesus Christ."

So, Joe and I had a little talk. He was a Catholic turned some sort of new age Protestant—he could still say the rosary and loved to sermonize. I had already been exposed to his ability. And me, well, I could read the Bible and remembered a few hymns and gospel tunes. We were lacking representatives of many other religions but thought those folks could help us out when we got started. In the morning, the plan was passed onto Miss Neena and Miss Violet. They were going to talk it up among the rescuees. We were going to hold a revival that very night.

Even an important concept like Separation of Church and State—one I think extremely important in most situations, has its place. Unfortunately, when we arrived at 7 p.m. the following night for our first full twelve-hour shift, we were swamped. My first shift had been the last for all the other staff. Eunice had been assigned to the day shift. Joe and I were in charge of the shelter and the orientation of four new nurses. Great nurses.

Amy was an obstetrics nurse who was flexible and assertive. She helped us with the occasionally manipulative patient. Sybil was a young nurse whose gentle and nurturing manner was loved and appreciated. Kate, a PhD ethics student and mother of six including triplets, calmed us down and kept us steady on busy nights. Armando, a psych nurse, cheered us with his theatrics.

That night there were admissions and discharges and we had to figure out how to move a four-hundred-ninety-pound patient in cardiac failure to a Baton Rouge emergency room. Our revival was postponed.

The next day we didn't sleep well. At ten in the morning, we were awakened by several groups of new volunteers. After Hurricane Rita, the State of Louisiana officials freaked out. "We *don't*, we *won't* have enough medical personal to handle this storm!" With a knee jerk response, FEMA, responsible for supplying medical corps reservists and volunteers, called up hundreds of new people—so as not to be blamed for being slow to respond ever again. The problem was the State of Louisiana didn't know exactly how much help was needed or the location of need. And what about transportation and provisions? So here, in Tent City, doctors and nurses sat with nothing to do and no place to go. Stuck for days, they were not happy. I was glad I arrived when I did.

One emergency room M.D. from Iowa got on the internet and found the Veterans Administration had sent mobile clinics south for use after Hurricane Katrina. These units had been sitting outside Baton Rough for three weeks. He got permission to use them, gathered a group of nurses together and left Tent City. I don't know where they went. New Orleans was abandoned. I heard they roamed along the Louisiana coastal road looking for towns that needed help. Everyone received an assignment eventually, but the miscommunication and political nonsense was disheartening.

The following evening, thick headed from lack of sleep, I read the Beatitudes and sang with a voice out of practice and scratchy from an oncoming head cold, "Farther along we'll know more about it. Farther along we'll understand why. Cheer up my brothers. Live in the sunshine. We'll understand it all by and by."

I learned that evening what our work at the shelter was really about—to comfort, to stand by, to be a witness, to say "Wow"

These people from New Orleans, from Lake Charles, from Slidell and Pearl River with their stories of survival and strength gave much more to us than we gave to them: Miss Neena who didn't evacuate for fear of being separated from her schizophrenic brother; Miss Violet whose son needed her after suffering a head injury; Anthony whose neighbor rescued him as the water swirled to the neck of his paralyzed body; and Miss Shirley, who while hanging onto her door frame as the water rushed in, blessed the bodies of the dead as they floated by. She hoped she could return to New Orleans to vote.

The "Professor" salvaged nothing but his collected works of Shakespeare, his Walt Whitman and his Emerson. Miss Amelia hoped she could return, if not to her house, to her fourth generation "sliver" of land. She smiled as she told the story of singing to the helicopters as they flew overhead, "Swing low, sweet chariot, coming for to carry me home." Miss Evelyn, a diabetic, sat in waist high water for six days waiting to be rescued as she whittled through her roof.

There was no anger, there was no blame. Steven, a homeless heroin addict with a tracheotomy, invited us into his bed sheet "home" for a cup of tea and thanked us for our help. On the last day of our stay, as the Louisiana State University Gospel Choir sang, *"Amazing Grace, how sweet the sound …"* Miss Annette grabbed my hand and said, "Miss Gloria, my tears of sadness and my tears of loss are flowing down the same tracks as my tears of joy and thankfulness. You thank those Yankee friends of yours for all their kindness, won't you?" She winked and kissed my hand.

Uriah's Hypothesis

The Yellow Beetle

At two in the morning, going west on Interstate 80, we came over a rise and were suddenly barreling down on the taillights of a yellow Volkswagen beetle. "Uriah! Watch out!" I yelled, grabbing onto my seat. All he could do was swerve. The Nova, powered by a V8 engine with the momentum of eighty miles per hours, went into a spin. Around and around and around we went and landed backwards in the median. Thank goodness we didn't flip over. The motor died on one of the spins and there we sat. I could feel my heart drumming in my neck. Zea was on the floor. I rolled her back onto the seat. She was still sucking on her pacifier and barely opened her eyes. Uriah tried to start the car, but the engine wouldn't turn over at all, not a sound.

"Who drives forty miles per hour in the middle of nowhere? It's more dangerous than going a hundred. I'll bet the idiot doesn't even know we're sitting here." Uriah rattled on for a few minutes—adrenaline pumping. A semi pulled up and the driver offered to take Uriah into the next town to call a tow truck. I wasn't crazy about staying alone out in the boonies. I thought we should wait until daylight, but the opportunity was there, so Uriah took it. I locked the doors and tried to sleep. I dozed between the passing of car lights.

In an hour, Uriah was back. The mechanic lifted the Nova's hood and quickly saw the disconnected battery cables. The battery must have tipped over while we were spinning. Uriah paid the guy twenty-five bucks and we were on our way. I stewed about the twenty-five bucks blown for no reason. Twenty-five bucks cut into our $250 royally and we had barely gone anywhere. Uriah was mad about the whole deal, including himself.

We usually ran out of cash before the end of every month, but unbelievably we had managed to save our tax return. Gas was only thirty-three cents a gallon and by camping and staying with friends and relatives, we could afford a short road trip to Colorado. I hadn't been adding anything to our income recently, trying to finish nursing school as quickly as possible by taking a full credit load.

Uriah was almost finished with a degree in psychology at Northwestern. I usually tried to do my share and had worked at the Paulina Street IGA right up to the day before Zea was born. I had to wear a silly dotted Swiss dress, so worn there was nothing left to the fuzzy dots but spots of crunchy glue. At nine months pregnant, I had to pull the waistband of the fitted dress above my belly—how glamorous.

After Zea was born, before I started school, I worked at a nursing home on Sheridan Road. Bad news. The place was filthy and reeked of urine. I worked in the activities department, but one day a nurse asked me to help her roll a lady over and I saw my first bedsore—down to the bone. Mostly, I threw beach balls at half-conscious old folks who were strapped into their wheelchairs. I quit the day the director of nursing called me into her office, had me shut the door, and tried to seduce me by telling me I'd never have sex with a man that was even close to as good as sex with a woman—too much for my practically virgin ears.

My work history went back long before those two jobs. After my Dad died—when I was nine—I ironed clothes and baby-sat for neighbors, giving my stepmom every penny so she could pay the school's tuition. She insisted my brother, sister and I attend the Dutch Reformed schools—an obligation, for her own reasons, she felt toward our mother.

Uriah thought it was impossible for me to work, to juggle caring for Zea, keep up around the house and go to school. He was working while he finished up at Northwestern. He worked as an orderly at Evanston Hospital and before that at a sail-making shop on Western and Division. He dreamed of working in the violin repair shop on Howard Street, but didn't have the necessary training. Uriah said we had to have a semblance of stability in our lives for Zea's sake.

Being broke most of the time was stressful for me, but nothing new. We usually cut it to the penny. If anything extra came up, we were shit out of luck. Once, Uriah had to have an abscessed tooth pulled and a bridge put in. The next month, until his next paycheck came, we ate popcorn for breakfast.

♭

We drove for fifteen minutes in silence, trying to process our "accident."

"Where the heck are we?" I asked. I reached for the ceiling panel and followed a line of little bitty holes backward until I found the overhead light and flipped it on.

"Alodie, come on. How many times are you going to turn the light on?"

"I have to turn on the light to read the map."

"We're east of nowhere and west of somewhere else. Does it matter?"

"Funny Uriah. And yes, it matters to me. I like to know where I am." I yawned. "I think the altitude's changing. I feel sleepy. Maybe I'm not getting enough oxygen."

"Maybe you're sleepy because it's three-thirty in the morning and we've been driving all night,"

"No, Uriah, it's different. You know how you get kind of lightheaded in the mountains. We must have crossed into Colorado, I'll bet we're somewhere between Julesburg and Sterling. What did the last exit say?" I asked.

"I have no idea. We're not in the mountains obviously. You're the one who reads exit signs."

"You can feel the altitude changing before you can even see the mountains." I stretched, pushing my feet hard into the floorboards so I could lift my butt off the seat. My legs were twitching as they always did when I was overtired. "When I was a kid, I remember getting out of the car to stretch somewhere around here." I yawned again, "My cousin Nick and I had a race down the shoulder. I could hardly breathe, no shit. Well, I must have missed the last exit, or else it was a ways back."

"Why don't you to try to sleep, Alodie?"

"I suppose I should try. I studied much later last night than I had planned. I sure hope I did okay on that microbiology test."

"You always worry, but then you do fine. Get some sleep."

I looked into the back seat to check on Zea. One leg and one arm were dangling over the edge. I got on my knees and eased her into a more comfortable position. She clicked her pacifier with her tongue. Two years old and she still had a pacifier. I was too busy with school to mess with the ugly few days we'd have if I took it away. Maybe before the fall term. Zea's platinum hair flashed in the occasional headlights of a passing car. I turned off the overhead light and closed my eyes. I never have been able to fall asleep in a car, especially when Uriah's driving late at night. He can fall asleep in a minute. When I feel the car start wandering over the center line, it's my turn to drive, and I mean right now. "How you doing, Hon?" I had to ask at frequent intervals.

"I'm fine," he said. "How about you?"

"My legs are twitching."

"Yeah, I noticed," he said. "We should stop pretty soon."

I agreed, "If we rest a little, we'll be able to talk coherently to Uncle Len and Aunt Edie. You think I should have told them we were coming?"

"Alodie, we went over this already," Uriah grumbled. "What would we have told them? We didn't know exactly when we were going to leave home or how long the drive would take. It's easier to drop in. Your aunt didn't have to plan anything or even clean the house." 'Dropping in' is a classic Uriah thing to do, but it makes me nervous. My stepmom compulsively cleaned up every little mess worried someone might drop over. She would risk me being late for basketball practice because we absolutely had to do the supper dishes before she'd drive me to school. It wasn't her butt that got kicked by the coach.

"We must be near the Colorado border, you think?" The question just slipped out of my mouth. I waited for Uriah to growl, but he didn't.

♭

My thoughts drifted backward through the day and to the chaos of our lives and our neighborhood. We needed this vacation. Uriah had most of the packing done by the time I got home from school that morning and at exactly twelve noon he slammed the trunk and we were on the road. I had a ten-day midterm break over the July Fourth holiday, and we couldn't wait to get out of the Jungle.

Our neighborhood was called, "The Jungle," by our friends. I suppose the old timers, they weren't all old—I mean the permanent residents, probably referred to the neighborhood by its official name, "Roger's Park," but I really don't know because we didn't mingle much with the people who grew up in the neighborhood or those who planned to stay. Roger's Park was larger than the most northeastern three or four blocks of Chicago with which we were familiar—the blocks we walked every day to the "L" station, the dollar theater, the BLTS deli on Howard Street, or to the Scrub and Suds Laundromat, Raspel's Bakery, LaChoza Restaurant or the IGA. Other than our daily trips two miles north to Northwestern University or however many miles southwest to Mayfair City College and to the various hospitals around the city where I did my nursing practicum, we survived on the few square blocks of our neighborhood.

We blended with the other transients who wore mostly tee-shirts, frayed blue jeans, and sneakers. When dressed up, I wore sandals or platform heels, creatively patched bell bottoms, gauzy tunics, or halter tops. I dreamed of wearing sandalwood beads, crinkled voile skirts and patchouli—and I would have if I could have found one, a skirt I mean, at the secondhand store. I had no idea how people got to smelling like the head shops in Old Town.

It had taken me some time to get used to living in the city, not that the string of towns where I grew up, towns whose borders were ill-defined, one suburb running into the next along the prehistoric sand ridge that once was the southern shore of Lake Michigan, were more utopian, but they were home.

Uriah grew up in the town of South Holland, Illinois. I grew up in Munster, Indiana—a border town. We went to high school together in Lansing, Illinois. This string of towns was settled by Dutch truck farmers who raised onions and cabbages and sent their children to Dutch schools. Our folks didn't drink—officially, or work on Sundays.

Our apartment was on the second floor in a cream-colored brick building on the corner of Jonquil Terrace and Hermitage Avenue. Across the street, just behind the four-story apartments on Hermitage Avenue, Chicago's elevated trains turned around. The screeching grind of circling trains was the background noise of our lives. The sooty air, stirred by the moving trains, stuck to our walls and windows. I tried to scrub the walls like my stepmother would have insisted on had she visited more often. But I only made the filth more obvious by scrubbing, leaving gray rainbows the length of my reach on the walls in every room.

The people in the neighborhood weren't Dutch. I was taught to be suspicious of anyone who didn't have a last name with a "Van" at the beginning, an "Inga" at the end, or a set of double vowels somewhere in the middle. I wasn't sure of what I suspected of the non-Dutch. My elders hadn't been specific. Outsiders were just plain trouble with a capital *T*.

I got over my ethnic wariness in a jiffy after meeting Flo, Maury, Gus and our other friends. But, wow, after the first night in our apartment, I was ready to pack up and go back home. In the middle of our wedding night, Uriah and I heard a commotion in the street. Looking down from our second-floor bedroom window, we saw maybe a dozen Hare Krishnas beating on drums and chanting. A lone woman with a gold ring in her nose was surrounded by men wearing queues, yellow robes and orange scarves which billowed in the winter wind.

"The Jungle." I guess the name had to do with the compression of the population and the density of the brick and concrete. The Jungle was stimulating and exotic, but stifling, oppressive and potentially dangerous. We wouldn't stay forever in the neighborhood. We were just passing through. The Jungle was our temporary home, the only one we could afford until we finished school. The Jungle was less than perfect—an environment made livable by the camaraderie of good friends and the ever-present avenue of escape to the shores of Lake Michigan.

♪

Uriah drove on for an hour maybe, until I could see the sky graying in the side mirror. Up ahead, we saw a fleck of yellow and red. As before, we came upon the VW within seconds. I wanted to give the driver—a girl about my age—the finger as we passed her, but I didn't. Uriah laid on the horn. The girl jumped in her seat, glanced over at us questioningly, and shrugged. She didn't have a clue why Uriah was so ticked off.

At the next rest stop, we pulled over. Uriah and I both fell asleep in a snap, but shortly after Zea woke up. There wasn't much chance of getting her back to sleep. She was pointing out the window at everything she saw. "Look-a, look-a," she said, over and over which she did every day, all day long. With no choice, I drove while Uriah napped. In what seemed like years, we reached Loveland, Colorado. As I turned the car into my aunt's and uncle's driveway, I nearly cried with relief.

Loveland

Uriah and I brushed our hair and smoothed our clothes in a hopeless attempt to look more presentable. I lifted my long stiff legs one by one from the car onto the driveway and groaned as I stood and stretched. The very spot on the cement where I now stood, just that one square foot, beamed up visions of my Colorado summer vacations.

I remembered the time I flew down the driveway on my first attempt to ride a skateboard. My cousin, Nick, had made the skateboard from a set of roller skate wheels nailed onto a splintery piece of plywood. "You're doing it! You're doing it!" Nick supportively yelled. And I did do it, until I reached the curb and landed on my tailbone and elbows.

I remembered how I had stood on the driveway to help Uncle Len eyeball the position of an old plow he had acquired to use for a yard ornament. The plow was placed among a couple of quartzite boulders he had crow-barred out of the mountains and rolled up a ramp into the back of his pick-up truck. "What do you think, Alodi?" Uncle Len had asked.

"More to the right. Yeah. The plow looks better centered between the windows. Try more of an angle." I moved right and left, back and forth. "Looks good to me Uncle Len," I said.

Uncle Len smiled and put his arm around my shoulder, "We're quite the team, aren't we." he said. Yes, we had been quite a team back then. I admired our work now, pointing it out to Uriah—plow and boulders just as Uncle Len and I had placed them ten years before.

I had missed my first kiss standing on that driveway, up against the garage in the shadow of the eaves. I had missed my first kiss because I left it up to a shy-boy to make his move. The first day or two after we stepped off the Union Pacific passenger train in Greeley, I'd pick out a boy, usually one of Nick's friends, and planed my summer's romance. I mostly kept my fantasies to myself, but that year I'd made a move on a Paul McCartney look-a-like who ignored me because he already had a girlfriend. I found out about the girlfriend from Nick after I'd made a flirting fool out of myself. Shy-boy was Paul's stand-in, an after-thought actually. He had been easy—flattered by the attention I lavished on him, but I was acting and he knew it. I wouldn't have kissed me either.

For a moment, I let the mountains soothe me with their forever presence in the west. I smelled the yellow of warm roses against the south wall of the stone house, took a deep breath of memory, and pulled forward the back seat of the car so Zea could tumble out.

"What do we do if no one's home?" Uriah asked, the same Uriah who preferred to drop in on people.

"We'll go around the back. The patio door is usually left open. If not, we can sit by the lake until someone gets home." I paused to think. My contingency plans hadn't gone this far. "If no one does come home, well, maybe we can find Nick. He lives somewhere in town." I led Uriah and Zea to the utility room door. If Aunt Edie was home, she wouldn't be near the front door. It was never used except by strangers. What is the use of a front door like that? I suppose it's intended to make an impression. Although I was developing a healthy suspicion of pretentiousness, I had been plenty impressed as a kid.

My father had been a foreman for United States Steel in Gary, Indiana. He had worked for thirty-five years in the heat of a blast furnace. He was in the Steel Workers Union, yeah, but he never made all that much money. The year before he died, a six-week strike worried him sick. My stepmother worked at her father's cabinet shop and picked up a job cleaning a motel. After my father died from bleeding stomach ulcers in 1962, my Uncle Len sent money to my mom—who was Aunt Edie's sister.

I think, but I don't know for sure, that Uncle Len continued to help us out financially. I do know he bought train tickets so we could spend two weeks of our summer vacation every year in

Colorado. Uncle Len was a doctor. I always figured he had oodles of money but had no idea really. Anyway, it was good of him to help us out. My mom needed a break. I loved Colorado. I loved hanging out with the rich relatives for a few weeks every year. The Colorado vacations were an escape from the stress that filtered through my mom to my brother, sister and me. The vacations were an escape from the day to day struggles of our existence.

Aunt Edie and Uncle Len's house, which was custom designed, was complicated. Wings jutted this way and that—great for roaming around while daydreaming. It was all on one floor except for the living room, which was lower by a couple of steps. I thought the sunken living room was so . . . Hollywood. One bathroom had two toilets, two sinks, and two showers. Extravagant it seemed to me. Aunt Edie said the boys didn't care much about privacy and with double of everything they could get ready for school without fighting over who got the bathroom first.

The house was decorated with pictures, artifacts and furniture from all over the world. It had been sent by the missionary parents of Uncle Len. The hammock on the patio came from Peru. The weave was so stretchy, three or four kids could sit sideways and swing. The oldest of my three Colorado cousins, Peter, had spent a year with his grandparents. His bedroom was filled with Peruvian masks, drums, blankets and Indian art of all sorts. I loved hanging around in his room, the ceilings were slanted, and he had his own fireplace.

As I suspected, Aunt Edie was nearby, in the utility room folding laundry. I watched her through the screen door for a second and gently knocked. Recognition came slowly, and not until I said "Aunt Edie, it's me Alodie" did she smile and say, "Well, Honey! I'll be. What are you doing here?"

A black lab, a dog I had known as a puppy, barked and slid as she came running in from the kitchen. "Hi Gracie. You sweet dog." I ruffled the dog's ears and said to Aunt Edie, "We stopped by on our way to see our friends who moved to Lyons. I hope it's okay."

"Of course it is. Did you bring your family?" she asked.

Surprised that she asked, I looked behind me. Uriah and Zea were holding back, a little uncomfortable barging in on a stranger. Aunt Edie wasn't a complete stranger to Uriah. He had met her once at a family gathering when we were still dating. He and my aunt probably hadn't spoken more than a few words to each other because there had been so many people around. That was before I got pregnant. I hadn't thought much about how that complication would affect my aunt and uncle's acceptance of Uriah, and I was put on edge when Aunt Edie reluctantly shook the hand Uriah held out in greeting.

I was so happy with my new life—being a mom, a wife, a nursing student. I was so far past the shock of being pregnant I hadn't anticipated a chilly reception. It hadn't occurred to me my welcome might be any different than it had ever been. I was the same Alodie my aunt had treated so lovingly every summer, but she hadn't seen me or Uriah since that family party three years ago.

My Aunt's demeanor changed subtly as she let her provincialism overcome what had seemed like her initial delight in seeing me. Her eyes swept the three of us. I was in a wrap-around skirt, toe-ring sandals, a blouse made from an old linen tablecloth. I wore dangling earrings. Uriah wore frayed blue jeans and sneakers. His beard was long, but his hair wasn't—very. Zea was dressed in several layers. She liked to wear all her favorite clothes at once. Under Aunt Edie's critical eyes, I realized Zea looked like a rag-a-muffin. The old-fashioned brown oxfords we had found the week before at the Salvation Army were practical but not very girlish. Her hair was sticking up every which way. As she took in the complete picture, my Aunt Edie dumped us quickly into a box which DIDN'T include her ideal of Young Republican, Youth for Christ, flag decal displaying, clean cut, good American kids.

"Are your friends hippies?" she asked out of the blue. "Are you going to that festival up in the mountains next week?"

"What?" I asked, confused. What was she talking about? I could feel Uriah bristle beside me. It was going to be a long afternoon.

Aunt Edie said she was busy. She had to finish the laundry and do some errands. "Uncle Len will be home around five. Supper's at six. Make yourselves at home," She said. "Swim in the pool if you like. If you get hungry later, there's lunch meat in the fridge. The bread's in the pantry. Help yourselves. Are you staying overnight?"

"We were hoping to if it's all right," I said.

"Sure, sure it is. You can sleep in Theo's old room. There's a crib set up already. Pete's littlest sleeps in it when she stays over."

We talked about the family back in Indiana and Illinois and Aunt Edie, temporarily anyway, forgot her misgivings about us. She ended up sticking around to fix lunch. Uriah, Zea and I took a much-needed nap after lunch, had a refreshing swim in the lake— not the pool—Uriah was a purest, and were ready by five to visit with Uncle Len.

As expected, Uncle Len dominated the evening. On every topic from the Kent State shooting to the Nixon/McGovern presidential race, to maintaining honor in Vietnam, my uncle held forth the voice of the Establishment and wouldn't let Uriah counter a word. I didn't even try. While the strawberry shortcake was being served, Theo called from medical school. After Uncle Len hung up the phone, the conversation shifted to what a great kid Theo was. Oh, yeah, what a great kid! My uncle was being a jerk, but he was nothing compared to my cousin, Theo. We wouldn't have stopped to visit at all if Theo had still lived at home. I get all worked up just thinking about it.

⚡

I would have perfectly happy memories of my summer vacations in Colorado if it weren't for my cousin Theo. We had so much fun—my brother, sister, and I. We'd swim in the pool, go boating and skiing, or drive into the mountains with the family for the day. My aunt and uncle and my two youngest cousins, Nick and Theo, would sometimes take us along on the family vacations. Peter had already left home. The adults would sit in the cab and the kids would pile into the camper-topped pickup while we toured Colorado, Wyoming or Montana. We went to Yellowstone and Mesa Verde National Parks, and once, all the way to Rapelje, Montana, where my stepmom's family had been homesteaders.

As I grew older, my cousin Theo started doing some mean things to me, like dunk me in the pool for too long. Once, when I was water skiing and he was driving the boat, he left me floating in the middle of the lake for at least an hour. I had started swimming and had almost reached the shore by the time he came back. I didn't climb into the boat. I wouldn't talk to him and just kept swimming. That kind of nasty behavior happened every year. My mom tried to reassure me that boys only teased the girls they liked. Theo wasn't teasing. I still hate him.

When I was thirteen, Theo pulled up my bikini top while he held me under water. I could hear him laughing from above. I couldn't get free from him, as much as I fought. I was starting to feel faint when Nick happened by to get his sunglasses. He yelled at Theo to stop, jumped into the pool and shoved Theo off me. Nick had to pull me out of the water. I was humiliated. Nick was so sweet, though. He acted like he never saw anything unusual and paid special attention to me after that. He'd take me cruising in his convertible or take me to the drive-in where he hung out with his friends. I avoided stupid Theo.

But, Theo's torment continued. A couple of days later I went next door to take a shower. My aunt and uncle's old house was next to their new one. The old house hadn't been sold, so we still used it that summer. While I was in the shower, I can even remember the Beatle's song I was singing. . . "She was just seventeen, you know what I mean, and the way she looked was way beyond compare ..." Theo had come into the house. He sneaked all my clothes out of the bathroom. I didn't hear him. When I stepped out of the shower, I was confused. Did I take my clothes off in the bedroom? I wrapped myself in a towel and opened the bathroom door. In a bedroom directly across the hall sitting on the bed next to my clothes was Theo.

I was afraid and furious. I spun in a circle not knowing what to do. He hissed in a low voice, "You let me squeeze your pussy and I'll give you your clothes." I screamed all the bad words I knew. He came at me. I slapped at him and kicked him and ran down the hall and out of the house trying to hold the towel around myself the best I could. By the time I reached the new house next door, I was bawling with anger. I went straight to my mom and told her what happened.

I thought she'd do something, but all she said was, "Don't tell anyone, Alodi. It will just cause hard feelings."

"Hard feelings?" I was stunned. "Aren't you going to tell Aunt Edie?"

"Maybe I will. I'll see," she said. I don't think my mom ever told anyone.

Theo disappeared. When he didn't come home for supper everyone started worrying. By dark, they began searching. Shit. I didn't have the guts to tell them what happened. I hoped Theo had disappeared for good. Uncle Len, somehow, found Theo hiding on the floor of an old motorboat stored in the shed. Poor Theo, what was the matter? Yeah, I should have told them all what the matter was, but I didn't.

⚡

After supper, Aunt Edie called Peter to tell him Uriah and I were in town. He invited us over to see the house he and his wife had bought the month before. We were given directions and were happy to get away for a while, although I suspected we were getting the brush off by my aunt and uncle. Peter and Uriah played guitars. Peter's wife toured me around the house. She was trying to grow moss on the stones of the fireplace. She misted the moss twice a day. Even so, the living room seemed a rather dry spot for moss, but I didn't know piddly about plants.

It was eleven p.m. when we quietly found our way to Theo's bedroom. With the help of a streetlamp shining through the sheer curtains, Uriah and I tucked a sleeping Zea into bed and snuggled together under the gentle slope of a mustard colored ceiling.

The gable end of the bedroom was glass from floor to ceiling. Uriah awoke at dawn and yanked back the curtains. The mountaintops were hazed with pink against the western sky. I woke at the sound of Uriah's deliberate rustling. "Let's get out of here, Alodie." He said. "We can leave a polite thank you note. We can use my early rising as an excuse. How about it?"

"Sure, okay." I yawned and stretched. What I really wanted to do was sleep until noon. I pulled on cut-off jeans, a halter top I had made out of two red bandanas, slipped on my sandals and rolled my hair into a knot. The sound of the toilets flushing wouldn't wake my aunt and uncle who slept on the other side of the house. I picked up both backpacks and made my way through the maze of hallways to the kitchen. I scrounged for a piece of paper and a pencil, scribbled a note of gratitude—maybe a bit on the gushy side—and placed it on the kitchen table. I met Uriah in the foyer, carrying a still sleeping Zea and we escaped through the front door.

The Hypothesis

Uriah had called our friends, Maury and Flo, after he had suffered through enough of Uncles Len's haranguing the night before. Flo said we could come a day early, but before hanging up she cryptically mentioned being a "threesome" now. We didn't know what to expect, a boarder? A child? A lover? Man or woman? Flo probably had a lover. I wondered how Maury was doing.

For the previous year or so, our friends in the Jungle had been redefining their notions about love. Not love exactly—relationships. We'd have marathon discussions on the topic, occasionally enhanced by a joint or two. Our friend, Gus, the most committed would-be communist among us, got us started by insisting we read Wilhelm Reich's, *The Sexual Revolution.* "Did you finish it yet?" he would ask.

The book brought into question the cultural norm of life-long monogamy. Was it the ideal relationship? Most of our friends were coupled, some married, some not. There were many singles rooming together. Uriah and I were one of the few couples who were married and had a child. The idea of experimenting with other kinds of relationships, or at least having an affair now and then, had a certain fascination. Uriah and I had married young, really young, and the idea of never having sex with anyone else was starting to feel like a jail sentence.

The opportunity for experimentation was everywhere. We were in such close proximity to our friends, and the crap of the time—the Vietnam War, the draft, discrimination and capitalization gone amuck drew us close ideologically too. Crazy Gus. He'd come visit me when Uriah wasn't home. "How's school going?" he'd ask, sitting on the arm of my stuffed chair. "I like your hair like this," he'd say, fingering my hair which was pulled into a ponytail.

"Sorry, Gus," I resisted playfully. "I'm not ready to jump into the sack with you because I read your communist propaganda." My real reason for not getting involved with Gus was that he was too close a friend to risk the possible consequences of a sexual entanglement. Uriah and I had talked about our marriage, and marriage in general for months, but I was a chicken to try anything when it came down to it. Uriah was brave, *is* brave. No kidding. He'll try anything— which is good because if it was up to me, we'd have a boring life. I suppose I'm insecure because my parents both died when I was a kid. I don't like things to change. Well, I do, but I get pretty nervous about it. When Uriah comes up with some harebrained scheme, I usually stall. I don't say "No," but I don't say "Yes," exactly either, at least not until the idea has time to ripen.

Uriah was ready to experiment before I was. I'd get squeamish and worry about the potential risks to our relationship. Aside from the common complaints of newly married couples, like farting under the covers and not putting the cap back on the toothpaste, we only had one difficult problem, we were falling into the husband/father, wife/mother roles of our parents, the roles our families and our community modeled for us. I felt stifled. Feed the kid. Do the laundry. Wash the dishes. Stuck at home with no life of my own, I begged Uriah to tell me what he learned at school, or what happened in the emergency room where he worked as an orderly. I should have had that job!

At the time, I'd given up the idea of going to nursing school— something I'd wanted to do since I was a girl. It was my greatest regret about getting pregnant. Thank goodness, Uriah realized I would become a drag to live with if I didn't find something interesting to do—and in a hurry. He's the one that practically forced me to go to school. He found out about free tuition at the Chicago City Colleges, and before I could say, "But . . . but ... but," I was taking night classes.

Uriah started pitching in—changing diapers and cooking, although he couldn't see dirt, so I still did most of the cleaning. I was starting to feel more sure of myself which gave me the courage to agree, finally, to the design of our experiment. We freed each other to go ahead in case an affair happened *spontaneously*, but we wouldn't go out looking for one. We promised to tell each other if anything happened—not the specifics, of course. There would be no lying, no cover-ups. That was the plan.

I freaked out occasionally. I didn't know what I was going to do if I got jealous. I anticipated Uriah would have the affairs and I wouldn't. All he had to do was to ask someone. Girls didn't, in spite of all their new bravado and feminist rhetoric, make the first move. Uriah told me this wasn't true. He said I was the biggest flirt in the neighborhood. Would you believe it? I didn't flirt. I really liked men, but what girl didn't? "Alodie, you know the way you *lean?*" he'd say, or, "Do you realize you had your hand on so and so's thigh half the night?"

"Come on, Uriah," I would counter, "I'm just a touchy kind of person." I held the notion I'd probably never, and he would always, get to have the fun. In the meantime, we got along great and I truly believed in Uriah's hypothesis—that I would never love him less by loving someone else. Love wasn't finite after all. A mother could love one, two, six, ten children all at once. Loving another man would be exactly the same thing.

♭

We wound our way through craggy coulees and canyons, ate soft bananas and stale wheat bread for breakfast, and chattered away about our first year in Chicago and the first time we met Maury and Flo. Uriah and I had been trying to adjust to city life, trying to come to grips with the *idea* of having a baby, then with the idea of *actually* having one.

We tried to find a church, but had been disillusioned with the guilt, damnation, racism and the elitist hypocritical dogma of the Dutch Reformed Church in which we were raised. Uriah had gone to a Quaker Meeting before we were married, but they didn't claim necessarily to be Christians and that bothered him. The Salvation Army seemed a bit naïve with their "Onward Christian Solders" theme and incessant ding-a-ling-a-linging. The Youth for Christ group on Northwestern's campus were vigilantly blind, making delusional claims, or just plain lying. They would make statements like, "I know I'm saved because Jesus spoke to me." Right. The Mennonites seemed the most rational and we attended meetings with them for a few months. But the more we associated with pure-hearted non-believers, our Jonquil Terrace friends, the less religion seemed necessary. We finally gave it up as irrelevant, destructive even, in my opinion.

*

Maury and Flo, what a pair. Gus from the apartment next to ours wanted to have a party but thought his place was too small. He invited several tenants over to see if we'd want to have a party together. During this initial meeting, Flo came dressed in an old 50s poodle skirt and sat cross-legged on the sofa. She had foregone the wearing of underpants and wasn't a bit modest either. It was hard not to look—very distracting. She was smart and loud and funny— but a good soul—definitely rough around the edges, a quality she cultivated.

Maury never said much. He was always stoned. After his Bar Mitzvah, he served as a cantor in an orthodox synagogue for years. Only remnants of his Judaism remained—Yiddish expletives. In Chicago, Maury had been a mail carrier. He claimed to climb into mailboxes along his route to smoke pot. We worried for him but there was no dissuading him.

That first party was crazy. We never did find out who posted an invitation at the university library. People were stacked up and down the steps—people we didn't know. When a friend of Maury's got drunk, Flo put him in the shower of her apartment with the nozzle aimed partly out of the window. Someone across the street called the cops because she saw water spraying from the second floor onto the sidewalk. The cops, searching for the source of the spray, came into OUR apartment—the doors to the entire floor were wide open—and banged on our bathroom door.

A friend of Uriah's started yelling, "Just a minute, for Christ sake! I'm taking a shit. I'll be right out." The cops went into Flo and Maury's apartment and asked about the water.

Flo, with arms around the cops' shoulders, said, "We're all drunk officers, and everything is just fine." We were all of drinking age, which was eighteen at the time, so drinking wasn't the problem. But the air in the building must have smelled of pot. A tenant from downstairs had a mountain of it on his kitchen table the night before. We had no idea where he had stashed it. Either the cops didn't want to deal with all of us or were too green to recognize the smell.

I was glad nothing really bad happened. I lost it when some dope threw a glass of wine against our living room wall. It was the first time I'd been drunk, and I was surprised when I couldn't get out of my chair to wipe up the mess. I just sat there and screamed, "What are you doing, you jerk? I don't even know you and you're trashing my apartment. Get the Fuck out of here." Well, that's how I remember it, but I was probably much tamer than that. I like to think I'm tougher than I am. Uriah frequently checked Zea, who slept through the whole party.

Maury and Flo were the first to leave the Jungle to see the world and seek their fortunes. They wanted to live off the land somewhere out west, ultimately to go where the buffalo roamed, but opted for affordability in the meantime. They built a wooden camper on the top of a pickup truck, christened it with cream soda, and were gone.

⚡

There wasn't a paved street in Lyons, Colorado. The wide dusty roads were lined with one story houses sided with white clapboard. White, white, white. "These houses are all the same, Uriah," I said. "Must have been only one carpenter in town."

"I think these might be houses bought in kits from Montgomery Wards in the late 1930s."

"Really? I asked. "I never heard of such a thing.

"My dad remodeled a house like this. He told me about it."

"White must be the only color paint Willy sells," I pointed to Willy's hardware as we drove through what must have been downtown. There was a Sinclair station with one gas pump, Grandma's Café, a post office and a church—also white clapboard. "Turn here Uriah." I held the directions for finding Mary and Flo's house. "Juniper Street, two blocks to Clyde, turn right, second house on the left. Picket or bent wire fences separated the yards from one another. Gates opened onto heaved and broken sidewalks which led up a step, maybe two into the wide and welcoming shade of a front porch. Grass struggled to grow in the rocky dust of the yards. Climbing roses tumbled over the fences and hugged the porch rails. Along with eddies of dust, the scent of the roses swirled through the town.

'There she is!" I yelled, pointing up the street. Uriah laid on the horn. Flo was scooting the last of her runaway chickens through the gate as we cut the engine. Her wavy thicket of dark brown hair was falling from a leather pick clasp. Breasts stretched an orange elastic halter to its capacity under white painter's overalls. She reached out her very tan arms.

"Oh, oh, oh," is all Flo said, squeezing us both at the same time. "Where is the little Zea? Oh, my God! Look at you, little girl. Come here." Flo pulled Zea from the car. Zea, caught up in the warm reception, gave Flo a big hug, but was quickly distracted by the chickens.

"Look-a, look-a," Zea pointed and began talking to the chickens, "B-a-u-k, b-a-u-k," she clucked, reaching her hands through the fence.

"We're not supposed to have chickens running around." Flo said. "Town ordinance. It's okay to keep them in cages in the back yard. I just hate to keep them penned up all the time, so I let them loose once in a while. Some stray dog freaked them out and they flew over the fucking fence." Flo opened the gate and prepared to kick back any chickens that might bolt again toward freedom. "Come in, come in." Flo gestured toward the house. "I just made some iced tea."

"So, Flo," Uriah hesitated at the gate and asked rather urgently, "What's this mysterious threesome all about?"

"Maury met a woman." A flash of unease crossed her face, but she continued all upbeat and happy. "Yeah, we're all sleeping together. Would you believe it?"

I did believe it and I wanted to be open-minded, but I was totally uncomfortable. The whole idea seemed *too* weird. No way would I sleep in a bed with Uriah and another woman. Leave it to Flo. She seemed completely accepting, at least she was trying to be. I didn't know what to make of the little catch I thought I heard in her voice.

Uriah asked, "What do you think of this other woman, Flo? Do you like her?"

Flo shrugged, "I don't know, she's all right. It's a temporary arrangement, you know, just to spice things up. I'll introduce you. Come on."

Once we got our backpacks untangled from the wooden beads that hung across the door frame, we entered the living room where the *other* woman, who Flo introduced as "Sasha Leone," was lounging on the sofa like Cleopatra. She didn't get up, she just put out her hand for us to shake. Sasha Leone seemed to expect a kiss from Uriah, but he passed. What kind of name was "Sasha Leone?" It had to be made up. God, hippies could be nuts sometimes.

"Let's sit out back," Flo said, as she handed us our tea. She led the way through the kitchen, down the back steps and into the yard. We sat under an overgrown grape arbor. "I'm dying to hear the scoop on the old neighborhood," Flo said, "What's Gus up to?"

"Baseball mostly," I said. "He keeps trying to get a team together. We went down to a park along Sheridan Road to watch him play a couple of weeks ago. You know, Flo, the one just north of Loyola University?" I got distracted by the picture in my mind. "The air pollution was so bad that day there was a warning on the news not to go outside if you didn't have to. It was nasty. Our eyes burned and we could feel the crap in our lungs. You're lucky you moved out when you did." Uriah rolled his eyes at me. *What?* I thought. *What did I just say or do? Change the subject? Was I dominating the conversation?* I do like to talk and sometimes it drives Uriah crazy.

"Gus is convinced there's no way to fix the country without a revolution," Uriah said, "But I don't know who beside him would show up."

"True, so true." Flo waved away a bee and laughed. Zea ran around the backyard chasing the chickens. Now and then, she let out a squeal as we talked about mutual friends. Finally, Flo stood up. "I miss everyone so much sometimes. We're meeting people here slowly, but it's just not the same."

"This grapevine needs trimming, Flo." Uriah said, as he leaned back and fingered the brittle leaves overcome by the shade above. *Now who was changing the subject?* I thought, but didn't feel any need to say so.

Flo replied, "Yeah, I know, it's a mess, but we're only renting and there are some grapes growing. See?" She pushed the foliage back to show Uriah the maturing clusters of grapes. "I better start lunch. Vegetarian okay?"

"I'll help you," I said, "What can I do?"

"You can cut up a zucchini and an onion and I think I've got a pepper we can throw into some beans and rice."

Cleopatra lazily slid into the kitchen, looked over the vegetable concoction we were working on, dug around in the refrigerator and then in the cabinets. "Nothing worth eating in this house," she grumbled. She grabbed an apple and went outside. Flo just shrugged.

After lunch, Flo suggested a walk to the post office. Uriah declined. "Think I'll take a nap with Zea."

"That'd be nice, Hon'," I said. "Hope she falls asleep before you do. I'll check in on the two of you when we get back."

Flo pulled a couple of addressed envelopes from a crack between the wall and the door trim and we walked out into the street. I looked toward the west, "I like the feel of this town, Flo, the way it's tucked into the foothills with the mountains looming overhead. Feels cozy—kind of protected."

"It's protected all right," she replied, "in more ways than one."

I purposefully didn't pick up on Flo's allusion to narrow-mindedness, well, I'm pretty sure that's what she meant. I continued. "And the dirt streets are quaint, but does the dust ever get to you?"

Flo scoffed, "You should try growing a garden here. Hardly worth the effort, it's so dry. I only got two fucking tomatoes last year."

"But don't you like living here? I'd like to be able to walk to the post office on dirt streets and maybe have a chat with a few neighbors on the way."

"A few is right." Flo said sarcastically. "Chats with the neighbors, if they happen at all, are not initiated by them, let me tell you. Alodie, you've never met such judgmental creeps."

"Oh, come on, Flo. Why do you say that?"

"Alodie, 'come on' yourself!" I've lived here for a year already.

I found it hard to believe that someone as friendly as Flo would not have made an inroad. I said, "Well, you're still strangers. It's a small town."

"Yes, and you dare not live by any convention but their archaic one."

"Well, Darlin'," I thought, but would never have said, *"Not many households include two women. Sexual experimentation in a small town is a little over the top."* I actually wished I was gutsier. What Flo and Maury were doing was kind of exciting, although it would be a lot more fun to have two men in the house than two women. Forgetting I had left Flo out of my internal conversation, I said, seemingly out of the blue, "I hate to be unkind, Flo, but Sasha Leone seems a bit self-absorbed."

Theatrically wiping her forehead with the back of her hand, Flo said, "Sweetie, would you get me my smelling salts. It's dreadfully hot in here. Could you open the window, dear?"

"Why do you put up with her?" Abruptly, Flo's expression changed, and she retreated into her feelings, which I couldn't read.

"It's complicated," she said. "You wouldn't understand."

I felt a little insulted, "You could give me a chance," I said.

"No, Honey. I just can't talk about it right now."

We walked past two or three houses in silence, then Flo said, "Alodi, I was thinking. Would you like me to watch Zea over the weekend, so you and Uriah could spend some time together? I mean, when was the last time you two were alone?"

I had a fleeting urge to say, *"Sure, and the weekend after that I can baby sit Cleopatra so you and Maury can be alone."* But of course I didn't. Instead I yelled, "Are you serious? Thank you!" I put my arm around Flo. "I think if we spend the rest of the week with you, Zea will be comfortable enough not to freak out. She's never been very clingy to Uriah or me. She'll be fine. I can't believe you offered! Are you sure?"

"Absolutely. I rarely get the chance to play 'the Mom'."

When Maury got home from work, he gave a beer to everyone and mumbled his hello. He was as quiet and distant as he was back in Chicago. Uriah plucked Maury's banjo. Flo and Zea sat on the steps watching a ladybug. Maury slouched on the porch swing and

Cleopatra wasted no time swinging her legs onto Maury's lap. I sat on the railing, studied the situation and concluded that Uriah's hypothesis about love was hogwash.

The Gathering

Three days after we arrived at Flo and Maury's, I squeezed my head and shoulders through the side window of the car and pushed myself to almost standing so I could wave goodbye to Zea and Flo. Flo tried to get Zea to pay attention to our leaving, to act as if she cared, but after a few obligatory waves, Zea began to squirm. Her eyes and thoughts shifted to the cat rubbing against Flo's shins.

It was the first time Uriah and I had left Zea with anyone but family and I was a little worried. Zea loved people, trusted everyone, and seemed to remember Flo from Chicago. Maybe I wished Zea was more clingy—no, that's not true. I was always happy she adapted so easily. We'd only be gone until Monday—three nights and three days. Flo would keep Zea occupied and she would be fine. We'd call now and then to make sure. I waved until we turned onto Main Street, squeezed back into the car and wiped my damp eyes.

I wanted to travel through the village of Estes Park and then to Rocky Mountain National Park via Route 34 and follow the Big Thompson River like I had done many times as a kid. The route went into the mountains from Loveland. I thought Uriah would be impressed by the narrow canyon which had only enough space between the sheer cliffs for the road and the river.

I got car sick more than once winding up the canyon. My cousins would deliberately speed around the curves, squeal the tires, and drive as fast as they dared just to make me sick. After I puked all over Nick's T-bird convertible, he slowed down. We passed a truck stop a few miles out of Lyons. Uriah said, "I'm dying for some meat, Alodie. The beans and sprouts we've been living on the last few days are killing me. You want another breakfast?"

Uriah reacted to my nod by performing a perfect three-point turn in the middle of a no passing zone. After he barbarically bit into his second patty of sausage and his carnivorous urges were diminishing, he pushed the dishes aside and opened the road atlas. "Alodie, there's no reason to go north to Loveland and then to Estes Park. Look," he smeared the map with a greasy finger, "Route 36 will take us right there from here."

"I know, Uriah, but I want you to see the Big Thompson Canyon."

"There'll be other canyons."

"Not like that one." I whined, but gave in. "Okay, but maybe on our way home we can circle through it if we have the time." Wishful thinking.

Our plan was to spend the night in the national park, head south and try to find the place where the Woodstock-like gathering was rumored to happen. No one we'd asked seemed to know exactly where that place was. I didn't know what all the mystery was about—maybe nothing was happening at all, or maybe the word was just starting to get around. We had missed New York's Woodstock and I really wanted to experience something like it. We would ask again as we got close to the supposed site, and if we missed it, well, a weekend toolin' around in the Rockies would be fun anyway.

The road became steeper as the foothills gave way to the mountains proper. When we pulled over at an overlook, we saw a posting for a ranch estate sale and flea market, not far off our route, and it had started just an hour before. We decided to check it out. We were poking around in the junk for about five minutes when Uriah spotted a unicycle. "Look at this, Alodie," he said. He pulled the unicycle from a pile of wagons, tricycles, and sleds. "I'm buying this."

"When are you ever going to ride the thing, Uriah?"

"I'll ride it around the neighborhood," he said. "What do you mean *when will I ride it?*" There was no further discussion. I didn't really want to discourage Uriah. It seem kind of silly to me, but his enthusiasm was persuasive. I noticed a vendor set up off to the side under a giant cottonwood tree. His trinkets were displayed on turned over cardboard boxes covered with old flour sacks. I walked over while Uriah was making a deal on his unicycle.

The man selling the trinkets was old, well, he might not have been very old, but he was scruffy. I imagined he was a real mountain man, a Grizzly Adams type, but as likely as not, he came from Denver. He had cut and bent old silverware into the most beautiful rings. I'm a sucker for jewelry and had to have one. I found one to fit my pinky, and except for unevenly chewed fingernails, I thought the ring made my hand look exquisite. We also bought an incomplete set of Currier and Ives plates and bowls—blue and while, painted with winter scenes.

The car was filling up. I couldn't help digging at Uriah a little. If he had taken the back seat out of the Nova as he intended so we could sleep in it, we would have to take all our new stuff out every night and put it back every morning after we camped. It was definitely better to have the back seat in place and set up a tent.

The time came when I thought we had spent enough money frivolously, and I became suddenly impatient to leave. Uriah paid for the unicycle and the dishes with a check. There would be a paycheck waiting when we got home. Hopefully, we'd get it in the bank before any checks written on vacation bounced. I hated fly-by-night handling of money. I was a skinflint and worried about our finances. Our attitude toward money was another way Uriah and I were different.

I was poor growing up. I was nine years old when my dad died, and afterwards, my stepmom worked two jobs to keep us in private, protestant Dutch schools. By the time I was eleven or twelve, I took in ironing and babysat my life away. In high school I worked every afternoon and on Saturdays at a dry cleaners. Almost all my money went to my mom. We all forked over our earnings—my brother, sister and me. I learned what was a necessity and what was extraneous. By nature, I'm not much of a consumer anyway, but my upbringing was reinforcing. I don't really know how to be a practical buyer. I always go for the cheapest brands. Uriah has taught me in the long run the cheap stuff won't last. It's just that when you only have a limited sum and you need something *now*, you get it at the lowest price and don't worry about tomorrow. The spoon ring purchase was out of character for me and I paid for it with guilt for a couple of days. But heck, we were on vacation. It was a souvenir.

Uriah's folks were reasonably well off. They never skimped. Uriah was taught by example that if he needed underwear he should go out and buy it. His family bought the good stuff and plenty of it so it would last. There was nothing stupider than having to run back to the store because you didn't get enough in the first place. Uriah's mother stocked the kitchen to overflowing. The candy cabinet was a chocolate lover's dream and the backroom refrigerator was bursting with soda. I ate my first steak at Uriah's house—half a steak. I couldn't eat a whole steak in one sitting. At my house we ate pot-roast.

The economic difference of our youth would show itself in petty arguments. I would freak out from time to time, for example, in the grocery store Uriah would want to buy candy orange slices when, with the same amount of money, we could buy four rolls of toilet paper.

Uriah did have hang-ups about money though—how it could be used by his father for leverage. Uriah resented his father giving him gifts and then attempting to control his lifestyle with the unspoken sentiment of "after all I've done for you." Our car was a good example of a gift with attachments. Uriah's parents bought us the brand new 1970 forest green Chevy Nova hatchback when we got married. Yeah, how cool is that? But I can still hear his father say, "Why don't you shave that beard. You look like an asshole." Really. That's what he once said. "With all I do for you," . . . and so on.

Uriah's father insisted on paying college tuition, although Uriah could have had a full scholarship. His dad wouldn't even read the scholarship application. Maybe he made too much money for Uriah to qualify anyway, but not even discussing it was one more way his father tried to hold the reins.

Funny though, how the car made our lives easier. Uriah wanted to take the back seat out almost as soon as we got it. We could use it as a mini-truck and sleep in the back when we went on road trips. I stalled him for the longest time, but pulling out the back seat was inevitable. When Uriah makes up his mind, well, it's just a matter of time. My veto power isn't eternal. Two years it held on the Nova's back seat which is a record for me. I added to my list of reasons Not to take the seat out as he added to his "better" reasons To take it out. I eventually gave in because of Uriah's determination and not for any *good* reason.

♭

We were off again with the unicycle clanking around in the trunk. We strolled the streets in the town of Estes Park for an hour, loaded up on groceries and entered the Falls River entrance of Rocky Mountain National Park at about four p.m. The first thing we did was try to find a campsite, but both the Aspen Glen and the Moraine campgrounds were full. We decided to go over Trail Ridge, watch the sunset, and then try a campground on the west side of the park. If we couldn't get in there, we'd hit the road and pull over somewhere. *Yes, Uriah, if you had taken the back seat out, we could just lie down in the back of the car.*

We hung out along Trail Ridge, got short on oxygen hiking around above the tree line, teased chipmunks and marmots and had a snowball fight. We cuddled and kissed in an alpine meadow among the mountain phlox and purple-tipped gentian as the sun went down between the summits of Mount Howard and Mount Richthofen. It was a good day. Lucky for us, there was one walk-in campsite still open at Timber Creek. We zipped our sleeping bags into one big one, made love, looked through the tent window at the stars, breathed in the rocky, piney air and slept reasonably well on the stony ground which we should have taken the time to brush off before we set up the tent.

Uriah, up early the next day as usual, was red-faced and blue-lipped when he woke me up. He had taken a dip in the creek still cold from melting snow. After packing up the tent, hiking back to the car and checking the map, we began our second day's journey. We followed Colorado Highway 34 south along the western edge of the national park until we came to a three-way crossroad near the town of Grandby. We had no clue which way to turn so decided to stop at a café in town for a late breakfast. Several backpacks and all sorts of camping gear lined the wall of the café. The place was crowded and buzzing with talk about "The Gathering." "The World Family Gathering," more specifically. Not long after our meal was served, a bouncy happy-go-lucky beach boy type asked if he could join us for lack of an empty seat.

"Sure, Man," Uriah said, holding out his hand. "I'm Uriah."

"Simon. Thanks," he said.

Because I was already sitting close to the window, Simon unhesitatingly slid in next to me. "I'm Alodie," I said.

"Hi, Alodie." Simon held out his hand. I had to wipe the egg yolk from my fingers. He gouged my new ring into my hand with a mighty grip. "Unusual name," he said.

"Yeah," I agreed. "Creative parents."

"People usually call me Sy," Simon qualified his previous introduction.

"Then Sy it is." I said.

"So, are you going to the big event?" Sy asked.

Uriah nodded, pushed a few hanging strands of hash-browns into his mouth, and said, "Hope to, if we can find it. You know where it's going to be?"

"Right here. Well close—ten miles or so east of town on the top of Table Mountain. Quite a hike up there I guess," Sy answered.

A frazzled waitress slopped a cup of coffee down in front of Sy. He quickly retracted into the sagging back of the booth. "People say there are parking areas outside of town and the organizers have arranged a shuttle to take folks the rest of the way into the national forest." Sy leaned past me to pull a pile of napkins out of a chrome container. "After that you're on your own."

"Are you still interested, Alodie?" Uriah asked. He looked like a dog dying to go for a walk.

"Yeah, why not? That was the plan."

"Care if I tag along with you guys?" Sy asked. "I hitched up here from Vegas and don't know anyone."

Uriah looked at me. I gave him a shrug and a nod. Sy seemed harmless.

♭

"Wow, a lot of people, huh?" Sy said as we pulled into a field set aside for parking. There was a steady migration walking to the northeast.

"What should we take with us?" I wondered. We didn't know if we were going to spend the night, or how easy it would be to come back to the car if we decided later to stay.

"No use carrying everything in now. Let's check it out first," Uriah said. Sy agreed.

We drifted into the stream of people converging onto the road leading into the mountains east of Grandby. The group was animated, talkative, excited. I thought the people were so cool. I secretly wanted to establish my identity as a Carol King, "Natural Woman," (except that I couldn't give up wearing just a little make-up.) Here were my comrades—the natural people. I always wanted to identify with a group, to be on the same wavelength with them, to be so close everything was understood without needing to search for commonalities. It was hard for me to get into any particular dogma or become a fanatic about anything. I'm a born skeptic. I never did connect with the religion of my family. I tried. Still, I longed to be a part of some cause, heart and soul. Sounds trite. At that moment though, the folks walking up the road were the ones I wished could be my tribe, my people.

They were peaceniks, cohesively gypsy-like, with flowing clothes and hair, lots of blue denim. The fragrance of patchouli, wafts of marijuana and the earthy smell of the mountains settled the group into a harmonious reverie. Word passed through the group that no "heavy" drugs were allowed, and the people were concerned. "Is marijuana a heavy drug?" they asked. The consensus quickly formed was, NO!

I was uncomfortable in spite of the ambiance—like as I do to know the plan and where I am. As small groups coalesced and separated, the same questions were asked over and over. It seemed only a very few knew what was happening.

"Where are we going?"

"Why did you come?"

"Isn't there supposed to be a shuttle up to the trail?"

You know it's a straight-up two-mile hike to the site on Table Mountain."

"What's supposed to happen up there?"

What do all these *Welcome Home* signs mean?"

"Were you stopped by any cops?"

"Barry says we're all reincarnated Hopi warriors or the Lost Tribes or something."

"Table Mountain is the center of the universe and July 4th is the Dawning of the Age of Aquarius."

"Who's Barry?"

"There'll be a ceremony up there to pray for World Peace."

"Isn't the camp on private land, like ten miles from the mountain?"

"Will there be any music?"

Finally, a flat-bed truck came barreling down the road, stirring up dust and splitting the group into two lines. With his head stretched through the window, the driver yelled, "Hop on. I'll be back in half an hour for more of you." A scribbled sign propped on the cab read:

> Rainbow Family of Living Light
> World Gathering
> The Welcome Home Shuttle

Uriah and Sy bellied onto the truck bed and then pulled me up. "Have you figured out what's going on?" Uriah asked.

"In bits and pieces," I answered. "Everything I've heard sounds pretty wacky."

Pulling himself more safely away from the truck's edge, Sy said, "I heard someone say there are flyers around which will tell us where to go and what the Rainbow Family is all about."

"Did you see anyone with a flyer, Alodie?" Uriah asked.

"I didn't see anyone," I said. "The blind leading the blind, it seems to me."

Uriah, forever optimistic, said, "When we get to the top of the mountain, someone's bound to know what's happening. And so what, Alodie, we're having fun aren't we?" I shrugged and smiled. I didn't want to wreck the mood, but I wasn't sure this was exactly fun. The truck stopped, the driver opened his door, stood on the running board and pointed over the cab. We jumped off the truck and stood in a cloud of dust until it cleared enough to see a barely worn trail beginning in the swale on the side of the road. We began our climb to the top of Table Mountain.

Uriah and Sy went ahead of me. I hiked with a couple of women from Santa Fe dressed in scarves and beads and braids. Part of the thrill on the climb was the camaraderie, meeting people from all over the country who longed for peace, thought Nixon was a paranoid liar, the war in Vietnam a mess and a revolution the only way out of the cultural and political quagmire. Every once and a while, I would catch up to Uriah and Sy, or they would slow down to wait for me. They were having a "profound" discussion according to Uriah about women's liberation, sexism, women as possessions, marriage, free love, etc. I stayed out of it though it made me nervous to hear Uriah tell a perfect stranger about his hypothesis. I don't know how detailed he actually was. Anyway, being "profound" was crucial to being hip. If you didn't dig into a subject to a painful depth, you were being superficial and bourgeois. We ground every subject into minutia.

I enjoyed studying the two of them, Uriah and Sy. From behind, they were somewhat alike, the same height at least. Sy was more slender. Uriah had a strong build—bulky arms and back—from physical work and gymnastics. His physique was inherited partly, his siblings all had muscular frames. Sy was slim and lithe. He didn't trudge, he pranced. He giggled and talked with his hands. Both men had wavy blond hair hanging loosely over their shoulders. Uriah had a reddish blond beard and a thick mustache. Sy was trying. Uriah looked and acted older. The difference between their ages, nineteen and twenty-one, seemed more than two years.

Uriah was idealistic and philosophical. He could also be melancholy and seriously determined. Sy seemed almost flippantly unconcerned, protecting himself, perhaps, from a previous hurt. He was light-hearted, probably reliable, but not necessarily answerable.

Sy told Uriah a bit about himself, but he only responded to direct questions. He grew up fatherless in Las Vegas. His mother worked at whatever job paid better than the last. His twin brother was a Buddhist. That's all we ever really got out of him. He was on the road to be on the road. What more was there? I think he was right. The whole point is to be on the road. Sy lived by the motto, "Be Here Now." And was good at it. I liked him from the start.

♭

After two or maybe three hours, we climbed over the rim of a crater. Stretching out in a wide circle, grasses and wildflowers swayed in the cool breeze. Exhausted, our Rainbow Family comrades were lying about, arms outstretched, appreciating the heavenly blue sky. We wandered a while and then lay down among the hundreds.

"If you mentally send heat up to a cloud, it will disappear—vaporize." A frail looking nymph of a woman pointed to an almost perfectly circular cloud. "Watch." We focused on the cloud. "I'll start on the east side," she said, "and work around the edges." After a few minutes, a few chuckles and other sounds suggested people thought the lady was zoning, but then the tone changed.

"Wow!"

"Far out!"

"Shit!"

"That was cool."

"Anyone can do it," the frail lady said. "Anyone."

Those who had brought camping gear set up their tents along the edges of the meadow. We just hung out not knowing what else to do. After an hour someone pointed. "Is that Barry?"

"Yeah, Barry's coming. He'll tell us what's going on."

Barry was a freak. Manic. On speed maybe. High on excitement at best.

"People, my people!" he shouted, jumping from one group to another. "Lost Tribes. You may spend the days on the Mountain, but we will not gather until Tuesday, the Fourth of July, when the moon is in the seventh house—The Dawning of the Age of Aquarius. We will pray for peace on that day. If you wish, come down the mountain and camp with us at Strawberry Lake."

Uriah sighed, disappointed. "What should we do, Alodie?" I was disappointed too, although the whole affair seemed rather crazy.

"Well, we can't stay," I said. "It's only Saturday. We can't leave Zea that long." I rarely felt Zea slowed us down or kept us from doing anything, but in this case, if we hadn't had the responsibility for a child, we could easily have roughed it until the Fourth of July and probably had the experience of a lifetime.

"Let's get off the mountain before it gets too late. What do you say, Hon?" Uriah grabbed my hand. There was no other choice.

Coming down Table Mountain we were the bearers of bad news for our reincarnated Hopi brothers and sisters who were still arriving. Sy came with us. He had to get his gear out of the car. The hike down the mountain was harder on our legs than going up. When we got to the county road, we waited for the shuttle with our backs against the hill and our feet against the road embankment. Uriah said to Sy, "We've got to leave, but you can come with us if you want to." I was hoping Sy would take Uriah up on the offer. I hated to part so soon with a newly made friend. I had taken a liking to Sy and it would be fun to have his company on the road. "We're heading back to Lyons tomorrow. We're staying with friends," Uriah added.

I asked with a hopeful smile, "Did you have any plans besides coming to the World Family Gathering?"

Sy smiled back, "No, not really. I'll probably head to Denver eventually. I stayed at a commune there for a couple of days on my way up here and met some cool folks. For now, I wouldn't mind traveling around with you, if neither of you mind."

I couldn't help reacting enthusiastically. "That's great!" I said, truly pleased.

The Flow of the River

The sun was close to the horizon by the time the Welcome Home shuttle returned to the base of Table Mountain and carried us back to the parking area. Because it was late, and we were tired, we dismissed the thought of going into town for food. We scrounged through our packs and found a few pieces of squished bread, a bruised apple, and some peanuts—enough to get us through the night. After eating and joking around about the weird day we had, Uriah and I set the pup tent up next to the car and Sy curled into the Nova's back seat.

The next day, Sunday, the three of us drove the back roads around the southern boundary of the national forest in no hurry to return to Flo and Maury's place. Twice, we chose lonely roads that dead-ended way up somewhere—making me anxious. Uriah thrilled on getting lost. "All we have to do is drive back down," he said. *Sure*, I thought. *If we don't get mixed up at the crossroads and lose our sense of direction.* Both dead ends were worth every bit of anxiety. The first, ended at a wild creek which bore through a granite canyon. White cedars and cinnamon ferns thrived in the spray. Uriah and I sat on a rock for a long time and watched Sy darting into the rainbows made by the mist. A second road ended at a glacier lake. The guys went skinny dipping. I would have gone too if it had just been Uriah and me. But I was modest in the company of others. I kept flashing on Julie Andrews spinning around in the grass somewhere in the Alps, but resisted the urge to sing, *The hills are alive with the sound of music.* How corny would that have been?

We did take one wrong fork in the road, but luckily didn't get too far before we noticed an abandoned pick-up we hadn't seen on the way up. Once back on mapped roads, I relaxed. Sy took a turn driving and turned the radio to full blast. I'll bet we heard the Eagles sing "Take It Easy" every fifteen minutes, and after half a day's drive we could sing every word, and did.

We talked over the radio about politics, a little. Sy was so upbeat, we weren't able to bemoan the state of the country under Nixon's rule for long. The Vietnam War was such a disaster. The draft was scary for both Uriah and Sy. They were both hoping to ride out their 1A status with high lottery numbers. Although not likely to be called, both had plans to avoid the draft. Sy was going to flee to Canada. Uriah was a conscientious objector and had all the paperwork ready for the draft board. Not from a tradition of conscientious objection, getting an exemption wasn't a sure thing, but his dad had vouched for him—and that was something. Uriah's dad had two brothers and a sister who had served in World War II. His youngest brother had died. Uriah's dad had stayed home to help his widowed mother run the family's vegetable farm. Uriah was surprised his dad vouched for him and probably had to stretch himself to agree. But then, who better would know Uriah was consistent in his beliefs against war than the guy who argued with him?

I was worried. What if the war escalated and higher lottery numbers were drawn? And what if Uriah's draft board didn't agree he was a C.O.? And what if I was left alone with a two-year-old daughter when I was only half finished with nursing school? How about it Uriah? But I didn't worry aloud because I didn't want Uriah to worry about me worrying. Uriah's faith in goodness was strong. My faith, shaken too much as a child, was structurally damaged.

That night we had to snuggle in close to stay warm. I was trying to sleep between Sy and Uriah, but Sy's back against my back was so distracting I couldn't help fantasizing about him long into the night.

We arrived in Lyons on Monday around noon. Zea was helping Flo make cookies at the kitchen table and pushed away the smother of hugs and kisses from Uriah and me. She was busy after all.

Flo seemed irritated with us for bringing Sy. I hadn't really thought about the intrusion. Flo and Maury's house seemed kind of a free-for-all, but apparently I was mistaken. I guess everyone should be able to control their own privacy. It seemed a given Sy would hang with us until the time seemed right to part. I may have had a fleeting uneasiness about bringing Sy to Flo's, but not enough to suggest we drop him off before we got to Lyons. When Uriah and Sy went back to the car to get two bags of groceries and a bottle of wine, Flo eased up a bit. Sy quickly started asking her questions about the chickens and soon they were laughing together like old friends. I was ridiculously jealous. Sy was smooth, but honest. He seemed a rare soul who all the women loved and men admired.

Cleopatra was gone. Flo and Maury both seemed relieved, although I may have projected my own relief onto their quietness. I was dying to know the nitty-gritty of what happened but refrained from prying. Flo had planned an after-supper party, figuring few of her friends would have to work the next day, the Fourth of July. They could party all night. Flo talked about the Dawning of the Age of Aquarius as an important alternative to the Fourth. After all, we wouldn't want to appear patriotic with all the crap happening in Washington. I don't know how serious she was, but it was as good a reason as any for a party.

And it was great. People had splurged and brought more than potato chips and dip. There were little salmon and cream cheese rollups. There was real red wine instead of Boone's Farm and Ripple, and people were drinking from glasses instead of passing the bottle. The pot was decent too. I didn't burn my lungs before I got high, and I didn't feel the least bit paranoid. The music was as expected for guitarists who had never played together and were bombed on their butts. I was surprised Uriah wasn't playing. He was engaged instead in a discussion with an exuberant Viking look-a like. A gorgeous guy whose name I didn't catch. The Viking waved a brown paperback in the air. I heard him, preacher-style, spouting the words, "reincarnation," "cataclysm," and "the white brotherhood," but I lost the drift of the conversation when I put Zea to bed.

I kept catching Sy's eyes from across the room. Then he came closer and starting bumping into my shoulder and I into his, until my *Should I?s* were overpowered by the tingling between my hips, and by my gasping little breaths, and by the heat rising up my neck. The question—*What am I doing?*—needled in and out of my awareness at first but did so less and less as the tension between us swelled and pulsed. By the time Sy hooked his little finger around mine and led me out the front door, I wasn't hearing any protests from other parts of me. No, by then I was out of my mind.

We walked along, fingers interlocked. I could feel Sy's heartbeat throbbing through his hand. Though no one was near enough to hear, Sy breathed into my ear, "I couldn't wait to get you alone outside. I couldn't keep my eyes off you. You are so … phenomenal."

The word "phenomenal" struck me funny and I jumped out of the moment to remember a psych patient I had cared for last semester. His pet word was "phenomenal." "Phenomenal outfit." "Phenomenal band." "It's phenomenal, Man." I hoped it meant more to Sy. Time seemed distorted and would have been distorted, I think, high or not. Dazed, I said something, but I don't remember what.

We were quiet for half a block or so, and then Sy threw up his arms and shouted, "I want to make love to you right this minute! Right here! I'll go mad if I can't. I'll go barbarian! I'll go Neanderthal!" I pulled him close to me by the back of his shirt and covered his mouth.

"You'll wake up the whole town," I warned.

"I don't care. I don't care. I'm going mad with love." Sy jumped and pounded his chest and spun in circles around me. Then, he grabbed my hands, spun me around a couple times, pulled me against him, took my head in both hands and said, "Alodie, I won't do anything, if it's not all right. Uriah said it was. Is it?"

I pulled away. Bringing Uriah into the moment jolted me. Had he and Sy discussed every possible detail? And was Uriah's permission necessary? Handy, yes, but not necessary. "Uriah said it was all right?" I asked.

"He did," Sy said.

I was irked. Wasn't I my own person? Couldn't I, shouldn't I make this decision myself? It was personal for God's sake. It seemed suddenly premeditated, as if the two of them schemed up the situation. "Did the two of you plan this?" I asked.

"No, Alodie. Of course not," Sy said. "I promise. We just talked about Uriah's hypothesis. You know, about loving more than one person. Making it with you didn't even come up."

"But maybe that discussion prompted you to get interested," I argued, but in a teasing way. I realized I didn't care all that much whether Uriah and Sy had discussed the hypothesis. The experiment should be more than talk and it seemed the testing was just about to begin.

Sy caught the change in my tone. "I was having major fantasies about you way before Uriah and I talked about much of anything."

"Oh really? And the trigger of your fantasies was …?"

"A pretty woman with a cool name, wiping egg yolk off her fingers to shake my hand."

"You're too easy, Sy."

"You're not mad anymore, Alodie? Don't be mad. I just really want this to be okay."

I looked into Sy's eyes. He was taking a risk getting involved in our experiment. I suppose he deserved some assurance Uriah wouldn't turn on him later. But right then, I needed to get Uriah out of my head. "Sy, I'm the only one here, and it's all right with me."

We kissed, shyly at first, then more and more fiercely. Lips and teeth and tongues and hands moved hard and desperately. We made our way, entangled and stumbling to the edge of the river. On a grassy sloping bank, we sank down on our knees. The pace slowed to the flow of the river, to the breeze in the cottonwoods. Fingers and tongues searched around curves, into warm hollows, caverns and niches, and would stay here or there when a sigh or a gasp or a head thrown back would be a clue to linger. And finally, after heaven had been reached from touch alone, to the rhythm of the crickets, we took each other in.

For quiet minutes we lay chewing on grass, watching the moon set behind the foothills, avoiding each other's touch long enough so we could start again with our lovemaking. Hours later, bungalows, telephone poles, and the arches of treetops took shape against the eastern sky. Morning was near. After many false starts, hating for the night to end, we stood. Wanting to be closer than was physically possible, Sy with his arm around my shoulder, and I with my arm around his waist, walked back to the house.

Stepping gingerly over last night's partiers, we found our way through the living room. I bumped into Flo and Maury's open bedroom door, and Flo whispered to me, "Have fun, Alodie?" God, she never missed a thing. I washed up a bit and gave Sy a parting kiss as he eased into a vacant recliner.

I tried to sneak into bed beside Uriah, but he never slept deeply as dawn neared and he asked, "Have you been with Sy?"

"Yes," I answered. Uriah palmed back my hair and kissed my forehead. I didn't touch him—I couldn't. But I smiled, closed my eyes and fell into my dreams.

Late in the morning, the hung-over household groaned its way back to life. I woke up scratching the backs of my knees; my butt itched like crazy too. What the hell? I pulled the curtain aside at the sound of laughter outside to see Uriah on the unicycle with Flo trying to hold him up, one hand on his butt the other hooked into the hammer loop of his pants. She was so blatant with her come-ons. I was probably misinterpreting. But she knew what had gone on between Sy and me and she might as well take advantage of the situation. Why wouldn't she think Uriah was fair game? But I wasn't really worried about Flo's flirting. Uriah wasn't attracted to her. He had told me that before. He didn't care for indelicate outspoken women and Flo was certainly that. Zea was throwing handfuls of rocks from the driveway onto the sidewalk. Her diapers were sagging around her knees and her hair was still flattened and fuzzed from sleep.

I rolled onto my back and quivered with visions of the night before. I pulled Uriah's pillow over my face and screamed into it "Shit! Shit. Shit. Shit!" I could only guess what the day was going to bring—consequences. But what kind? Would the experience have been worth it? God, I wanted to be with Sy again. I wondered how Uriah was feeling. I hoped he was as okay as he seemed. How was I going to handle the two of them together? How would they act with each other?

I tormented myself with worry for a while longer until my itching backside drove me to the shower. The recliner was empty. I could hear Sy joking with Maury in the kitchen. As I dried myself off, I looked at my skin. It was streaked with pink lines. I was allergic to all kinds of detergents, maybe it was the sheets. There was a knock at the bathroom door.

"Alodie, you in there?" It was Uriah.

"Yeah, I'll be right out," I said.

"Maury's got breakfast on the table. Hon, can I come in a minute?"

I hesitated, because I didn't know how to face Uriah. I wasn't feeling guilty exactly, just weird—sad somehow. Uriah had never touched me like Sy had touched me, as if I were a sapphire held carefully in his hand—a treasure he turned over and over, noticing every cut, every sparkle. Making love was different with Uriah. Maybe it had just become more routine; it wasn't new or exciting anymore. I couldn't believe I was comparing the two of them, how awful. Relationships aren't just about the quality of lovemaking. Even so, before Sy I didn't have a problem, now I did. I loved Uriah for a mile-long list of qualities. The man could talk to me for goodness sake! But still it was going to be hard to go back to our usual way of loving each other. I quickly got dressed.

"Lodie, what are you doing in there?"

"Sorry. Sure, come in."

Uriah opened the door a crack so as not to expose me to the living room and squeezed into the tiny bathroom with me. "So?" he asked, an unexpected grin on his face. I couldn't help grinning back.

"What?!" I said. He seemed like a mother trying to get the scoop from her daughter after a first date.

"Well, how was it?" he asked.

105

"I'm not telling you. Get out of here." I shoved him gently against the door.

"Are we okay, Alodie? You still love me?"

"Of course I still love you, silly." I kissed Uriah's cheek. "You going to be okay with Sy?" I asked.

"I'll be fine," he answered. "I'm glad this thing finally happened—the first test of our hypothesis. True so far?"

"You told Sy about our hypothesis, didn't you?"

"Well, yeah. We spent a lot of time together climbing up that mountain. So, is it?" he repeated.

"Is what?"

"Our hypothesis. Is it true so far?"

"So far. Yes … No … I'm not sure," I said. "I can love Sy without loving you any less. But I love him differently, and I don't know what that will mean. We'll talk about it sometime soon." We held each other tightly for a minute before Maury gave the second call for breakfast.

A Fair Share

Uriah squeezed himself out of the bathroom. I untangled my hair, hung the towel perfectly on the rack, took my pajamas to the bedroom and fiddled around, procrastinating my entry into the kitchen. Finally, after I had stalled long enough to be conspicuous, I held my breath as I tried to slide unnoticed onto an empty chair at the table. There were "good mornings" all around, and then the conversation went on as if no one knew about last night or didn't really care one way or the other. Flo wasn't letting on, which I appreciated for Uriah' sake. Still, I had trouble looking anyone in the eyes and focused instead on my omelet. Sy and Uriah began a theatrical telling of the hike up Table Mountain and I relaxed, almost forgetting the new complexity of their relationship.

Eventually, because I couldn't help myself, I looked smack at Sy and he sent back a wink. I thought I'd die. That one little wink sent me into a frenzy. I wanted to grab the boy and drag him—anywhere. I took a couple of quick breaths, then a long one, and hoped no one noticed the flush rising to my face. Maury had put enough jalapeno peppers in the omelet to save me if I needed a reason for blushing.

After the straggling overnighter's left the house, plans were made for the day—the Fourth of July. Flo, Maury, Uriah, Zea and I were going to picnic at Maury's favorite meadow in the mountains. Sy declined. He was going to check out an old van the Viking wanted to buy. I was disappointed, but thought it was wise on Sy's part.

The drive into the mountains was pleasant, except that my skin was crawling. A series of rashy looking lines had erupted behind both of my knees. My shoulders and butt were unbearable. Poison ivy, no doubt. Last night I was too distracted to consider poison ivy. By the feel of my skin, I'd need several bottles of calamine lotion before the worst was over. I sat in the middle of the back seat. Uriah held my hand and I nuzzled my nose into his beard. I loved the smell of his skin. I tried not to be overly affectionate. The line between reassurance and overcompensating was blurry. I hated how I was calculating my every move. Zea thrust her hand in and out of the open window to test the strength of the wind. Flo was pressed in close to Maury on the front seat. She was *definitely* overcompensating.

Maury was acting like nothing had happened. I had gained enough insight into the dynamics of three-some-ness to know "out of sight, out of mind" wasn't possible. And why *did* Sasha Leone leave? Maury had moped around. Cleopatra had pouted. And, Flo had been what? Patient? Resigned? Maury's nonchalance was fake. The turbulence of a messy relationship doesn't instantly calm. More than likely, Maury was slicing his consciousness into competing voices, and at the moment, the voice of denial was merrily chatting about a farm he'd one day own. Internal schizophrenia. I recognized the symptoms.

Maury's meadow was expansive and yet safely held by the surrounding mountains. We combed through waist high grass and fondled the ripening fuzzy plumes. Zea peek-a-booed through waves of bear grass and bluestem. She toed the icy stream which was brushed with the violet of lupine, the yellow and white of toadflax and the scarlet of paintbrush.

No one talked much. Gradually, Maury and Flo went on ahead. Uriah and I lagged behind with Zea. We discussed the plan for the rest of the trip. A couple of guys Uriah knew from school were at a music camp in Aspen. Offhandedly, they had invited us to visit. Uriah, always literal, decided to take them up on their offer. Sy would come with us, and then we'd drop him off in Denver when we started home—like we promised.

I assumed Uriah knew my relationship with Sy wasn't over. I had taken but a nibble of what I wanted from Sy. And what did I want? More of him. More of what happened last night. "Uriah," I asked, "Are you still open to the experiment?"

With endearing dumbfoundedness, he said, "Well, sure. Aren't you?"

"I think so," I said. "It's confusing. I'll see how it goes." I wasn't being honest. There was more to the sentence. What I was thinking was, *I'll see how it goes AFTER I spend as much time with Sy as I can and until I HAVE to leave.* I squeezed Uriah's hand and kissed his neck. "I love you, Hon," I whispered. No doubt about that. My confusion was how to manage both of them, Uriah and Sy, and give Uriah a fair share of my thoughts.

The picnic basket was filled with cashews, gigantic figs, pomegranates, tofu, sprouts and pita. We munched languorously. Light darted randomly across the split log table sieved through a canopy of pine needles. The wind whizzed in the branches overhead. Zea squinted and blindly pointed to the tops of the ponderosa pines. "Look-a, look-a, Mum." I grabbed Zea and hugged her until she squirmed. God, how I loved her.

As she put the picnic basket in the trunk, Flo asked, "Does anyone want to drive into Boulder or Longmont to see fireworks tonight?" Three apathetic groans were the noncommittal response.

"I was planning to do some laundry and get our packs organized," I said. But I was also hoping to escape with Sy for a little while.

Flo wouldn't drop the fireworks idea and said, "You can't deny Zea a chance to see fireworks. She's two years old, she'll love it. Come on you poops."

"She'd be just as happy with a couple of sparklers," Uriah said. "It will be pretty late, and the noise might scare her. We can pick up sparklers on our way home."

Flo wasn't satisfied. "Maybe Sy and the Viking will go with me. Let me take Zea. Come on."

"What do you think, Uriah?" I asked.

"Sure, why not."

I looked at Zea who had gone quiet. "She's asleep," I said. "She'll be fine tonight if we can keep her from waking up for a while."

When we got back to the house, Uriah eased Zea from the car and carried her up the front porch steps. The beads in the doorway caught on Zea's dangling arm and she stirred just a little. When laid on the bed, she rolled over on her tummy, put her butt in the air, click-clicked on her pacifier and returned to a sound sleep.

After starting a load of clothes, I looked around nonchalantly for Sy. I asked Maury, and then Uriah and Flo if they had seen him. I covered my obsession by saying he might want some of his clothes washed. Sy and the Viking weren't back yet, apparently. I sat with Uriah and Flo under the grape arbor for a few minutes and then said, "I'm going for a walk. I won't be gone more than half an hour. Could you hang the laundry when it's done, Uriah?" I had given Uriah a task on purpose because I didn't want a companion. I wanted to be alone for a while to quiet the chatter in my head.

"It's kind of late, isn't it?" Uriah looked at the sky to judge the time.

"We'll have to let it hang overnight." I said.

The white clapboard houses, the heaved and broken sidewalks, the spread of roses climbing on cracked and bent fences barely touched my consciousness. Retracing the path Sy and I had taken the night before, I replayed our lovemaking over and over in slow motion. Then, I moved forward in time creating a fantasy in which Uriah and Zea went home leaving me behind to drift around in the mountains with Sy until either my want of him dissolved or I desperately missed Uriah and Zea. My microbiology class kept knocking me back into reality. I had to finish and pass my summer classes to graduate next June. There was no alternative. Sy would disappear in three more days. Maybe he had disappeared already.

I kicked the dirt, bent to release a stone from my sandal, slapped at a horsefly and wished for Sy. *Get over it, Alodie,* I thought. *Fun, that's all it was—like eating a piece of German chocolate cake. Buck up. Get over it!* I walked a few more blocks to the edge of town where the road ran parallel to the river. *We must have been right along here*, I thought.

The evening quiet caught my attention but there was another sound—a rustle. I closed my eyes to listen but heard only the hum of the river. I looked for a place where the weeds were compressed. There. I knew it. Red stems, three leaves, in the grass and clinging to cottonwoods—poison ivy. I walked a few more yards, when I was snared around the waist and flung in a full circle. My sandals flew off, my wrap-around skirt separated, my teeth gouged my tongue and I fell backwards onto Sy.

"Sy! Darn it! You scared the piss out of me! Where did you come from?" I asked. He slapped his hand over my mouth and rolled us over as a unit. He brushed a leaf off my forehead. He put a shushing finger to his lips. And, as Sy dug his arm between the earth and the small of my back I rose to his lift—bone against bone.

"Sy, we've got to get up. We can't stay here." I fought his strong hold on me, stood, and reached out to pull him up. "Look." I waved my hand across the bank.

"What?" he asked. He seemed irritated by the interruption.

"Poison ivy."

"Oh, wow, and a lot of it. I'm not allergic to it—not very. I've only had it once," he said.

"Well, look at this." I lifted my skirt to show him the backs of my knees.

Sy cringed, "Ouch."

"A bit of imagination and you'll know where else I've got it."

Sy sucked in a breath. "Ooooh." He took my hand. "Come on," he said. "I want to show you something."

"What?"

"Just come on."

"How did you manage to get behind that cottonwood tree without me seeing you?" I asked.

"Jake lives around the curve up there—see where the road splits off from the river?"

"Who's Jake?"

"You know, the guy you called "The Viking" last night. I was walking back to Flo and Maury's when I saw you coming this way. I ducked behind the tree before you saw me. Scared you, huh?"

"Yes, you scared me."

He dropped my hand, pulled up my hair and kissed my neck. "You're kind of cute when you're mad."

"Oh yeah?"

"Yeah," Sy whispered in my ear. "Your freckles jump off your face."

I couldn't think of what to say to that, I just shook my head and smiled.

We left the road and followed a path along the bank. Around the next bend, the incline sharpened and the river narrowed. The restive water fractured against the rocks. We inched our way over a rotting bridge and along a sliver of a ledge into a coulee. Hidden from the drying heat of the sun, a delicate stream poured over a shelf thirty feet above. Star moss cushioned the stony walls and maiden hair ferns danced in the spray. Sy stripped down to his skivvies and spiraled through a pool lined with water cress and into the obsidian water at the base of the falls.

"How did you find this place?" I called across the water.

"Jake took me here this afternoon." I watched Sy dive and surface while I side-stepped my way around the pool. I reached my hand into the downpour. Warmer than expected, I took another step, and for thoughtless moments let the falls smooth over me. Then, I saw Sy's rippling image in front of me through the wall of water.

"You're all wet," he said, and traced a figure eight around the contour of my breasts. He untied the knotted tails of my blouse.

"No, Sy." I restrained his hands, kissed him and turned away.

"What's up?" he asked.

"Nothing."

"You feeling uneasy?

"Not really, just seems like Uriah should be here. He'd like this place."

Sy cupped my face with cool palms. "Okay," he said.

"Thanks, Sy." I fell into the well of his indigo eyes and felt surrounded by him. "Thanks for understanding. We better get back. I don't want Uriah to worry."

As Sy and I turned the last corner toward Flo's, we saw Uriah coming toward us on his unicycle. "Go, Uriah!" I shouted, just as he sideswiped a fence and fell forward. Uriah dropped the unicycle and walked to meet us.

"You're all wet, Alodie," he said.

"Yeah. On my walk, I met Sy coming back from the Viking's house. He showed me the most beautiful little waterfall on the other side of the river. You would have liked it."

"You were gone a long time," Uriah said.

"Was I?" I hoped Sy would help me out, but he just shrugged. "I'm sorry, Hon. I didn't have a watch."

"Flo and Maury took Zea to Longmont. They're going to meet some friends and see the fireworks. We could've gone along." Uriah said.

"I wasn't in a great hurry to get back because you didn't seem interested in going with Flo," I said.

"Plans change, Alodie. I stayed behind because I didn't want you to wonder what happened." There was more to Uriah's reason for staying behind, but he wasn't going to admit it.

"You could have left me a note," I said.

"Right!" he snapped. When Uriah was upset, he chopped at his words, but didn't say what was on his mind. Often, he didn't know exactly what he felt until I quizzed him. He had every right to be annoyed with me, but I didn't want to discuss it in front of Sy, so we walked to the house in silence.

Sy, instinctively, if not purposefully, tried to ease the tension by telling us about the crazy old fool who tried to sell the Viking a motor-less van. The guy had been using the van as a cage for his pet snakes.

After settling on the front porch, Uriah and Sy started talking about the principles of riding a unicycle. Not interested, I went to hang my skirt and blouse on the line in the backyard. The laundry was still in the washing machine. I decided not to complain to Uriah and hung it myself. I pinned the last pair of boxer shorts to the clothesline and cut through the house to the front porch. "What do we do about supper?" I asked.

"I'm dying for some meat," Sy said, rubbing his stomach.

"Maybe we can find something open in Longmont," I said. "But it is the Fourth of July."

"Something will be open." Uriah stood up. "Maybe we'll run into Flo and Maury." Uriah left a note on the kitchen table and we took off.

The only restaurant we could find was a dive. Cigarette smoke hung in layers and the smell of rancid grease was all but gagging. Surprisingly, the food was good, home-cooked and fresh. We gave up the long-shot notion of trying to find Maury and Flo and drove back to Lyons. I went to bed around nine o'clock. I was beat. A couple hours later, I heard Uriah tuck Zea into her makeshift bed of blankets piled in the corner, and then he climbed in with me. I felt bad for him, so I did my best to love him up and keep my thoughts on task.

Aspen

The next morning I was awakened by Flo's voice outside the bedroom window. "I can't believe you did this, Uriah," she was clearly angry.

"It's fine, Flo. Look. I left as many grapes as I could. Doesn't it look better? Next year it will have even more grapes."

"But Uriah, it's not our grapevine."

Uriah rationalized, "The landlord will be happy you're taking care of the place."

"Maybe, if the thing lives," Flo said. "You shouldn't prune a grapevine in the middle of the summer." And as an aside, she mumbled. "So much for shade."

Uriah wouldn't give in to the idea he had made a mistake. "If you give it plenty of water," he explained, "the vine will be just fine."

I couldn't believe it ... yes, I could ... Uriah had pruned the grape vine. He was so sure he was right all the time. He could be so thick. He just failed to factor in the concerns of others. There was no telling him anything once he made up his mind. I got up to smooth

113

things over—try to pick up the pieces of Uriah's error, but by the time I used the bathroom and went into the yard, Uriah and Flo were hugging. I stayed out of it, although it took effort not to apologize for Uriah, just to make sure everything was cool.

The wash was damp from a heavy dew, so we hung around until eleven o'clock. We packed the Nova and gathered around the car.

"I'm sorry we didn't get to say goodbye to Maury. Hug him for us, will you, Flo?" I asked.

"Sure I will." Flo picked up Zea. "Bye little Zea girl." With tears in her eyes, Flo said "I'd like to be back in Chicago by Christmas, if Maury will go for it."

"You're serious?" Uriah asked. "You want to come back?"

"Well yeah, for a while—until all of our friends start to leave. What do we have out here anyway?"

"It would be great to have you back," I said. "The neighborhood's not the same without you."

"Thanks for everything, Flo." Sy said.

"You be good, Sweetie," Flo pinched Sy's cheek.

A couple more rounds of hugs and goodbyes and we were on our way to Aspen.

♪

There was no direct way to get from Lyons to Aspen. I studied the map and chose a route south to the interstate. Uriah, preferring the back roads, argued with me for a few minutes, but there just wasn't a good alternative this time. I sat in the back seat with Zea. She got cranky and we had to stop often along a road that snarled through miles and miles of foothills. I read *Hop on Pop* three times before Zea fell asleep. After a short distance on the interstate, we again found ourselves snaking through the mountains. This time, with Zea asleep, we could relax and enjoy the scenery.

It was probably a mistake to let Zea sleep for the rest of the trip. When we arrived in Aspen at seven o'clock, she was a spitfire and unlikely to fall asleep until late. Uriah inquired about the music camp and his friends from Northwestern at the main lobby of one of the hotels. The desk clerk knew nothing about a music camp. We searched a telephone book for hotel listings and after a few phone calls and a wild goose chase around town we found the lodge where his friends were staying. They weren't in their rooms when we arrived and it was getting late, so Sy decided he would try to find a place for us to stay. Camping in town would be difficult and we didn't want to drive any more to find a campground or even a place to pull over. After an hour, which seemed endlessly longer to me, Sy returned.

"There's a way to sneak into the back of the lodge where your friends are staying," he said. Sy was excited. He bobbed and weaved like Muhammed Ali. "There's a storage room with a couple of beds in it."

"Great," Uriah said. He picked Zea up and headed toward the car.

I wasn't so sure about this plan. "Sy, how did you find out about this room?" I asked.

"I went to the bar downstairs and saw a couple of girls in hotel uniforms. They were having a beer after work. I got chummy and before long had them feeling sorry for me. They showed me the room and said they'd leave it open for us. There's a service entrance in the back that's always left open."

"So what if we get caught?" I asked.

"Alodie, what are they going to do to us if they find us. Kick us out. So what?" Uriah was getting impatient with me, but I still resisted.

"Arrest us for trespassing maybe," I replied with the same sarcastic tone Uriah had used on me.

"Nah. They won't, Alodie," said Sy, "We'll give then a sob story about arriving in town late, hotels all booked, and Zea needing a place to sleep—and then we'll hightail it."

I caved, "Okay, let's do it."

Sy took Zea and me to the room and then went back to the car to help Uriah with the sleeping bags. I had all I could do to keep Zea quiet, but the room was down the hall from the occupied rooms so our only concern was the night staff, but they were unlikely to wander down to our end of the building in the middle of the night. With a sideways glance, I noticed Zea rubbing her eyes.

I snuggled her close and sang her favorite lullaby over and over until I was as close to sleep as she was.

Uriah fell across a bed behind a stash of broken chairs. Sy took off to check out the action around town. Still in my clothes, I rolled over on the bare mattress. Uriah whispered to me. "Alodie. Come over here, Babe." I thought about feigning sleep, but no. Uriah and I needed to get back to normal. I was feeling uneasy—not about what *was* happening between us—but what *might* happen. I went to him. His hands were strong. I felt safe with him. I kissed the hollow at the base of his neck. I kissed all two of his chest hairs. I kissed his belly button. I ravished every inch of him. When I was through, I kissed his lips. "You know, Uriah," I said, "I'll never love you less."

"I'm sorry I got mad at you yesterday about staying so long on your walk," he said. I put a finger to his lips, but I didn't answer.

Out of a dream, I heard my name. "Alodie?" I rolled over and felt across the bed for Uriah. He wasn't there. "Alodie, are you awake?"

I moaned, "What?"

"It's Sy. I want to sleep with you."

"Where's Uriah?" I asked, my eyes still closed.

"He couldn't sleep, I guess. He just left."

"What time is it?"

"Four o'clock."

"Oh," I yawned, "Uriah wakes up really early sometimes." I drifted off for a second.

"Alodie, let me sleep with you." I slid over in the bed and felt Sy's hand slip through my thighs.

Troubled in Mind

"Alodie. Wake up," Uriah jiggled me. I panicked, but held perfectly still. Shit. Sy and I fell asleep together. I didn't mean for Uriah to come back and find the two of us in bed—majorly inconsiderate. Not daring to look, I slid my arm across the bed. Sy was gone. Thank goodness he was more careful than I was.

I yawned and stretched. "Ouch! Shit! I'm stuck to the bed."

"What?" Uriah asked.

"Darn poison ivy. It must have broken open and dried during the night." I gradually ripped the back of my knees, my tailbone and my right shoulder from the mattress. I stood up and twisted around to check my legs. "Oh, God. Would you look at this?"

Uriah sucked in his breath, "Oh man, Alodie." We heard banging in the hall, Uriah looked at the door. "We better get out of here before everyone wakes up and the maids start cleaning."

"What time is it, Uriah? It must be early."

"Six-thirty or so."

"Oh, Hon. Why so early?"

"Come on, Alodie. I've been up for a couple of hours already."

"Let's go back to bed for an hour or so." I laid back down. "No one will bother us. The room's abandoned."

"No, come on." Uriah took my hands and pulled me back up.

"Okay, okay."

Hearing us, Sy stirred on the other bed. "Hey, guys. How are my favorite married people this morning? *Was he being sarcastic?* I thought. I looked at his face. *No, he was just being sweet.*

Uriah smiled. "We're doing just fine except I can't get Alodie out of bed."

"I'm up, I'm up," I said. We gathered our belongings and Uriah carried Zea, still asleep, a block and a half to the car.

"You know, we might as well eat now before the restaurant starts to fill up. What do you think?" Uriah asked. "There's a café around the next corner. After breakfast we can see if my friends are up and hang with them for a while—maybe hear some music."

"Sure," Sy said, and excused himself to take a leak.

I wondered if going out to eat again was a good idea. "How are we doing for money, Uriah?"

"Pretty well. We'll be fine. Don't worry about it." I had to trust him because I didn't have charge of the money on this trip. By my calculations, we were probably down to about $75 and would need all of it to get home.

Sy caught up to us and as we entered the café Uriah held Zea out to Sy. "Sy, here, take Zea will you? I want to catch that guy who's leaving."

I hadn't noticed any one in particular, so I quickly turned around. Through the glass door I saw a lanky teenager—maybe sixteen—wearing denim painter's pants and a white t-shirt. I followed Sy to a booth. "Who was that?" Sy asked.

"Beats me."

Zea wiggled and stretched, opened her eyes, reached up and touched the tip of Sy's nose. "Good morning, Zea," he said. Zea squirmed suddenly, checking for Uriah or me.

"I'm right here, Sweetie," I said. Zea calmed right down and turned toward the window.

"Look-a-look-a, peep, peep," she said, and pointed to a sparrow jumping along the top of a bicycle rack.

"Pretty bird, huh?" Sy asked Zea. "Can you say, pretty bird?"

"Puddy bud," Zea replied. Sy tickled Zea under her chin. She giggled and pulled away to stand on the seat and watch the sparrow.

Sy looked at me. "I'm going to miss you, Alodie." He reached over the table. I reached back. He turned my wedding band around and around. "I hope I can be like you and Uriah if I ever get married. But shit, I really wish you weren't attached." I couldn't respond, I mean, what could I have said? I didn't wish I wasn't married, but I sure did want to stay with Sy. I just stared him in the eyes and bit my lip.

A greasy haired waitress slammed her coffeepot on the table and glared at us with bulging fisheyes through her magnifying lenses. "You ready" she barked.

"Absolutely," Sy saluted and we ordered immediately.

I reached again across the table, but Sy didn't reach back. Instead, he rubbed my leg with his. I said, "Wish we didn't have to go to Denver today. I wish I could spend another day with you." Sy motioned to the door with is eyes.

"Sorry," Uriah said as he sat down.

"I ordered for you," I said to Uriah. "The waitress was a bit demanding. Two eggs and hash browns okay?"

"Sure."

"Who was that guy?" I asked.

Uriah explained. "I met him this morning on my walk. He was hanging out on the street waiting for the café to open. His name's Ezra. He's an Amish kid. He left his community this spring."

Addressing Sy, I said, "Uriah's fascinated with the Amish. I think if he had insisted on staying religious, we might have become Amish."

"No way," Sy said.

"Seriously," I continued. "Uriah's a conscientious objector and really digs the whole 'small is beautiful' bit. It's not hard to picture Uriah out in a field trying to get a couple of horses to drag a plow through the mud. You think?"

"Alodie, stop." Uriah was serious. "I was telling you about this guy. We got talking and he told me his construction crew could really use some help."

"How did you know he was Amish?" I asked as an afterthought.

"It came up during the conversation. Alodie, will you just listen?" The snap in Uriah's tone made me realize I was being sarcastic.

"Sorry."

Uriah continued, "I thought more about what Ezra had said on my way back to the lodge. Wouldn't a job out here be a cool possibility for next summer? When I saw Ezra just now, I wanted to get more information. We could come out here after you graduate."

"Maybe," I shrugged. Another one of Uriah's schemes, but this one sounded practical. I wasn't going to make a decision on the spot, though. "We'll have to think about it."

"I didn't expect you to agree this minute," Uriah raised his voice. I didn't think what I said should have provoked a reaction like that and I stuck my tongue out at him.

"You're being a creep, Uriah." I didn't really mean to say that, but Uriah was bugging me.

Sy eased the tension by carrying on the conversation about working in Aspen. I ate the rest of my breakfast in silence.

We met Uriah's so called "friends" at the lodge, but they gave us the brush off. They had classes all morning and then rehearsals. The community concert wouldn't be until the end of the week. *Well,*

119

EXCUSE us. The little snots. I thought. But Uriah hardly knew these people. What was he expecting? Trying not to lay a trip on him, I just asked instead, "Now what?"

"To Denver, I guess," Uriah said.

"To Denver," Sy agreed, walking between Uriah and me, he put his arms around our shoulders.

Sy took a turn driving with Uriah in the front seat. I was in the back again with Zea. I checked the map.

"Are we in any kind of hurry?" I asked. "There isn't a quick way to get across the mountains without backtracking the way we came. That means Interstate 70 most of the way to Denver." I flattened the seam of the road atlas to look more closely. "There is a scenic route that goes south a bit before it picks up Route 285 to Denver. Let's see ... there's a reservoir a little off the route, but not too far. It might be fun to stop there for a swim. What do you two think?"

"We're not in any hurry," Uriah said. "Are you, Sy?"

"Not at all. Let's do it."

Uriah and Sy talked and laughed. Nothing heavy, just good-natured banter. This whole trip was amazing. How could these two guys be getting along like this? Uriah was tense though, and he was taking it out on me, which was fair I guess, although I never would have been in this position if it wasn't for our cockamamie hypothesis. I couldn't catch everything the guys were saying because the back speaker of the radio was right behind my head. Twice, I asked Uriah to turn it down—which he did, but not enough to improve my ability to hear what he and Sy were talking about. The first time "Take It Easy" played, we all sang along.

The second time it played, I begged Uriah to change the station. The song was just too fitting and I found it depressing. I had a world of trouble of my own on my mind.

All I did was daydream about Sy. I couldn't help myself anymore. Sitting kitty-corner from him in the back seat, I could watch his profile, his expressions. I was obsessed with him and getting crazier by the minute knowing it was going to be over by that evening or at the latest the next morning. Over.

In a pipsqueak town called Johnson Village, we picked up a few groceries and made it to the Antero Reservoir around noon. Access was difficult and we drove onto several roads barricaded just shy of the water. Eventually, we found the public access road and were glad we persisted. Apparently, after the reservoir was built and the land flooded, the public access area was revamped—planted with a variety of pines, firs and spruce in groves. The native plants were reintroduced in arboretum orderliness.

Zea was restless. Uriah took her to the water's edge to play while Sy and I dug out the gear and set up the pup tent. We had decided not to continue on to Denver. The distance was too far and Zea had tired of driving. We would have arrived in Denver well after dark and then would have to figure out sleeping arrangements. Sy suggested we camp again, and Uriah agreed. I was secretly relieved we would have a few more hours with Sy but fretted over who was going to sleep with whom. Sy interrupted my mental chatter with talk about where he'd go first if he could just up and go anywhere in the world tomorrow. He asked where I would go, but I hadn't thought about it much, unlike Uriah who was always dreaming about traveling the world.

The cheese we bought at the Johnson Village grocery was moldy. Sy rescued what he could with his pocketknife and I threw the scraps to the stellar jays. The crackers were stale and the apples were mushy, but the peanuts were good. We wrapped the sandwiches in a brown paper bag and began hiking down the path to the reservoir's edge. Sy danced around me in circles. "Alodie, Alodie, my favorite coyote."

"Coyote?" I laughed.

"It rhymes doesn't it? You try thinking of a word that rhymes with Alodie."

"Me-LO-dy, but that's dumb."

"How about bloaty?" Sy snorted.

"Thanks a lot."

"Roadie. Doty …" I said.

"I've got one," Sy gleamed, "Truman Capote."

"I'm your favorite Truman Capote?"

"Come on Alodie. Help me out here. I'm on a roll."

"I'm at the bottom of my rhyming barrel, Sy."

"Cody, Brodie, Don Quixote."

"Brilliant. You're a rhyming genius, Sy." He swung me around by the waist and took off at a run into the woods. "Where you going?" No answer—to pee I supposed. Sy didn't come right back. I kept walking. After a few minutes, I began to wonder what the heck Sy was up to. I kept looking back, but there was no sign of him. Out of the corner of my eye I saw movement. I looked into the trees but saw nothing. I went a few more paces, then saw another flicker in the tress. I bristled with the image of a cougar jumping out at me. Maybe some critter attacked Sy. "Right, Alodie, a cougar," I said aloud. But where was he? Then, I heard an eerie sound in the woods—kind of a wailing sound. It had to have been a bird, a hawk maybe. I tried to spot the bird among the branches, but the needles were so dense I couldn't find the source of the sound. Then, I saw movement again. Just as the—whatever it was—slipped behind a tree, I caught a glimpse of red. Not the color of a cougar, but of the bandana Sy had tied around his forehead. "Sy, you shit!" I darted into the woods after him. He stayed just beyond me hiding behind tree after tree. Finally, hidden on the ground behind a huge rotting stump, he grabbed my ankle and tumbled me to the ground next to him.

"Some cougar you are," I said.

"Cougar?"

"Never mind. You made me smash the sandwiches."

He drew his finger down my forehead, over the tip of my nose, across my lips, around the curve of my chin, and down my throat to the center knot of my halter top. Then he flicked me in the nose.

I jumped on top of him and held his hands to the ground. "Now, you die," I said. I pulled his bandana over his eyes, jumped up and started running. He stood up fussing with his headband, he tripped over a root, got up again and stumbled forward. The water was in sight. I scrambled out of the woods and into Uriah's arms.

"Save me!" I yelled. "There's a blind cougar after me!"

We all went swimming. Zea played along the shore. The cold water soothed my poison ivy, which, in a few places behind my knees had cracked to the point of bleeding. When our lips turned noticeably blue, we found a grassy spot in the sun and ate lunch. I sat with my back against a boulder and sang Zea her favorite Mary

Poppins's lullaby until she fell asleep in my arms. "Stay awake, little girl."

I watched Sy and Uriah hike to the dam. They stopped now and then to point at the water or the sky. All I could hear of their conversation was expressed in their hands.

Sy, Uriah and I sat evenly spread around a fire for an hour or so after dark. It would have been nice to be closer to either Uriah or Sy, but I couldn't figure out how not to make either of them feel rejected. Clouds had rolled in and the air was cooling down. We were all tired from lack of sleep the night before. What I really wanted was to spend this last night with Sy in the pup tent, but I didn't think Uriah would go for it, especially after the irritation he'd shown that morning. He had been relaxed and calm, though, during the afternoon. When Uriah got up to get a blanket from the car to cover Zea, I followed him. "Uriah?" I asked. I bit my lip. "Uriah?" I repeated, not knowing how to say what was on my mind.

"You want to sleep with Sy in the tent," Uriah said. He knew me well.

"Yes, I would." I replied. "It's our last night. I'll probably never see Sy again after tomorrow."

"Don't you think you've spent enough time with him? What about me? I mean, we're a family, right?"

"Yeah, but it's not that simple, Uriah. Sy's new. It's just a bit more exciting to be with him right now."

"I suppose, Alodie, but what bugs me is that you're ignoring me. Do you have to stop loving me to love Sy?"

"I haven't stopped loving you, Uriah."

"Do whatever you have to do, Alodie."

"Okay, but Uriah, where will you sleep?" I asked.

"On the ground somewhere."

"Will you watch Zea?"

"Yes. I'll put her in the back seat and sleep near the car."

"What if it rains?" I asked.

"What do you care? I'll deal with it."

"Uriah, don't be mad."

"I'm not mad, Alodie. I'm tired of you being somewhere else in your head. You're neglecting me."

"I know, but I can't help it."

Uriah turned away and said, "We're going home tomorrow, right?"

"Yes," I replied," We're going home."

Sy wrapped his red bandana around a flashlight and hung it from the frame of the tent. We snuggled under an unzipped sleeping bag and I forgot about the other side of my life.

Denver

At dawn Uriah unzipped the flap of the tent. Without looking inside, he called softly, "Hey, Alodie. Sy. Let's get going." I knew it was hopeless to dissuade Uriah from his plan—even though it was only five o'clock in the morning. I sat up.

"Okay, Hon'," I replied. Sy hadn't heard Uriah. I watched his sleeping face. We had slept erratically. Every move, every uneven breath had stirred an awareness of the other. Just an hour before, we had finally given in to sleep. Uriah clanked the unicycle against the top of the open trunk. He was packing. "Sy?" I kissed his bare shoulder. "Sy, come on."

He put his arm over his eyes. "I don't want this day to be here, Alodie." I bit my lip and looked away.

While Uriah drove north on Colorado 285, Sy dozed in the front seat. I wasn't feeling quite right—maybe a little feverish. Uriah stopped for gas and I went to wash up. Zea had awakened by then and came with me to the bathroom. She pointed to my legs, "Mommy. Ou-weee," she said. I touched the oozing behind my knees. As I washed my face, I noticed a fine rash on my neck. Then, I noticed it on the underside of my arms. I had a rash everywhere. The poison ivy must have gotten into my system. I was going to need some help to get over this. We'd have to stop to see Uncle Len on the way home.

Uriah put a box of powered donuts on the roof of the Nova and opened the passenger door for Sy while he carefully slid into the seat balancing a flimsy cardboard box that held six cups of coffee. I bumped the seat accidentally when I climbed in and Sy barked at me. "Jeez, Alodie. Watch it."

His irritation jolted me. Before I could apologize, he added. "I caught your stupid poison ivy."

"You told me you weren't allergic to it."

"How could I NOT get it, we were practically glued to each other."

I was totally hurt and embarrassed for Uriah. I didn't understand Sy's blaming me. He rolled around in the stuff too. But if he had caught it along the river, he would have developed the rash when I did. I felt like I should defend myself, certainly not take the blame, but I apologized instead.

"Is it bad, Sy?" I asked. No reply. "I'm so sorry," I said again.

We drove in silence. Maybe Sy was as miserably sad as I was. Maybe he was as frustrated. Maybe he was as tired.

Sy had trouble finding the commune where he wanted to be dropped off. He had lost the address and the phone number and tried to rely on his sense of direction. We ended up driving in concentric circles around a Denver city park which Sy remembered being a few blocks from the house. Our circling method worked. Four blocks out from the park we pulled up in front of a hodgepodge of a house, the outside stairway and after-thought entries hiding the classiness it once had. The front porch was furnished with saggy couches and chairs, a grill and several bicycles. From the porch ceiling wind chimes and mobiles ding-a-linged and danced. Sy invited us in. "Should we just barge in?" I asked.

"Sure, why not."

"Do you even know these people?"

"Enough." Sy knocked on the half-opened door and walked in. Uriah, Zea and I followed, hesitantly. A chandelier, dulled by unpolished years, hung in the entry way. No one was around.

"Maybe you should wait here until I find somebody," Sy said, and climbed the banistered stairs.

"Alodie, why don't we just go," Uriah said. "We could just skip the goodbyes." I looked at him, horrified.

"We can't just leave without saying goodbye."

"Why drag it out, Alodie?"

I whispered a shout, "No, we're absolutely not leaving!"

When Sy came back after about ten minutes, he had his arm around an angelic nymph of a girl with a river of red curls almost to her waist. "Alodie. Uriah. This is my friend, Camille," Sy said. Uriah held out his hand.

"Hi, Camille." I caught a subtle flick of Uriah's eyebrows. I mumbled a hello. Who was this girl anyway? I was suddenly crazy with jealousy. I hated Camille.

"Would you like something to eat before you go?" Camille asked.

Yes, but NO, I thought. *How can I sit at a table with this woman?* But before I could decide what to say, Uriah graciously declined. I was beside myself. I was angry and hurt and humiliated and embarrassed. Did Sy care for me at all? Did he take advantage of Uriah's openness and our crazy hypothesis? Was he just jerking me around? Desperate, I asked, "Sy, could I talk to you a minute?" He hesitated. I walked out the door allowing him no option. "Please?"

I led Sy around the house to the backyard. When I was more than a safe distance to avoid the risk of being overheard by Uriah, I spun around and jeered at Sy. "Who is this Camille person? Is she your girlfriend? Was she on your mind the entire time you were with me?" I wanted to slap Sy. I wanted him to comfort me. I made a move toward him, but he held me away.

"Alodie, please. I came to Colorado to find Camille. I met her when she passed through Vegas on spring break. We hit it off. I didn't tell her I was coming, and when I got here last week she had gone to Wyoming for her uncle's funeral. I was hoping I could find her and thought maybe something would come of it, but when she wasn't here I took off into the mountains." He looked at the ground and wiped the back of his hand across his eyes. When he looked back at me his eyes were true. "I wasn't thinking about Camille when I made love to you, Alodie. If you weren't married to Uriah, I would have forgotten all about Camille. Put yourself in my place. What would you have done? This thing happened between you and me. It was great, but it has to be over, Alodie, it has to be." My breath was trapped in my chest. With his thumb, Sy wiped a tear from under my eye.

Uriah and Zea came around the corner of the house and Uriah said sharply. "What are you doing, Alodie? Let's go. We've got to get at least halfway through Nebraska today." But then he looked at Sy and softened. Sy grabbed Uriah's hand and they embraced.

"Thanks for letting me in, man."

"Yeah," Uriah replied. "Good to know you."

Sy kissed me on the cheek. I could only smile goodbye. Uriah took my hand and led me to the car.

Don't You Dare

Everything about me was miserable. I was one giant itch from head to toe. My mind was numb and my heart was actually hurting like a punching bag swung back and hit me square in the solar plexus. The only thing I didn't feel like doing was puking, but even that I might do if I kept staring at the tiny holes on the Nova's roof panel. I blurred my eyes so the little holes merged into lines and shapes and then back again into their diagonal crisscross. I couldn't see the tiny holes at all when tears welled up and distorted the light. A salty stream tracked down my cheek and onto my chest.

Uriah reached over and put his hand on my shoulder. "I'm sorry, Alodie."

"Why should you be sorry, Hon'? About what?"

"About the whole situation."

"No, don't be sorry, Uriah. I let myself get way too involved."

Uriah chuckled, "Too bad the first test of our hypothesis wasn't with some jerk you could have an easier time unloading."

I thought for a moment and replied, "Yeah, but then this experiment wouldn't have happened. Maybe it would have been easier on you if the three of us hadn't been together quite as much."

"I don't think so," Uriah said. "I like Sy. I'm glad I met him. Better to know what was happening than for you to be sneaking around." Uriah smoothed back a strand of my hair. "You going to be okay?"

"It's going to take a while."

Uriah drew his hand back to the steering wheel. "Get me out of Denver, will you, Alodie? What highway am I looking for?"

I thumbed the tears out of my eyes and reached into the back seat for the road atlas.

"Mommy, cry?" Zea asked. She was wrapping her doll in a red bandana. Sy's bandana—another burst of tears.

"Yeah, Honey. Mommy's crying," I studied the map through a blur. "Did we pass the exit to Interstate 76?" I asked Uriah.

"I don't know," Uriah shrugged.

"What road are we on now?"

Uriah pointed to a green sign overhead. "There's an exit for Broomfield, Highway 287."

"We missed I-76," I said. "You know what though? I really need to do something about this poison ivy. Would you mind if we stopped to see Uncle Len? Maybe he'll give me some cortisone. I don't know what else would help. We can cut back to I-76 from Loveland."

"Are you sure you want to go back there?" Uriah asked. I could tell from his tone that he certainly did not.

"I have to do something about this stuff. It's all over me and in me. Uncle Len will be in his office. We can just stop there and not go to the house."

Zea was whining, so I pulled her over the seat into the front. I reached for her *Hop on Pop* and read it three times before she tired of it. We played, "I Spy." Uriah and I recited as many nursery rhymes as we could think of and then sang the "Itsy Bitsy Spider," "Sugar Babe," and "Freight Train" until at last we were in Loveland. Keeping Zea busy had distracted me from Sy. I felt a little better. Uriah was being unbelievably kind.

Uncle Len was on his lunch break when we arrived at his office. He had gone home for his usual sandwich and swim. We decided to go to the house instead of waiting for Uncle Len to return. "Alodie, don't get trapped into staying, okay?" Uriah said.

"I don't want to hang out either. I'll be honest and say we really need to get home and settled before school starts again. I hope Uncle Len has something he can give me at home. He stocks a drawer with drugs in the bathroom. I was snooping around one day when I was a kid and found them."

"Did you ever try anything?"

"Right, Uriah. I was a good girl back then."

"Unlike now?" I gave him a playful punch as we pulled for a second time into Uncle Len and Aunt Edie's driveway. We knocked, entered the house and called for Aunt Edie and then Uncle Len, but no one answered. Uriah and I found Uncle Len in his rose garden on the south side of the pool. I explained the case history of my poison ivy with the exception of how I got it. I'm sure he noticed the telltale clues when he took me into the bedroom to examine me.

"Are you pregnant, Alodie?" Uncle Len asked with a matter-of-fact tone.

I was taken aback. Why would he ask? It was none of his business. I snapped, "No, I'm not pregnant." I had no doubt about it because I was sure to take measures after Zea was born. My bristling at Uncle Len's question was not really aimed at him. A wave of horror came over me when he asked. Wouldn't that have been a mess? Sy never had asked me what I was using, and he never offered. I had never even thought about the risk of getting pregnant.

Uncle Len caught my tone and the look of worry on my face. "I'm not prying, Alodie. I want to give you a hefty dose of cortisone and I couldn't do that if you were pregnant."

"I'm sorry, Uncle Len. No, I'm not pregnant, nor am I planning to be for a while."

"Okay, then. Here you go." He rummaged through his drug drawer but came out with nothing. "I'll have to write you a prescription." I flinched. We were down to the last of our money. Uriah would have been humiliated if I asked Uncle Len for a handout. Having samples on hand was different than asking. I didn't say anything.

"I'll make a note on the prescription to charge me. You must be getting low on funds after travelling for a couple weeks."

"Yes, we are actually. Thank you, Uncle Len." I gave him a hug and a kiss on the cheek.

"Careful now. You shouldn't go around kissing people in your condition." I smiled; if he only knew.

"We're going to scoot right out," I said. "We'd like to get at least as far as North Platte today. I have to be in class on Monday morning."

"Sure. I understand, and, I have to get back to the office."

"Say hello to Aunt Edie for us?"

"You bet."

I drove while Uriah napped in the back seat with Zea. There were long stretches of the highway I didn't see at all. I was floating in and out of the scenes that had made up the last ten days. For all I knew, I would implode or explode with the pain of knowing Sy—whenever I remembered him—forever. I had purposefully not asked Sy for his address or telephone number. I didn't want to be tempted to call him, but now I was in agony over that decision. On and on I drove. And, when Uriah woke up, on and on he drove. Zea sensed the distance between Uriah and me, the unusual silence and talked quietly to herself while playing with her toys in the back seat.

At six o'clock we arrived in North Platte, Nebraska. A banner over Main Street read, "Welcome to the National Rodeo Championship." We parked in an alley for lack of a place on the street. We walked from hotel to motel. There wasn't a room available anywhere. We felt conspicuous. We didn't fit in. Our dress represented a way of life so different from the people on the streets we could have come from Mars. We were ignored or sent side-long glances and snide remarks, "Goddamn, Cong-loving hippies."

"Let's just leave, Uriah. We can take turns driving," I said.

"You're exhausted, Alodie, and you don't sleep well in the car. I'm going to take the back seat out when we get home just for situations like this."

"Don't start in about the back seat, Uriah. Please," I whined. I *was* exhausted. He didn't respond. We walked past a restaurant called, 'The Branding Iron.'

"Let's ask in here," Uriah said. "Maybe a local will know a place where we can stay."

Standing in the foyer, I signaled to a waitress as she flew by with a steak the size of a Frisbee. "Excuse me, Ma'am. Do you know if there are any places left to stay in town? Any place will do. A YMCA? The Salvation Army? A hostel? Anything?" I asked.

"No, there's nothing like that—hmmm. If you're not fussy, there's an old hotel down the end of Main Street. People live there, but they might have a room or two. I doubt the cowboys stay there 'cause you have to share a bathroom and the boarders are a little, well, you know, nuts."

"Doesn't matter at this point," Uriah replied. "What's the name of the place?"

"The Two Star Hotel," she laughed. "Three blocks over," she pointed west, "and a couple or three to the right. You'll see it."

"Thanks a lot. Sorry to hold you up," I said, relieved.

The old hotel and saloon looked like they were lifted from a 'Gun Smoke' TV set. The bar was turned into the front desk. The tenants were hanging around, playing cards and smoking. They all glanced up as we entered. A man with tobacco juice running from the corner of his mouth stood up as we approached the desk. "Can I help you folks?" he asked, politely enough.

"I hope so," Uriah said. "We really need a place to stay for the night."

"Yep. I suppose everything's booked 'cause of the rodeo," the man said. "Yep. We got a room if you don't mind sharing a bathroom. There's a tub in a different room the lady here can use. Yep. There's a lock on the door. The bed's a little saggy, but the sheets are clean. Yep, might find a cot for the little one."

"That would be great," I said.

"Where ya'll from?" the man asked, wiping his mouth with his sleeve.

"Chicago," Uriah said. "We're on our way home." While Uriah continued the conversation and took care of the money end of the arrangements, I went to get the back packs. We went up the two flights of stairs to the room. The room was as expected, dingy and decrepit, but I didn't mind. I fell backward on the bed. "I want to go to sleep this minute," I said," but I need a bath."

"Why don't I take Zea for a walk," Uriah said. "Maybe we'll go to the arena and look at the horses or down to the river. I'll bring back some food. You okay staying alone?"

"I'll be fine," I replied, "If the locks work." I dug in the backpack for the last of my clean clothes, took a towel from the top of the bureau and went to the tub room. A deep old-fashioned tub with claw feet and a brass faucet all but filled the room. I ran the water, which was steaming hot, and although it smelled of sulfur, was inviting. I eased down, gritting my teeth as the water touched the areas of skin dealt havoc by the poison ivy. I closed my eyes and soaked. I wanted to stay in the tub and never come out. I wanted to wish away the last two weeks. No, I didn't. I couldn't interpret what had happened. I felt so changed. I soaked and soaked. It was just too soon to make any judgement. I didn't feel guilty or sorry. There was more good that came of it than bad, wasn't there?

Uriah seemed okay. He didn't seem hurt—too badly. Some hurt was inevitable. We'd have to discuss all that and anticipate the crazy mix of feelings if another situation for experimentation came up. Or, maybe we should abandon the hypothesis altogether. The thing with Sy just happened. I hadn't wished it to happen, and I didn't want to wish it away. No verdict was necessary. Sy wouldn't worry over it. He'd let it be what it was.

A knock on the bathroom door interrupted my thoughts. "I'll be out in a minute," I said.

"No hurry," a woman's voice said on the other side of the door. The water had become chilly, although I hadn't noticed until I ducked under to rinse my hair.

The light coming into the bedroom window had a pink glow. I watched the sky until the sun dipped below the horizon. I lay down, gave up resisting the sinkhole in the bed's center and fell asleep before Uriah and Zea returned.

"Hon'?" Uriah nudged me. "Do you want any supper?"

I opened my eyes but didn't sit up. "Yeah, I'm pretty hungry. What do you have?"

"Baloney sandwiches and orange juice."

Still half asleep, I took a bite. "Thanks. Tastes good."

Uriah tucked Zea in and told her a story about a squirrel monkey he had as a pet when he was a kid. When Zea fell asleep he said. "I'm going to take a bath, Alodie. I'll be back soon. Will you wait up?"

"I'll try." I struggled to stay awake but rolled over and slept soundly until the next morning when a kiss on the cheek from Uriah woke me.

"Hey, Babe. Time to go. How you feeling?"

"I don't know yet. Better, I think. I slept well anyway. How about you?"

"I ended up on the floor because I couldn't help rolling over onto you. I was kind of hoping you'd wake up. I miss you."

"I'm sorry, Uriah. I didn't feel you come to bed or roll into me. Come here." I pulled Uriah down to me. "I miss you too." We sat on the bed in silence and rocked in each other's arms.

As we neared Lincoln, Nebraska, around noon, Uriah pointed down the highway. "Look," he said.

"Look," Zea said. We both smiled.

"Is that a yellow Volkswagen on the shoulder up there?"

"Looks like it." We looked at each other.

"Couldn't be," I said.

"Yes, it is. Look. The girl's trying to hitch a a ride. Her car must have finally died. I wonder where she was."

"At the World Family Gathering, you think?" I asked.

Closing in quickly, I could see the girl—tall, tan, a black braid down to her waist, wearing a tight red t-shirt and the shortest cut-off jeans I'd ever seen. Just as I started saying, "She won't have any trouble getting a ride," I felt the slightest shift in the V8s RPMs. "Don't you dare, Uriah!" I yelled.

"Why not? The girl's in trouble."

"The girl almost killed us two weeks ago."

"She was having car trouble."

"Obviously." I couldn't believe it. Uriah started braking. "Uriah, I mean it. Don't you dare stop!"

"Alodie, we can't just leave her stranded."

"Yes, we can."

Trade Offs

I am the most scentless woman on the planet. Unscented deodorant, Ivory soap, basic Suave shampoo. I've succumbed to using Crisco for skin cream. Geez, I smell like me. The reason for giving up my earthy patchouli and ylang ylang essence is because my husband of 45 years—come December—has developed an allergy to me.

For the last year, maybe two or three—time gets distorted in the silver years--shortly after we climb into bed together, my husband's eyes begin to itch, his nose begins to run, and sometimes he starts coughing violently. These symptoms begin simply when we look longingly at each other in the moon light across our queen size bed. When the occasion becomes more romantic, well, I've heard of older men dropping dead from overexertion, but I've never heard of an older man dropping dead from allergic suffocation! But the risk is all too real.

My husband has really been a good sport about his allergy to me. He tries to make it not about me, but about him. He says, well, I guess when my juices get flowing, they flow from every opening I've got. But I feel sorry about it. He rarely spends the night with me anymore. To alleviate his asphyxiation, after I fall asleep, he drags himself upstairs to sleep on the couch.

A year or so ago, in an attempt to narrow down the cause of his allergic reactions to our togetherness, I confiscated and stashed away his double-sized feather pillow. While this action helped ease his allergies where he had used the pillow out of bed—like propping it behind him while watching a movie or leaning back on the pillow when he read a book, his allergy to me continued.

A good marriage is built on trade-offs. Forty-five years of togetherness—point made. One morning, I stood at the end of our bed debating whether the bedding could wait another day or two to be washed. There lay his two non-feather pillows. There lay my two pillows—hmm—foam and feather, foam and feather. No, it couldn't be! My favorite pillow, like from forever? Is he allergic to my pillow? No, it couldn't be. I stripped the sheets off the bed, the cases off the pillows. I pulled the brown Egyptian cotton case off my beloved pillow and saw in the morning light a tiny downy plume puff through a seam into the air. A feather. Yes. Oh no. After all these years, I anticipated yet another tradeoff to continue our wedded bliss.

That night under the half-moon light I looked longingly across our queen-sized bed at my husband's golden thinning hair. I snuggled a little closer. I kissed his cheek. I wrapped my legs around his. I waited. I looked across the moon-lit room at my downy pillow, my companion, my comfort all these years and said good-bye. And for the first time, in a long time, my husband slept with me the whole night through.

The next morning, I dug into the back of the bathroom cabinet, found my patchouli ylang-ylang goat's milk soap, my heavily scented deodorant and my favorite shea butter skin cream, dowsed myself and took a slow deep breath.

Polly Spooner and the Whispering Cottonwood

1. Her Majesty

T aking care that the sparkling side of the stone would glitter in the sun, Polly Spooner jabbed the geode between the ridges of her cottonwood's rhinoceros bark. "Oh, my beautiful Whispering Cottonwood," Polly always began her request this way, "please grant me a wish today." And then, she waited, and waited, and waited, pressed her head against the bark until it hurt, and strained to hear a voice murmur above her.

When she had concentrated so hard on the sound of the leaves that she no longer could hear the vrooming of cars, the churning of the garbage truck, the distant clanking of the factory, or even the organ on the ice-cream truck, she made her wish. Polly always made two wishes—one for now and one for later. She always ended her request with a deal. "I promise, Your Majesty, when I am fifty years old, I will do as you wish in return."

Satisfied she had wished as mightily as she could, Polly eased her pony-tailed head away from the leafy giant. She smoothed her daisy print sundress and wrapped her arms around bent knees. In the spring, she liked to watch the cottonwood seeds, like tiny parachutes, drift and spin on the breeze, but now in the summer, she watched the silky clouds dance along on the west wind.

Polly named her tree, which stood in the park across the street from her house, "The Whispering Cottonwood" because of the muttering sound the glossy heart-shaped leaves made in even the slightest whisk of a wind. Sometimes Polly called the tree the "*W-i-sh*-pering Cottonwood because it was her favorite place to wish. Her friends wished upon stars or wished when they blew out birthday candles, but Polly had discovered her wishes came true, when she brought a magic stone to the Whispering Cottonwood, sat snuggly between its root arms and sang her favorite song, "Buffalo Gals."

For a year after her first mom died, Polly lived with Aunt Johanna. When the moon was full, Aunt Johanna would grab Polly by the hand and they would run outside into the back yard. Aunt Johanna would spin Polly around and sing, "Buffalo Gals won't you come out tonight and dance by the light of the moon." They would laugh and fall dizzily on the ground and look for faces in the moon.

The tree trunk was polka dotted with Polly's stones. "Here's a beauty," Polly said to herself the day she found the sparkling geode. A gravel truck had dumped its load next to her ragweed hideaway. Her hideaway was at the edge of the neighborhood. Drainage ditches ran along both sides of the road. Polly had pulled out the ragweed from the bottom of the ditch to form a perfect circle. The plants which rimmed the circle towered over her.

"Come on down here. Now, don't you break." She pulled the ragweed tops toward her hand over hand. Then, with clothespins borrowed from her new mom, Trina, she secured the tops together making a cozy ragweed tent.

Sometimes Polly would sneak off to the hideaway to escape her brother, Hank, when he was having one of his hissy-fits, or to escape her sister, Betty Lou, when she was having one of her sissy-fits. Sometimes Polly had to escape when Trina was worrying, but usually Polly would go to her hideaway just to play.

Polly sang "Buffalo Gals" one more time, took a deep breath of late summer air and elbowed herself from the soothing hug of her cottonwood's roots.

"You better get out of here unless you want to get clobbered by a baseball!" Skippy, the nastiest kid on the block yelled across the park as a group of neighborhood boys gathered to play hard ball. Max, Dickie and Hank joined in, "Yeah, no dumb girls in the park during the game. Go play with your dolls."

As Polly turned to leave, she stuck out her tongue and snapped back, "I hope Crabby Mr. Tackiss steals your ball." She fled when the boys started after her. She saw her father climb out of his shiny black '57 Chevy and ran toward him. "Dad, help. The boys are after me!" Polly grabbed the leg of her dad's pants and spun around behind him.

In his quiet way, he said, "You almost knocked me over, Spot."

"Daddy, can we see 'The Swiss Family Robinson?'" A family gets shipwrecked on a deserted island and live in a tree house!"

"I don't know, Polly. Your mom doesn't like us going to the movies."

The enthusiasm faded from her face, but then a smile appeared. "We can talk her into it, Dad." Seeing "The Swiss Family Robinson" was the wish she had made under her cottonwood tree and she knew it would come true. They walked to the house along the flagstone path. Polly looked over her shoulder and sent a double wink of thanks to her Whispering Cottonwood.

"Who are you trying to wink at, Polly?" her dad asked. Polly pretended to zip her lips shut between her thumb and fingers. She never told anyone about her magic cottonwood tree, not even her father.

2. The DDT Parade

The next day after a booming thunderstorm, Independence Park was flooded. The drainage ditches were overflowing. Polly Spooner cut through the alley behind the row of houses on her block. A few days before, she had noticed a rusty tin pail behind Skippy's garage. Polly didn't think it was stealing to take the discarded pail, but she still felt a little guilty when she grabbed it, so she ran as fast as she could to her hideaway hoping no one would see her. The long green grass in the ditch swirled just like Polly's hair when she pretended to be a mermaid at the Wicker Park Pool. The rippling grass tickled her feet. Polly stood in the ankle-deep water and pulled her rifle from a pile of leaves along the bank. Using it as the stick it really was, Polly edged bottles, broken cups, empty cans and scraps of wood toward her. "Huckleberry," Polly said aloud, "We better build our kitchen on higher ground."

Then, in a lower voice, she replied, "That's right, Tom. There's no tellin' when the river will flood again." Polly rearranged the kitchen and then used the stick to go fishing.

"That's a mighty big catfish ya got there, Tom."

"Yes sirree. We ain't gonna go hungry tonight."

Polly heard a whistle blow. Instead of calling the twins home by yelling to them like all the other mothers, June's and July's mom blew a whistle. Three blasts. Lunch. June and July must have come home from church. They went to church on Saturday mornings to get ready for first communion. Polly didn't know what "first communion" was. The twins went to church on Saturday nights too, for mass. Polly knew "mass" was just a different name for church.

Maybe the twins could play for a while after lunch. Polly threw her rifle up on the bank, hastily kicked a few leaves over it and pushed through the old beach towel strung up for the door to her hideaway. Polly skipped toward home. June and July were climbing down from the Scotch pine tree in the park. The bark of the tree was rubbed a smooth yellow-orange from the heavy traffic of climbers. Polly waved. "You want to play after lunch?"

"Let's ride bikes in the new subdivision," July suggested.

June and July were Polly's best friends. They lived two doors away. Even though they were identical twins, Polly could tell them apart because July had a little scar on the tip of her chin. June was sassier, and often reminded July that she was the oldest. June was born on June thirtieth, three minutes before midnight. July was born two minutes after midnight, on July first.

Polly sniffed the air. Stinky. The sunlight dimmed as the smoke from the Gary steel mills grayed the sky. Polly noticed the leaves on the neighbor's silver poplar were turning inside out showing the white of their undersides. More rain. Polly licked her finger, held it up and turned slowly around. Her dad said whichever direction the air felt the coldest on her finger, that would be the direction of the wind. Polly had no doubt, definitely North.

Polly let the screen door slam. "Take off those muddy sneakers, Polly, and wash your hands." Trina turned from the stove with a pot lid in her hand to check on Polly still in the utility room. Polly heeled off her shoes before entering the kitchen. "I was just about to call you in for lunch. I've got hot dogs boiling. You know where your brother is?"

"Out back. I think. I heard him hammering on something. Where's Dad?"

"He went to the hardware store. He should be home soon."

Standing on a chair, Betty Lou poured a cup of sugar into a pitcher of Kool-aide. "You're spilling sugar all over the place!" Polly grabbed the cup from Betty Lou's hand. "Here, let me do it."

"No, I'm doing it."

"Polly, let her be," Trina said.

"Jeez Louise," Polly griped.

"That's naughty talk, Polly. You don't say anything with the name of Jesus in it. Thou shalt not take the Lord's name in vain."

Polly felt a twinge of guilt. It seemed she was always sinning without meaning to. She washed her hands at the kitchen sink and noticed the vines that hung on the cabinets on each side of the sink needed water. Polly liked the ceramic apple and pear pots in which the vines were planted. "I'll water the plants, Mom."

"Okay, be careful."

Polly was already dragging a chrome-legged, gray and red vinyl chair across the linoleum. She climbed on the chair and filled a glass with water. "You're such a pretty little plant," Polly said, missing the smile on her mom's face. "Did you make these pots, Mom?"

"No, I only painted and glazed them."

"I wish I knew you when you did ceramics."

A year after her first mom died, Polly's dad married Trina. Polly looked at Trina and thought, *She's pretty. Her cheeks are peachy and her blond hair curls just right.* Polly tried to imagine her old mom's freckled face and auburn hair, but she couldn't see her clearly. Polly asked her cottonwood to help. That wish hadn't come true—yet. *Maybe Her Majesty was busy and didn't hear my wish,* Polly thought. *I'll ask her again tonight.*

Ceramics had been Trina's hobby. She had decorated the house with flowerpots and figurines. Trina had a lot of jewelry too. Sometimes when she wasn't busy, Polly and Betty Lou would sit with Trina on the edge of the bed, open the top dresser drawer and try on the jewelry.

"This piece is from my Grandma Vander Kamp. It's from Holland and very old," Trina would say. Or, "This one was a gift from Agnes, a friend of mine from Chicago."

Trina was never married before she married Polly's dad and had a life of her own. Polly was nosy and tried to find out about Trina's secret past. Sometimes Trina would tell, and sometimes not. Like the time Polly asked, "Did you have any boyfriends before Dad?" That was a mistake. Trina stood up, tisked and walked away!

After lunch, Polly went to the bathroom to wash the ketchup from her hands. In the mirror on the back of the bathroom door, Polly looked into her own root beer brown eyes. Her dark blond bangs were snarled and a summer bloom of freckles dotted her face. She rubbed a smudge of ketchup from her chin. Polly heard a familiar roar. She stepped into the bathtub and looked through the inch of open window below the star-etched glass. She located the source of the sound from across her backyard and the alley, through the neighbor's yard to the block beyond. It was the Mosquito Truck!

Polly wiped her hands on her hips and ran into the kitchen. "Mosquito Truck!" she yelled. The procedure was automatic. Hank, Betty Lou, Trina and Polly exploded like fireworks to close every window in the house. "Can we follow the truck, Mom?" Hank asked.

"Yes, but not too close." Hank slapped his cap over a bristly crewcut and darted outside. Polly followed slamming the screen door. Betty Lou started screaming. "Wait for me! Wait for me!"

Simultaneously, Skippy, June and July from down the street; and Kip Tippy, Max and his little brother, Marvin, from across the park emerged on blue, red and green bicycles to follow an old army jeep. The jeep, now painted red with a tank and a sprayer mounted on the back, was The Mosquito Truck.

The bug-spray smell of DDT was already overwhelming the stench of the steel mill smog. The troupe raced toward Independence Park Boulevard and on to Potomac Avenue. Other kids merged from all parts of the neighborhood. "Here it comes!" Hank shouted. Ready and waiting, the bicyclists took a deep breath as the whine of the blower deafened them. A dusty man standing on the back of the jeep dumped another bag of gray powder into the mouth of the blower. Polly's eyes stung and her nose tickled. She liked the smell of DDT. The Mosquito Truck driver waved and took the lead. A DDT parade! The solidarity of it all thrilled the participants. Lifted their spirits. Life was good.

Later that evening, Polly sat on the front steps holding a pink cellophane candy wrapper over her eyes. She didn't bother to look for the real sunset. She knew the red ball of the sun couldn't be seen over the little Cape Cod houses-built row upon row on the flat land of northern Indiana. Polly wandered to her Whispering Cottonwood. Sleepy, with a bit of a headache, Polly pressed her head against Her Majesty. This time she sang a different song, "Zippity-do-dah, zippity-ay. My, oh my, what a glorious day." She thought dreamily about her mother and wished she would remember her forever. As Polly gazed into the canopy, a sigh, barely discernible, floated down from the rosy sky through the rustle of the leaves above.

3. Lemon Balloon Moon

"It's your turn to get into the tub, Polly." Trina stood up and stretched, then gathered the empty popcorn bowls from the end tables and the hassock. The Lawrence Welk Show was on TV. Polly watched a dancing couple spin around in front of the orchestra while bubbles floated up behind it.

"Dad? Why do they blow bubbles around the orchestra"?

Polly's dad reached down to pet their beagle puppy, Ginger. "They're supposed to be champagne bubbles."

"What's champagne?"

"It's a fizzy wine that people drink at weddings and other celebrations. I guess Lawrence Welk wants us to get into a celebrating kind of mood."

"Polly!" Trina called again.

"Polly, did you hear your mother?"

"Yes, but you said I could wait until the Lemon Sisters sing," Polly tiredly whined.

"Quick. Run upstairs and get your P.J.s. The Lennon Sisters usually sing right after the next commercial." Polly's dad gave her a wink as she dragged herself to the bottom of the stairs. She smiled grudgingly.

Polly was afraid of boogie men. On Saturday nights she had to go upstairs by herself to get her pajamas before her bath. On most nights, Hank, Betty Lou and Polly went upstairs to bed at the same time and she felt a little safer. Polly was usually able to fall asleep

143

quickly after checking for boogie men in the closet and under the bed.

She took a deep breath, puffed out her cheeks and climbed the stairs as fast as she could. She always startled at her reflection in the window at the top of the steps, but still held her breath. Polly knew that if she could hold her breath, run across the game room, flip the light on in the bedroom, grab her pajamas from under her pillow, flip the light off, tear back through the game room and down the stairs, the boogie men wouldn't have time to snatch her and carry her away.

Polly heard the Lennon Sisters singing when she hit the bottom step. "By the light of the silvery moon, I'll sit and croon . . ." *What does "croon" mean?* Polly wondered.

"Polly. Where are you? The tub's full."

"I'm coming!"

After a soothing soak, Polly climbed once more up the stairs slapping her slippers in time as she rhymed, "Croon, prune, cartoon, raccoon, saloon." Snuggled cozily in fresh sheets, she could hear her sister's steady breathing. On the other side of an imaginary line, one Polly was not allowed to cross, Hank tossed. He burped and farted under the covers. He practiced a lot. Because he was a boy, and the oldest, he was going to get his own bedroom downstairs as soon as Trina found a place for her extra furniture.

Polly thought of a few more rhymes as she squinted to make the "lemon balloon moon" sparkle as it floated past the south facing window. She closed her eyes to hear the August crickets chirp more clearly. As she felt herself sinking deeper into the mattress, a tingly feeling wiggled its way up her back. When Polly opened her eyes, the bedroom looked the same, but there was a soft glow in the room. She sat straight up. Goosebumps sprouted along her arms. She listened hard past the thump of her heart and thin gasps of her breath. A quieting pushed away Polly's fear as she sensed a hand smoothing her hair. Then Polly saw, drifting across Hank's imaginary line, her first mom, draped in a white lace nightgown. She kissed Hank on the cheek and floated back across the room to touch Betty Lou's forehead. *Did you have a candle before? How come I can't see your feet?* Polly's misgivings were eased by her mom's smile. Polly smiled back and watched as her mom gradually disappeared like a fog in the morning sunshine. "Don't worry, Mom. I'll remember you," Polly said, as she turned over on her tummy and nuzzled her face into a cool spot on her pillow. *I will always remember you.*

4. Jeopardy

Polly Spooner opened the door of her parents' bedroom just a crack so the light from the hallway wouldn't fall on her dad's face. Sunday morning was her dad's day to sleep in. She reached around the door frame and groped along the back of Trina's dresser feeling for the hard, smooth cold of a glass ashtray. It held her Sunday school pin and the attached first, second and third year gold bars of perfect attendance. When the light was on, she could see herself in the ashtray. Her school picture was glued to the bottom and covered with soft felt. It had been a gift for Trina on Mother's Day. Polly was glad Trina didn't smoke cigarettes or the picture would have been pretty icky by now.

"What are you doing, Polly?"

"I'm sorry, Daddy, I'm trying to find my Sunday school pin."

"It's okay, I was awake." He rose up on an elbow. "I was thinking we could go for a hike after dinner today. Neither the White Socks nor the Cubs have a game."

"Can we go to the ditch where those big tubes cross over?"

"Sure. Good idea."

"Can June and July come with us?"

"If it's okay with their parents."

Trina was crabby. On the way to church, she said, "Your dad should get up and come to church with us. I don't even know if he's saved. He's probably drinking again like he did after your mother died." Polly felt sad inside when Trina said bad things about her dad. She felt a little better when the congregation sang, "He Leadeth Me, Oh, Blessed Thought." Following the instructions Aunt Johanna gave her, she made a perfect rabbit out of her lace handkerchief. While the preacher gave the sermon, Polly remembered the vision of her first mom. *Was it real? It seemed real. I was me and the room was the same. I felt her touch my hair.* She startled when the preacher yelled, "All have sinned!" He pounded on the pulpit and threatened, "The souls of those who do not come to the house of the Lord are in jeopardy!"

"Jeopardy?" Polly whispered, "What's jeopardy?"

After church, Polly went into the basement for Sunday school. Mrs. Van Doodle said with a stern voice, "All rise!" and tapped her baton on the music stand. Polly sang with all her might, "Jesus wants me for a sunbeam to shine for him each day." She saw herself with beams of light shooting out all over the place while she guided Jesus along a dark path.

Polly smoothed the back of her dress so she wouldn't hit the cold steel of the folding chair with her bare thighs, but when she sat down instead of cold steel, she hit the hard floor. "You dummy!" She got up and kicked Albert 'Spit' De Groot in the shin.

"Polly Spooner. Shame on you." Mrs. Van Doodle scolded. "You shouldn't call people names and you certainly shouldn't kick them."

"But . . ."

"Now sit down!"

Polly fought back tears of anger during the next song, and when Spit started kicking the bottom of her chair during the Bible verse, Polly turned around and pinched his leg. "Ouch!" he yelped.

"What are you two doing now?" asked Mrs. Van Doodle.

Before Spit could say anything, Polly explained, "He pulled my chair out from under me and now he's kicking it."

"Albert, is that true?"

"No," Spit said, saliva foaming at the corners of his mouth.

"It is too, you liar."

"Polly, you shouldn't accuse anyone of lying."

"He is, though." Polly was so angry she blurted, "You should do something, Mrs. Van Doodle!"

"If Albert did wrong, he will have to answer to God. As far as you're concerned, Miss Spooner, I'm going to have a talk with your mother."

Polly felt sick to her stomach. *I'm really gonna get it.* She sniffed tears up her nose.

When Trina turned onto Delaware Parkway, Polly saw her dad sitting on the front steps with a pipe in one hand and a coffee cup in the other. He was freshly shaved, his thinning mousy brown hair slicked back with Brill-crème. Even before the car stopped, Polly opened the door and ran to her father.

"Daddy, Spit De Groot pulled my chair away and Mrs. Van Doodle yelled at ME! It wasn't fair." She paused and asked, "Dad, are you saved?" Her father reached out to her and she collapsed in his arms. Polly sobbed on his shoulder. "Where were you all that time after Mom died?"

He stroked the back of her head but didn't answer.

Polly took a deep breath and looked up. "Dad, what does 'jeopardy' mean?"

He chuckled, "It means a dangerous situation, Spot."

Hank pressed his face against the inside of the screen door. "What's wrong with you, Cry Baby?"

"None of your business, Stupid."

"That's enough," Polly's dad said.

"Mom says you have to come in and set the table," Hank ordered.

Polly hugged her dad tightly around his neck. He said, "Go ahead, Polly. Do what your mother says."

"Oh, Pol-leeeee." The twins came over that afternoon to see if Polly could play outside. Only on the Sundays when it was okay with Trina, could she put on her play clothes and go outside.

"My Dad's gonna take us on a hike over the ditch, can you come?"

"I'll go ask," June said, skipping away with her black pigtails bouncing. July squeezed through the screen door that Polly was holding open and slipped inside. She quickly slid onto the piano bench. Every chance they got, the twins would play, "Heart and Soul," or the "Chopsticks."

"Everybody ready?" Polly's dad took Betty Lou's hand and started down the flagstone walk to the street. The usual neighborhood gang had gathered. "Do you all have your parents' permission?"

"Yeah. Sure."

"Okay. Let's go."

They walked for three blocks and Betty Lou asked, "Daddy, why does Dickie McCoy live on the other side of Hart's Ditch?"

"Well, I guess his parents bought some land from the farmer over there."

"But how do they get their car over here? Dickie always walks across the foot bridge."

"They have to drive to 45th street to cross the ditch."

"Why does Dickie walk so funny?" Kip Tippy asked.

"He had polio." Hank said with authority.

"Isn't that why we take those sugar cube things for?" Skippy picked up a rusty bolt from the ground and tossed it into the air.

"Maybe Dickie didn't get those sugar cubes from his doctor," Hank grabbed Skippy's bolt on its way down.

"Hey, Idiot." Skippy punched Hank in the shoulder.

"Maybe Dickie got sick before the vaccine came out." Polly's dad speculated.

"Does his leg hurt?"

"It probably did when he was sick."

The water in Hart's Ditch was higher than usual. "P.U.," Marvin pinched his nose.

"Why does this ditch stink so bad?" Max walked to the edge and looked at the oily rainbows on the water's surface.

"It's a drainage ditch and sometimes the sewage from the toilets and sinks overflows into this ditch if there's a lot of rain," explained Polly's dad.

"Where does the water go?"

"To the Calumet River and out into Lake Michigan."

"Icky!" July made a face. "Mr. Spooner, didn't Rosey Jones drown in here?"

"Yes. Are you June or July?"

"July, Mr. Spooner. You can tell us apart by my scar." July fingered the tiny scar on the point of her chin. "I fell off my bike."

"I'll remember to look for that." Polly's dad continued. "Rosie Jones was sledding down the bank and broke through the ice. She got stuck under it. That's why you kids aren't allowed to play here in the winter. Sometimes the water warms up and the ice is unpredictable."

"Unpredictable," Polly repeated. She liked big words.

The group walked on and talked. Polly's dad pointed out his favorite sassafras tree. "There aren't many of these trees this far north," he said. "But there were where I grew up in southern Illinois."

"You sure know a lot, Mr. Spooner," Skippy said

"Here we are. Now you kids be careful. Cross one at a time."

"Why are these pipes so big, Dad?" Hank asked.

Polly's dad paused to think. "I really don't know what they're for."

"But Daddy, what are the pipes for?"

"Polly, I said I didn't know."

"But . . ."

"Polly. I don't know!"

Polly was jolted by a new awareness. Didn't her dad know everything? If he didn't know, then who did? "Maybe nobody knows what they're for."

"You stupid," Hank mocked. "Whoever put them here knows what they're for."

Polly had to admit that sounded reasonable.

"Hank, be nice to your sister." Polly lagged behind the group.

"Polly, come on." Her dad encouraged. "It's your turn."

"I'm scared."

"Look. All the other kids are balancing and doing just fine. The pipes are plenty wide to walk across."

Polly put one foot onto the pipe. Her heart began to race and her knees felt wobbly. "I can't, Daddy."

Ever since the side of Hank's tree house broke off with Polly tumbling after it, she was nervous about being up high. "I'm going to crawl across," Polly announced. "I can crawl."

"That's a good idea, Polly."

"Look at the sissy," Skippy pointed and shouted from the other side.

Polly didn't reply but bit her lip and concentrated. Polly's dad followed her, carrying Betty Lou piggy-back. Polly placed one hand safely on the far bank which was held from washing away by crushed rock—clean, white limestone. Polly's eyes were drawn to the squiggles and curlicues in the rocks.

"Daddy, look at these funny rocks."

Her dad bent over Polly. "Oh boy. These rocks are full of fossils. Do you know what fossils are, Polly?"

"No."

"A long time ago little creatures died and their bodies left impressions in the bottom of the lake where they lived. The bottom of the lake turned into stone. When the men at the Thorton Quarry dig into the ground, they are digging up the old lake bottom."

"Fossils." Said Polly, raking them around with her hand. "You know everything, Dad."

Her father kissed the top of her head, "I know some things."

Polly's eyes fell on a perfectly shaped snail fossil in a smooth piece of limestone. She tucked the rock into the pocket of her pedal pushers.

Two hours later the troupe trudged back home through Independence Park and spread out to their own homes. Polly stopped off at her Whispering Cottonwood. A mourning dove cooed in the top of the tree. She dug the fossil from her pocket and pushed the rock into a gnarly groove. She skinned the side of her thumb. "Ouch!" Polly sucked off the blood. When the bleeding stopped, she said, "Oh, my beautiful Whispering Cottonwood, please grant me a wish today." Polly pushed her head against the tree, but she couldn't think of a wish so she asked. "Your Majesty, did you tell my old mom to come visit me last night? Was it really her?" Polly waited and waited. Her mind started to wander back through the day and then she heard an elusive voice. She cupped her ears. "What did you say? I didn't hear you." Polly concentrated on the sounds around her and thought she heard a voice faintly say, "Yes-s-s-s."

5. Purgatory

"Let me have that stupid bird!" Skippy said, grabbing at the robin Max and Marvin had gently placed in a shoebox filled with grass. The neighborhood kids had gathered in the park to study the bird.

"Don't touch her Skippy, she's hurt."

"That bird's gonna die. You can't keep a bird in a shoebox."

"How do you know?" July asked.

"Yeah, maybe she's just dizzy and hit a window really hard or something." Hank said.

"She's not dizzy. Come on, let me have her."

"No, leave her alone!" Max yelled.

"Gimme that bird."

"Quit it, Skippy," Polly pushed him away.

"You gonna make me?"

"Cut it out, Skippy," Hank stepped forward. Skippy picked up a stick. Polly backed away, but instead of coming after her, Skippy knocked the shoebox out of Marvin's hands and grabbed the robin.

"This bird's gonna die. Watch this." To the horror of the bystanders, Skippy pried open the beak of the bird and forced the stick into its mouth. "The stick's gonna come out of its butt!"

"Stop it! Stop it! You'll kill it!" There was a swirl of arms and legs and fists and feet and flying baseball caps that ended in a big pile of children on top of Skippy.

151

"Why did you do that?"

"You're mean."

"You're going to purgatory for that."

"Hell even."

"You're horrible."

"I'm telling your Dad."

"Go ahead."

"I will."

"You're all a bunch of babies. It's just a stupid bird." As the last child rolled off the pile, Skippy stood up and flung the robin still on the stick into the roots of Polly's cottonwood tree. "It's just a stupid bird," Skippy repeated, as he ran toward his bike, gave it a running start and rode away.

$\flat$

"But, Mom, I don't want my hair cut. I like it long."

"Polly, I'm not going to be fussing with your hair every morning before school."

"I'll comb it myself."

"You can't get it smooth enough or braid it behind your head." Trina was determined, but so was Polly.

"I can do braids on the side. You're not making Betty Lou cut her hair. That's not fair, Mom."

"Polly, no more arguing. Come here. I'll braid your hair on top away from your head a little. The beautician will cut it at the rubber band and you can keep the braid. That will be neat, won't it?"

"I guess so."

"Now scoot along. The beautician's name is Doris. Just knock. She's expecting you. You know the house, right?"

Polly rode slowly around the neighborhood taking detours and stalling. She rode up Revere Court and Bunker Hill Drive. She stuck her tongue out as she drove past Mrs. Van Doodle's house on

Potomac Avenue. Polly stopped at the beautician's gray house and hid for a minute behind the mock orange bushes that in the spring smelled so good she would pull down the branches and stick her whole face in the flowers.

Polly had never been in a beauty shop before. There was a strong ammonia smell that went right up her nose like the window cleaner Trina used. There were big helmets on stands. The sink had a notch cut out of it. Doris said, "Okay, Honey. Hop right up here. So, it looks like you want me to save your braid. That will make your hair pretty short. It will be cute. I'll give you a Pixie."

"What's a 'Pixie'?"

"A pixie is a little elf or fairy. You know, like Tinker Bell in Peter Pan. You'll like it, you'll see." Doris placed a plastic cape around Polly's neck and secured it with a hair clip. She spun the chair around so Polly couldn't see into the mirror and picked up the scissors. The crunching sound the scissors made when cutting through the thick braid made Polly cringe. Doris handed her the beautiful braid, blonder at the tip than at the blunt, newly cut end. She held the braid while Doris finished trimming and buzzed the back of her neck. "This is called 'shingling.' It's the special way to cut a Pixie." Polly sat quietly. "Are you ready?" Doris asked excitedly. Polly held her breath as Doris spun the chair around again. Tears filled Polly's eyes. "What do you think?"

Polly sniffed, "I look like a boy."

"Oh, no, Honey. You look adorable. Here. Hold the mirror and check the back." Polly hesitatingly did as she was told, but didn't say a word.

Polly rode around the neighborhood four times before going home. Her head felt much lighter. The wind blew her hair all over, but it fell perfectly back into place when she slowed down. Rounding the last corner, Polly pedaled hard. Lifted her braid into the air and yelled into the sky. "Beware, Captain Hook! Here I come!"

♭

Early the next morning, Polly Spooner jabbed a stick into a tin can and smashed a piece of puffball mushroom into the brew she and June were concocting to poison Skippy. "The red berries on the vines behind the little store are poisonous. We should go get some."

"Are you sure they're poison?" June asked.

"My Dad said they are. They're called 'nightshade' and they can stop your heart."

"Good. If we put enough red berries in it, it will look like jam."

"We'll put it on a Saltine and then he'll eat it."

"Yeah, and then he'll be dead and stuck in purgatory forever."

"June, what's 'purgatory'?" Polly had wondered about this word during the fight with Skippy.

"Don't you know? If you're naughty, you get stuck there to pay for your sins before you can go to heaven."

"Don't bad people go straight to hell?"

"They go to purgatory first. If they're good in purgatory they can go to heaven. I guess it's like a second chance."

"What do people have to do in purgatory?"

"Dig ditches and stuff."

Polly got very serious, "June, no one can know about this poison for Skippy except you and me. If anyone finds out and tells, we'll have to go to jail." June grabbed Polly's arm. "I won't tell, I promise. Come on. Let's go pick the berries. Do you have any crackers at your house?"

"I think so."

♭

"Polly, where have you been? You know you have to practice your piano lessons before you can go outside."

"Sorry, Mom. I forgot."

"Well, get right to it. Half an hour, and don't forget your Hannon finger exercises."

"Okay."

"And Polly," Trina added, as she lifted a basket of wet clothes and pushed open the screen door with her back, "I read in the paper that the road is going to be tarred and graveled today. So, watch out for the trucks and make sure you and your sister stay on this side of the street."

Polly wanted to be the best piano player in the world. Polly's dad bought the piano for her first mom, but she was too sick to play it very much. Polly carefully pointed to each note on the bass cleft and then searched for the matching piano key. She liked the song, 'Oh, Danny Boy'. It was the same melody as a song she sang in church called, 'Good is the Lord, and Full of Kind Compassion'. When she was done practicing, Polly pounded out on all black keys and sang, "Peter, Peter pumpkin eater. Had a wife and couldn't keep her. Put her in a pumpkin shell and there he kept her very well."

Polly looked out the front screen-door to see if Skippy was in the park across the street. Nope. Betty Lou and the twins were raking up freshly mown grass into lines that would serve as the outline of a house. Men in tall boots, holding shovels, rakes and hoes were gathering at the corner. Polly walked to the end of the flagstone sidewalk. "Betty Lou, June, July, look." She pointed to the corner. "The tar machine is coming." The first steaming machine had arrived. The men were adjusting the arm that would evenly spray hot tar along the width of the street. "Hurry up!"

The gravel truck backed up behind the tar machine. Betty Lou and the twins screamed and ran across the road leaving their rakes behind them. Children were appearing from everywhere. Those who lived across the street sat in a line along the edge of the park. The children on Polly's side sat in a line in their front yards. Hank, Dickie McCoy and some other boys came from between two houses, but Skippy wasn't with them.

The tar machine revved its engine and shiny black boiling tar sprayed onto the street. The gravel truck drove backwards and slowly dumped small mounds of gravel in the middle of the road. The men in boots slugged along pulling the gravel from the piles and smoothing it out in the tar. Suddenly, Skippy came flying around the corner on his bike. He gave a whoop and hollered,

"Watch this!" He stood up on his bike and rode right behind the tar machine. But the hot tar was slippery and Skippy's back tire spun out. Skippy hit the road and slid into the cut grass at the edge of the park. When he stood up, he had tar and dead grass stuck all over him. A big cheer went up from the neighborhood. "Ha, ha. Serves you right. That's what you get."

Four doors down, Skippy's mom saw what happened. She ran out to the street and waved to the tar machine driver to stop. Skippy and all the kids in the park crossed the street in front of the machine. Bawling like a baby, Skippy was now the center of attention. The children congregated in his yard. "Get this stuff off me, Mommy," Skippy cried.

"I don't know how to get it off."

Crabby Mr. Tackiss wandered over from his house and said, "You'll have to wipe him down with gasoline. That's the only thing that will cut the tar."

Hank leaned in, "We have a can of gasoline in our garage. You want me to get it?"

"Yes, will you?" Skippy's mom asked. "I'll get some rags. Will you kids help me?"

Skippy's mom gave gasoline-soaked rags to everyone and they scrubbed harder on Skippy than they had ever scrubbed anything before.

Polly couldn't visit Her Majesty that evening because the street was still sticky. As she climbed the steps to the back door, she remembered the poisonous brew she and June had made for Skippy. Polly retrieved the tin can from its hiding place behind the garage, walked into her backyard and drop-kicked it right into Crabby Mr. Tackiss's rose garden. "Oops." Polly said and ran into the house.

6. Negotiations

"**M**iss Dykema, this is my sister Betty Lou. Is she in your class?" Miss Dykema scanned her list. "No, Polly."

The year before, Betty Lou went to kindergarten at the public school five blocks from home. Polly's dad thought it was silly to spend a whole bunch of money just for a half day of kindergarten at the church school, but promised Trina that Betty Lou could go to the church school when she started first grade. Today was Betty Lou's first day. Trina had cried when Betty Lou climbed the steps of the bus. "Jee whiz," Polly mumbled under her breath. "What is the big deal?" Polly had promised Trina she would take Betty Lou to her room.

Polly led Betty Lou to the next first grade room. "Mrs. Terpstra, this is my sister, Betty Lou. Is she in your class?"

"Hello, Betty Lou. Let me see." She read the 'S' names, "Schaap, Sikma. Stegenga. No, you're not. It's nice to meet you, though."

"Come on, Betty Lou. Quick. I'm going to be late." Polly pulled her sister to the last first grade room. Standing in the hall outside the room was Mrs. Van Doodle. "Oh, no. Mrs. Van Doodle must have changed grades." Betty Lou stopped and glued her feet to the floor. She wouldn't budge in spite of Polly's tugging.

"I won't go. No! Mrs. Van Doodle is an old witch. Mommy said I would have a nice teacher."

"Well maybe she'll be nice to you."

"No, she won't. She's crabby and mean."

"You have to. Now come on!" She gave her sister one more yank and managed to pull her a few steps further. Mrs. Van Doodle was watching the commotion and walked toward the girls.

"Good morning, Polly."

"Good morning, Mrs. Van Doodle."

"Good morning, Betty Lou." Betty Lou looked at her feet. "Betty Lou, can't you speak? I said, 'good morning'."

"She's a little scared because it's her first day," Polly explained.

"I wasn't talking to you, Polly."

"Sorry."

"Good morning, Betty Lou." Betty Lou lunged toward the door, but Mrs. Van Doodle grabbed the shoulder of her new dress. "When a teacher says, 'good morning' you must say 'good morning' in reply.

"Come on," Polly begged, "Just say it." *Oh no, she's going to cry.* Betty Lou's bottom lip came out in a pout.

"Children who won't obey their teachers must go see Mr. Miff. Polly take your sister to Mr. Miff's office and explain your sister's behavior."

"But I'll be late for . . ."

"Don't argue with me!"

"Yes, Mrs. Van Doodle."

Polly led Betty Lou through the halls, up the stairs to the new wing and into the principal's office. The secretary smiled. "May I help you?"

"My sister won't talk to her teacher because it's her first day and she's scared. Mrs. Van Doodle got mad and sent us here."

"Oh, Sweetheart, don't worry. I'll get Mr. Miff."

Mr. Miff was wandering around the halls making sure the first day of school was going smoothly. It took several minutes for the secretary to find him. "Come into my office girls." Mr. Miff walked slowly ahead of them, dragging his right leg. "What seems to be the problem?" By this time, Polly was frantic.

"Mr. Miff. I'm going to be late because my sister wouldn't say 'good morning' to Mrs. Van Doodle because she's scared. And I tried to make her but she wouldn't. And so, Mrs. Van Doodle sent us both to the office and now I'm going to be late."

"Shhh." Mr. Miff put his hand gently on the top of Polly's pixie head. "It's okay. Sometimes the first day of school is difficult, especially for new students. Come on, girls. Polly, I'll explain the situation to your teacher. Betty Lou, would you like to take a little walk with me? I'll show you the playground."

After school, Polly went to Mrs. Van Doodle's room to pick up Betty Lou. "Good-bye, Betty Lou." Mrs. Van Doodle said. Polly held her breath and took Betty Lou's hand.

Betty Lou smiled and said, "Good-bye, Mrs. Van Doodle."

✦

"I don't know where your father is." Trina drained the potatoes into the kitchen sink. "He should have been home an hour ago. Let's just start."

"He'll be home, Mom. Maybe he had to go to the hardware store for something."

"That wouldn't take this long. I'll bet I know where he is."

Polly began to worry. *What if Dad did go to the bar after work? Maybe he's drunk. Maybe he'll never come home again.* She poured the milk and then pushed the white eyelet curtains back to see if her father was coming around the corner. "Here he comes, Mom. Here he comes." Polly opened the utility room door. Her dad had a worried look on his face as he unzipped his coveralls. He was a foreman at the Gary steel mill—in charge of blast furnace number 261. "What's the matter, Daddy? How come you're late?"

"I'll tell you about it later. Looks like supper's on the table. Did you wash your hands?"

"Yes, Sir." *He doesn't seem drunk.*

Polly's dad looked at Trina. "I'll be right back. I have to wash up." His face and hands were smudged with soot.

"So, Hank. What did you learn on your first day of school?" Polly's dad asked questions about school every night.

"John F. Kennedy is going to run against Richard M. Nixon for president."

"Ver-schrik-kel-ijk!" Trina said in Dutch. Polly thought it was nifty that Trina could do that. "Kennedy's a Catholic. If he wins, the Pope will be running the country."

"In this country there is a separation between religion and government."

"Yeah," interjected Hank, "It's called 'Separation of Church and State'."

"Very good, Hank. You've been listening." Hank puffed up with pride. Polly's dad continued, "Mr. Kennedy will not make decisions based on his religious beliefs. President Eisenhower doesn't either."

"At least President Eisenhower believes the RIGHT things."

"In your opinion, Trina."

"Yes, in MY opinion. It sounds like you would like to see John Kennedy win the election."

"I think he would understand the concerns of working-class people like us."

"I've always been a Republican and I ALWAYS WILL BE!" Trina said in an unusually loud voice.

Polly didn't like the feeling of this conversation "What's a Republican?" Polly didn't wait for an answer; she changed the subject. "Miss Puddinga has gigantic hands and her breath smells like coffee."

"Does that affect her ability to teach?" Her dad smiled.

"What do you mean, 'affect?'"

"Can she be a good teacher with big hands and bad breath."

"I guess so. Yeah. She's pretty nice."

"What was the Bible verse you learned today, Polly?" Trina asked. In church school, Polly had to learn a Bible verse every day.

"Go to the ant, thou sluggard, consider her ways and be wise."

"What does it mean, Polly?" Her dad spooned a second helping of mashed potatoes onto his plate.

"Well. Umm. I don't know."

"Didn't Miss Puddinga explain it? Were you listening?" Polly squirmed. She had been daydreaming during Bible class.

"I guess it means that if a slug were an ant, it would be smarter."

Hank burst out laughing. "Oh, for pity's sake. That's not what it means."

"Hank, be respectful of your sister. Can you explain the verse?"

"Sure. It means that a lazy person can learn how to act better from an ant."

"No. It doesn't." Polly argued. 'Wise doesn't mean to act better, it means to get smarter."

"Same thing."

"Is not."

"Okay. Okay." Their dad seemed irritated. "You're probably both right. You should always work hard and do the best you can. That's the wise thing to do. And you should listen to your teacher, Spot."

"Do you know the book, chapter and verse?" Trina asked. "So, you can look it up later?"

"But why would I want to look it up, if I memorized it?"

"You're not sassing your mother, are you?" Polly looked at her dad in surprise. *Did I just sin again?* He explained, "You might want to read the rest of the story. And, in order to do that you would need to know the book, the chapter and the verse number." There was a pause in the conversation. "How was your first day, Betty Lou?" Polly stiffened. She hoped her sister wouldn't tell what happened with Mrs. Van Doodle. "It was fun," she said. "I really like the playground."

While she chewed a stringy piece of pot roast, Polly thought about Mr. Miff. *How did he get Betty Lou and Mrs. Van Doodle to be friends? He must be a magician or something.* Polly felt so relieved she and Betty Lou didn't get punished that she laughed.

"What's so funny?" Hank asked.

"Nothing." Polly's mind wandered to a song she had learned in music class that morning, 'The Erie Canal.' "And, she knows every inch of the way, from Albany to new Bu-a-fa—lo—oh."

"You're not supposed to sing at the table," Hank scolded. "Or talk with your mouth full."

Was I singing at the table? "I was humming."

"Same thing."

"Is not."

"Is too."

"Now, stop." There was a seriousness in her dad's voice that frightened Polly. "There is something I need to talk to you about." No one moved.

"What's wrong, Daddy?"

"The steelworkers went on strike today. That's why I was late. I was at a union meeting."

"What's a strike? What's a union? Is that like the United States?"

"Quiet now, I'll explain."

"For how long?" Trina started ripping the corner of her napkin.

"I don't know. It depends on the negotiations."

"The negotiations?"

"The steelworkers belong to a group called a 'union.' The union picks some men that talk and make deals with the bosses and owners of the mill to make sure we get paid enough money. The talks are called, 'negotiations.' Sometimes the talks are about whether the working conditions are safe, or that we get enough money to help us out if we get sick or hurt. The union feels the bosses aren't helping us enough and won't listen to us anymore. We won't go to work until they change some of those things. That's called, 'a strike.' The steelworkers are stronger when they stick together as a group."

"You quit work?" Hank asked, eyes wide, beginning to understand why this was bad news. "But Dad, if you quit your job, you won't get ANY money."

"I'm not quitting my job. I'm just not going to work. If the steelworkers strike, the owners don't make any money either. They'll have to close the mill. It's a risk. We hope they give in before we give up. We hope they'll give us at least some of what we're asking for."

Polly's dad pushed back his chair and sighed. "I agree with the union demands. We've been asked to work overtime so much that we're getting tired. More accidents have happened. We don't get paid enough for overtime work and it takes us away from our families. You know how often I'm late for dinner." Polly snapped a look at Trina.

"I'll get a paper route," Hank offered.

Trina started clearing plates. "I'm sure I can work again at my father's cabinet shop. I'll have to give up taking in ironing—that's okay."

"You can teach me how to iron." Polly wanted to help too.

"Thank you, Polly. Maybe you are old enough to iron." Trina smiled and put her arm around Polly's shoulder.

"I can clean the bathroom," Betty Lou said.

"Thanks, Sweetheart."

"What are you gonna do, Dad?"

"Well there will be many union meetings to attend. I may be able to help out at Uncle Bud's furniture factory."

"Or, maybe you can work at the cabinet shop too." Polly's dad took Trina's free hand. "We'll be all right, but we won't have quite as much money for a while." Polly was excused from helping with the dishes. Her dad and Trina did them together so they could talk.

Polly went to visit her Whispering Cottonwood. The dead robin with the stick in its mouth was lying right in the spot where she liked to sit to make a wish. The bird was stinky and there were maggots coming out of its eyes. *What am I supposed to do now?* Polly stared at the robin for a few minutes, and then picked up the end of the stick. The carcass was stiff and balanced on the other end. Slowly, using baby steps, she walked to the honeysuckle bushes. She laid the bird down on the grass while she cleared a space underneath. She gently placed the robin in the shade of the bush and covered it with the grass Betty Lou and the twins had piled up for their house. "Good night, little bird. Sleep tight."

Polly picked up another clump of grass and spread it between the roots of her tree. She didn't have a pretty stone, so she pulled a penny from her pocket, wedged it into the bark, sat down and pushed her head into the tree as hard as she could. "This is very important, Your Majesty, so listen carefully. Oh, my beautiful Whispering Cottonwood, please grant me a wish today. When I am fifty years old, I will do as you wish in return." Polly Spooner wished for her family to have enough money and for her dad's union to get what they wanted. She hummed 'Buffalo Gals' for good luck until she saw a flicker of orange. *What was that?* And then she spotted a robin hopping from branch to branch in the top of her tree.

7. Extras

"But Auntie Jo, it's really cold outside. When we went out for recess, I almost froze my fingers off." Polly pretended to shiver.

"All right. You can stay inside, but the next time you come over, take your hat and mittens along."

The weather had turned cold earlier that afternoon. The wind whistled around the house and blew red, yellow and orange leaves in every direction. Aunt Johanna wanted help picking the last of the tomatoes and to cover the marigolds, pumpkins and gourds so they wouldn't freeze that night. Ever since the strike started, Betty Lou, Hank and Polly walked the block from school to Aunt Johanna's house on the days their mom was working, and their dad was at a meeting.

Aunt Johanna pulled on her garden gloves. "Get your homework done and no funny business."

"Yes, Auntie Jo."

"Quick," Hank said. "Is she looking?" Polly stood to the side of the window and pulled the shade down when Aunt Johanna turned away from the house. "They're in here." Polly opened Mr. Miff's closet door. Mr. Miff had moved into Aunt Johanna's house as a 'boarder' when he took the job as principal of the church school the year before. He dragged his right foot because he had a wooden leg. He had been injured by a grenade during World War II. Aunt Johanna told Polly that Mr. Miff had several extra legs in his closet. Now was Polly's chance. She had convinced Hank and Betty Lou to help her.

"Look at this one!" Hank held up a leg with a shiny black patent leather shoe on the end. Here's one with a boot on it."

"Polly, help me. Here. Strap this one to my knee. Betty Lou, check on Auntie Jo."

"She's still out there."

Hank bent his knee and held his foot behind him while Polly tied the straps around Hank's waist and thigh. She giggled, "Look, you have two knees."

Mr. Miff's leg was cut off above his knee, so now Hank had Mr. Miff's knee and his own.

"Put these others on your arms and you can be a camel." Polly moved quickly to secure the other two legs. Hank started walking around on the three wooden legs and one of his own making all sorts of animal noises. But he had trouble balancing on the wooden legs and finally tripped on the rug next to the bed. He pulled Betty Lou and Polly down on top of him. They squealed and laughed and joked. . . Bang! The back door slammed.

"Shhh. Hurry up. Get these off of me!"

"I can't. Hold still."

"Open the shade, Betty Lou. Straighten the rug." Betty Lou pulled on the shade and it snapped all the way to the top.

"Children?"

Stamp. Stamp. Stamp. The door opened. Polly and Hank had no choice but to smile at Aunt Johanna from a pile of wooden legs with Betty Lou leaning over them.

"Oops," Polly said.

"Oops?" Repeated Aunt Johanna. "Oops?" Then Mr. Miff entered the room and looked over Aunt Johanna's shoulder. He bellowed like the big bad wolf, "What are you doing with my legs?" Polly, Betty Lou and Hank stiffened with fear. With her hands on her hips, Aunt Johanna's frown turned slowly into a smile. Mr. Miff laughed and choked and finally sat on the bed so he wouldn't topple over too.

♭

"Betty Lou, don't pour the water all in one place. Here, I'll show you. See, like you're sprinkling salt on your scrambled eggs." Polly turned the old vinegar bottle sideways and pretended to salt Mr. Tippy's embroidered work shirt. Water dribbled evenly from the holes in the aluminum dampening cap which Trina bought at Kresky's Dime Store. "Now, you try."

Betty Lou slowly fingered and read the wet letters, "M-r-r T-i-p-p-y. What does Murr Tippy mean?"

"Capital 'm', small 'r', period, stands for mister."

Betty Lou traced the letters again. "It says, Mister Tippy!" She began dampening the shirt as Polly had instructed. "That's good. Now fold the shirt and roll it up really tight."

"How come?"

"So, the water goes all through the shirt and stays wet until I can iron it."

"You have to finish this whole basket before we can go to Grandma and Grandad's house?"

"Yes."

"Why?"

"Because Mrs. Tippy is expecting it by noon."

"This shirt looks like a sausage." Betty Lou put the rolled shirt in Polly's ironing basket.

"Now, why don't you get a rag and dust the piano. We can help Mom finish the rest of the housework."

"I have to go to the bathroom."

"You always have to go to the bathroom."

"I do not."

Polly rolled her eyes.

It was a special Saturday. Trina's family was having a 'Get Together'. The children didn't have any grandparents until their dad married Trina. All of their real grandparents had died long before they were born. They not only acquired a new set of grandparents, they also got five new sets of aunts and uncles and, best of all, nineteen extra cousins. Some of them were coming all the way from Colorado. Great Uncle Fred and Aunt Susie were coming from Montana for Grandad's seventy-fifth birthday.

"How are you doing, Polly?" Trina asked.

"I'm on my last pair of pants."

"Oh, but Polly. I forgot to put Hank's Sunday shirt in our ironing basket. I found it just now when I was putting the laundry away. Would you mind pressing it so Hank can wear it tomorrow? Betty Lou, would you sprinkle it for Polly?" Betty Lou had returned to the living room and was watching 'Mighty Mouse' on television.

"You can see the TV from the kitchen."

"No, I can't."

"Do it during the next commercial."

While she waited for Betty Lou to sprinkle the shirt, Polly turned the knob on the television. It had been Betty Lou's Saturday morning to watch her favorite shows, but no matter which Saturday it was, Polly always switched the channels in time to sing along with Roy Rogers and Dale Evans as they rode their horses, Trigger and Butter Cup, down the poplar-lined lane of the Double R Ranch. "Happy trails to you, until we meet again. Happy trails to you, keep smilin' on 'til then." Polly sang in her most clear, most beautiful voice. "Happy trails to you, 'til we meet again."

Polly's dad and Hank came into the kitchen piling rags, soap and car wax onto the table. "We're ready to go when you are."

"The car is spic and span. Right, Dad?"

"Yes, and waxed for the winter. It's a gorgeous Indian Summer day."

"Why is it called Indian Summer, Dad?" Polly asked. She was anxious to get outside, but carefully finished ironing Hank's shirt, pushing the point of the iron between two buttons. Steam rose up and the iron hissed. Polly's face was flushed from the heat.

"Indian Summer is a period of nice weather that comes after the weather has already turned cold."

"I know, but why is it called, 'Indian Summer'?"

"Well, maybe the American Indians counted on one more warm spell to finish getting ready for the winter or traveling to warmer places, but you know, I really don't know for sure. Maybe we should look it up in the encyclopedia tomorrow. Do you remember how to spell 'encyclopedia', Spot?

"E-n-c-y-c-l-o-p-e-d-i-a." Polly's dad had taught her to spell all kinds of words using special rhythms. She spelled her favorite, "M-I-double S, I-double S, I-double P-I. Okay, I'm done." Polly said, putting the second shoulder of Hank's shirt onto the clothes hanger. She admired her work.

Trina looked over Polly's shoulder and kissed the top of her head. "I think you iron better than I do, Polly."

Polly felt proud. "Thank you, Mom." But then she thought maybe it was against the Ten Commandments to feel proud. *I hope I didn't sin again.*

⚡

"Do you know there are sixteen boys and only six girls?" Polly held her fingers extended after counting all of her new cousins. "That doesn't seem fair, and those boys are always spying on us and teasing us."

"That's because they like you, Polly." Trina said. Polly wondered if that were true.

"They don't act like it."

Granddad and Grandma Vander Kamp lived only two miles away. Trina tied her see-through shimmering scarf carefully over her hair. "I can't wait to see Sylvia."

Polly's dad parked the car behind three others in the driveway. He pulled a comb out of his breast pocket, looked in the rear-view mirror and slicked back his hair.

"Dad?"

"Hmmm?"

"I think you comb your hair too much."

"Why's that, Spot?"

"Because it's coming out in front."

Polly held her dad's hand and walked a little behind him as they entered the breezeway. Polly was still getting used to being the new cousin. Sometimes the boys would tease her about being adopted—which she wasn't. They were so stupid. Once, she even got a stomachache. Her dad said she was just a little nervous and it would get better. The breezeway was a closed-in porch between the garage and the kitchen with windows on both sides. Polly could look into the backyard and see Granddad's raspberry patch, his peach trees, and his flower beds that today were buried under piles of dead leaves and grass. She could look across the front yard at the mulberry, box elder and silver maple trees that grew on the east branch of Hart's ditch.

Polly looked at the honey spot on the ceiling of the breezeway. The first time she had met her new grandfather, they had supper in the breezeway because it was hot in the house. The tip of the honey bear was plugged so her granddad squeezed hard, and, S-P-L-A-T, honey shot all the way to the ceiling. Even though Grandma tried to scrub the honey spot off, it left a little circle above Granddad's place at the table.

"Hey, Paint. Come out here." Polly's new cousin, Boo, yelled through the screen door. Most of the cousins had nicknames. Boo's nickname had been shortened from 'Boo-Hoo.' His older brothers said Boo cried all the time when he was a baby. Even though her dad already nicknamed Polly, 'Spot', because of her freckles, her cousins named her, 'Paint' at her parent's wedding party. She didn't mind the nickname. Having a nickname made her feel like she belonged to the family. Anyway, Polly liked her freckles. Her first mom had freckles and Aunt Johanna said, "A face without freckles, is like a sky without stars."

Boo continued, "Uncle Fred and Granddad are having a tomato fight. They're rotten and flying all over the place. Come on!"

Polly dropped her dad's hand and forgot about feeling nervous. She pictured her Granddad plastered with tomatoes. She and Boo ran around the back of the garage to the side garden. Cousins were lined up along the edges hooting and hollering. "Get him, Uncle Fred. Watch out! Holy Cow!" A giant soggy tomato missed Uncle Fred and went sailing into the sidelines. The cousins jumped back. Pretty soon the tomatoes were gone, and Granddad grabbed an over ripe cucumber from the trellis on the garage. "Hey, old man, take this!" He flung the cucumber at Uncle Fred who had just reached down to pull a left-over carrot out of the ground. The cucumber hit a boy Polly didn't know. *Must be a Colorado cousin,* she thought.

"Granddad, you're asking for it," he warned. The Colorado cousin ran to the compost pile along the fence and picked up a worm-eaten cabbage. "Take that!" The cabbage knocked granddad's cap off. Within seconds, cucumbers and cabbages and carrots and squash and pumpkins and dried sweetcorn and peppers and dirt were thick in the air. Polly almost peed her pants, she was laughing so hard.

Where are the girls, anyway? Polly looked around the yard when the vegetables were gone. Everyone was exhausted. She saw her dad sitting alone under a peach tree. Polly ran over to him. "Dad, did you see the vegetable fight?"

Polly's dad didn't seem to hear her, "Huh?" he said and picked a piece of something out of her hair and stared across the yard.

"What's the matter, Daddy?"

"I miss your mom."

"Well, she's probably inside somewhere talking to Aunt Sylvia."

"Polly, do you like your new mom?"

"Sure."

Polly's father whispered as he stood up, "I hoped you would."

"Ollie, Ollie in free!" Polly looked around to see who was 'It'.

"Looks like you better hide, Spot." He smiled and nudged her off.

"See you later, Daddy."

Polly didn't hide. Instead, she ran into the house to look for the girls. The aunts were cutting up potatoes, onions and carrots for beef stew. The uncles were playing cards in the living room. Polly hoped her dad would find them and play too.

"Where are the girls?" Polly paused and added, "Grandma." She like to say 'grandma', but it didn't come out naturally.

"Da girls are in Aunt Jane's bedroom." Polly liked her new Aunt Jane. She had gone to nursing school in Ohio and worked at Michael Reese Hospital. She took the South Shore train all the way to Chicago every day. Aunt Jane knew all kinds of things.

"Did you know," Aunt Jane was saying when Polly entered the room, "When men dry dishes they turn a plate over to wipe the back, but when women dry a plate, they wipe the back without turning it over. Men and women do lots of things differently because their brains are different." Polly tried to picture in her mind how her dad dried dishes, but she couldn't remember because he hardly ever did. Aunt Jane continued, "You girls need to think like scientists. Observe and study everything and go to college."

"I'm going to college," Polly said. "My Dad says I'm really smart."

"He's right, Polly. Aunt Jane took her nurse's cap out of its box. "I wonder how you look in my cap? The other girls have already tried it on." Polly looked in the mirror.

"I think I'll be a nurse someday."

"I bet you will."

The afternoon passed quickly. The family ate supper together in the basement. The ping-pong table and the pool table were set with dishes and there were four card tables set up besides. Granddad said a prayer and then Grandma dished up the stew. Some of the cousins started moaning about the whole-wheat bread.

"Don't you have any Wonder Bread, Grandma?"

"No, vee haf no Vonder Bread."

Uncle Fred teased, "Da viter da bread da sooner yer dead!"

Aunt Sylvia had covered the entire birthday cake with candles. Aunt Jane, Aunt Sylvia and Trina lit the candles together. Granddad tried, but Uncle Fred had to help blow out the 75 flames.

The cousins played 'doctor' after supper. Grandma's steam-press was the operating table. The boys started arguing about whose turn it was to be the doctor, so Polly went upstairs. She found her dad and Trina sitting in front of the fireplace which was built against the end wall of the breezeway. The fire was dying and the coals were glowing

"You look tired, Polly," Trina said. Polly leaned against Trina's shoulder. "I'm not tired." As Trina fingered the hair around Polly's ear, she could feel her eyes begin to close.

8. Sunday

The next morning Polly opened one eye and rolled over. She pulled her stuffed dog under her chin and smelled the fake fur on its matted white head. She liked her dog, but Betty Lou's was golden-yellow with long straight hair that tossed around like the eighth-grade cheerleaders' pom-poms. Polly tried not to like her sister's stuffed dog better than her own because Mrs. Van Doodle said you shouldn't want anything other people have. It was called 'coveting', which was also called 'envy', which was against the Ten Commandments. Polly pretended her poor ugly dog was an orphan she rescued from Captain Hook's ship and would be her loyal friend forever.

"Let them sleep, Trina."

Polly could barely hear her parents talking at the bottom of the steps.

"One Sunday without church won't hurt them."

"What will people think?" There was a long pause. "People already wonder why you never ..." Polly couldn't hear what else Trina said.

"They had a busy day yesterday and got to bed late. Let them sleep."

The latch on the door at the bottom of stairs clicked.

"Mmm." Polly stretched. Betty Lou wasn't in her bed. The sun was warm on Polly's cheek. *It's late. We missed church?* Polly sat up and threw her silky flowered bedspread back. It slid to the floor. The smell of coffee and her sister's giggling drew Polly to the kitchen. "Aren't we going to church?"

"No," her dad said. "We're going to have waffles for breakfast and then we're driving to the Indiana Dunes."

Even though Polly really had to pee, she stayed in the kitchen doorway. "Why? We usually go to the dunes on Decoration Day."

"Because it's another beautiful autumn day. The changing leaves will be at their peak." Polly's dad lifted the cover of the waffle iron.

"It's not Saturday night. Why are we having waffles?" Ginger scooted under Polly's nightgown and licked her toes. "You silly dog. What are you doing inside?"

172

Hank came up behind Polly, "What's going on?" he asked, rubbing his eyes.

"We're going swimming," Betty Lou said.

"Swimming?"

"No. we're not going swimming, Honey. The water will be too cold. We'll just play on the beach and climb Mount Tom."

"We're going to the dunes? What for?"

"To see the leaves," Polly replied.

"Get dressed you two. Your mom will be home soon and then we'll go."

The car whizzed under the green signs on Interstate 80. Trina read every sign, "Cline Avenue, Burr Street, Grant Boulevard."

"In a few years, we'll be able to go further east, as far as Interstate 65, but the clover leaves aren't built yet," Polly's dad explained. "For now, we have to drive the rest of the way on Highway 12/20. I remember when we drove all the way on Route 6 and Highways 12 and 20, before any of the Interstate was built."

"There it is, "Hank said, "I saw it first."

"No, I saw it before you did, but I didn't say anything." Polly searched between the pines and giant oaks for another glance at Lake Michigan.

"Did not."

"Did too."

"Here comes Ripley Street," Trina pointed to the blue sign on a railroad bridge over the road.

"Indiana Dunes State Park," Polly read the brown information sign. "Exit here."

Polly's dad put a dollar in the box at the ranger's station. They snaked through the tree covered dunes and eventually arrived at the huge parking lot. In the summer the parking lot was filled with people in bathing suits and rubber flip-flop sandals. They carried picnic baskets, beach towels and toys, but now there were only three abandoned cars and one with a couple of teenagers sitting on the hood kissing.

"Polly and Skippy, sittin' in a tree, k-i-s-s-i-n-g."

"Shut up, Hank"

Trina reached back and grabbed Polly's knee. "Polly Spooner, you never tell anyone to SHUT-UP."

"Polly. Hank. Put your heads down on your laps and I'll tell you when you can look up." Polly's dad jerked the car to a stop.

Polly hated to have her head down when she wanted to look at the pavilion and the lake to see how big the waves were. She pinched Hank's knee. He punched her thigh. Before she knew it, her dad pulled her out of the car and stood her up against the shiny black fender. "We're going to have no more fighting today. Do you hear me, Polly?"

"Yes, Sir."

Hank was peeking. Polly's dad saw him and went around the car. He opened the door, pulled Hank out by the arm and said, "If I hear you teasing your sister again today, you're going to sit in the car until we're ready to go home. Do you understand me?"

"Yes, Sir."

"All right then. Where should we go first?"

"To the beach!" Betty Lou grabbed Trina's hand. "Okay, Honey. Don't pull my hand off."

"Dad? Where is this water coming from?" Polly and her family took their shoes off and waded across a stream swirling into Lake Michigan.

"It's just a little creek that drains the land around the dunes."

"The water is so clear. Look. There's a crayfish." Hank nudged it with his toe.

"Watch out, Hank." Betty Lou stepped back. "It might pinch you."

"The water is so clear, but how come it looks like root beer?" Polly asked, watching a school of minnows darting away from the bank.

"It must come from some kind of algae, or maybe tannin from the decay of the oak trees and leaves on the dunes." Her dad took Trina's a hand to help her up the sandy bank.

Polly had more questions, but just then, Hank shouted, "I'll race you to that big hunk of driftwood." Polly, Hank and her father ran down the beach splashing in the cold foam as the waves crawled up the shore. Polly was fast. She could run faster than any other girl in her class, but she couldn't catch Hank. Her dad slowed down to run with her.

"There's the sign for Mount Tom," Hank pointed.

"Let's wait for your mother and Betty Lou. We'll go up together."

Polly trailed behind her family as they climbed Mount Tom. She was studying the trees and picking up leaves of different shapes and colors. She knew all the trees because she had a book called, *Trees: A Guide to Familiar American Trees*, that Aunt Johanna had given her on her seventh birthday.

Polly's father was busy helping Trina and Betty Lou up the steep slope. Hank was climbing up and running down and asking why everyone was so pokey.

"I'm getting really hungry." Betty Lou threw a stick into the lake.

"Me too," Hank said, smashing in the remaining side of his sandcastle. The waves were getting larger as a biting wind blew in clouds from the north.

Polly lay back in the sand and tried to see animals in the clouds. "We didn't bring any food for a picnic. What are we going to eat?"

Polly's dad and Trina were sitting together on a dead log. "Well, I thought we should go to Parkmore for fish."

"Really?"

"Hurray!"

"But we can't afford it, can we?" Trina didn't seem very excited. "Besides, we shouldn't buy on Sunday."

"But we have to eat. I'm starving," Hank argued. Polly's dad rubbed his forehead.

"Can't we Mommy? Please?" Betty Lou asked.

Polly sighed, but didn't say anything.

"It's the last day Parkmore's open. It's closed for the season after today. I thought the kids . . ."

"Okay, okay. Let's go. What's one more Sunday rule broken?" Trina didn't look all that mad. When Betty Lou, Hank and Polly began to dance in a circle and sing, "Parkmore, Parkmore, siss-boom-bah," she couldn't help but laugh.

The waitress hooked the tray snuggly against the driver's side window. The smell of the deep-fried fish, butter-dipped toast, french-fries and coleslaw blew into the car. Polly's dad first passed around the napkins and plastic forks. Polly and Hank set their mugs of root-beer on the shelf in the back window. Then came the plates piled high with crispy food. Polly ate and ate. She didn't say one word; it was so good.

Before Polly went into the house. She visited Her Majesty. The crinkly, yellow heart-shaped leaves were feathering down. There were enough leaves on the ground to make a pile between the roots. Polly lay on her yellow cushion and looked up into the blaze of color above her. Because so many leaves had fallen, the sky showed through, gray and thick. Polly shivered. "Oh, my beautiful Whispering Cottonwood, please grant . . ." Polly stopped. She had no wish and started over. "Oh, my beautiful Whispering Cottonwood, thank you for making this the best Sunday I've ever had." She closed her eyes and started to sing 'Buffalo Gals' but she was interrupted by the touch of something cold and wet on her nose. She opened her eyes. A giant snowflake kissed her eyelash. Like tiny white butterflies, the snowflakes flew around her. Through them, she thought she heard something say. "S-n-o-w."

9. Thump, Thump, Swoosh

Polly Spooner pounded the frame of the twin's green screen door. "Oh, J-u-n-e. Oh, J-u-l-y." It was Wednesday after school. A dirty mop-water sky had drizzled and sleeted and snowed all day, but now patches of blue sky were breaking through the clouds. A pink car, with what looked like wings along the trunk, pulled up to the house. It honked, braked hard and slid on the gravel driveway. The twins and their mom piled out.

"Do you like our new Plymouth?" July asked, trailing a finger along the fin of the fender. I think it looks like a rocket."

Marge, the twin's mom, leaned back into the car to get her purse. "We bought it to celebrate," she said.

Polly thought for a moment but couldn't find any reason to celebrate. Stepping off the porch, Polly risked sounding stupid and asked, "To celebrate what?" she asked.

June came up the walk swinging her lunch bucket. "Don't you know? John F. Kennedy won the election!"

"But he's a Catholic and a Democrat."

"So are we," July said, doing a fancy cheerleader jump. "Gimme a K, gimme an E, gimme an N . . ."

"Do you want to sit in our car?" June asked Polly. "Can we, Mom?"

"For a minute. Keep your feet off the seats."

June pressed the steering wheel. The horn blew through the neighborhood. "Hip, hip, hurray!" she yelled.

After a few minutes of admiring the creamy leather seats, the cranberry carpet, fancy buttons and knobs, Polly asked, "Do you want to see my secret fort?" That's what she wanted to do when she went to the twin's house in the first place.

"Huh? Where is it?" The girls wondered in unison.

"In the drainage ditch at the end of Delaware Parkway."

"Sure. We'll have to change out of our school uniforms. Come in and wait, it's kind of cold out here."

Marge stood at the kitchen table clipping a picture of Mr. Kennedy from the newspaper. She lit a cigarette. "I never thought

177

I would see this day. And, it's about time." The radio was turned up and as Chubby Checkers sang 'The Twist', Marge began to dance. "Do your parents like Kennedy, Polly?"

"I don't know," Polly lied. Trina had slammed the breakfast dishes onto the table when she heard the news on the Moody Bible Institute radio show. Polly's dad was still sleeping when she left for the bus, although she knew he would be pleased. No one at school seemed very happy. Miss Puddinga prayed, "Bless the country in these troubling times."

The twins danced down the steps. They grabbed their jackets and earmuffs and all three girls squeezed through the door.

"You girls get home before dark."

"Yes, Ma'am."

Arm in arm they skipped down the street and sang, "Ooh—ee—ooh—ah—ah. Ting. Tang. Walla-walla, bing-bang." Polly didn't know all the words to 'The Witch Doctor', but she knew the chorus and hummed along on the verses. The twins knew all kinds of neat songs from the radio. Polly wasn't allowed to listen to WLS—Chicago.

Polly's fort was a mess. The snow from Sunday had turned into rain on Monday and had washed the remains of dead ragweed and soggy leaves into the bottom. "Look at all these dead birds. Poor things," Polly said sadly, as she pushed through the old beach towel that had fallen halfway to the ground. "What kind of birds are these?"

"They're kind of purple-ie," July said. "And shiny." She flipped one over with her foot.

"My science teacher says that all the birds in the WHOLE WORLD are going to die because of DDT," June said.

"All the birds?" Polly thought June was exaggerating.

"What's DDT?" July wondered.

"DDT is the stuff they spray on mosquitoes," June answered.

"You mean like what comes out of the mosquito truck?"

"I guess so," June speculated.

"Are we going to die too?" July asked.

"Nah. We're too big to be poisoned by mosquito spray." June kicked a bird into a rusty pail.

"How come it kills the birds?"

"Because they eat bugs and ALL the bugs are dead."

"No, they aren't." Polly thought about the last time she saw bugs—maggots on the dead robin Skippy had killed.

"Well, the mosquitoes are dead, and a lot of birds eat mosquitoes."

"I'm glad the mosquitoes are dead," July said. "I hate mosquitoes."

"I hope all the birds don't die," Polly worried.

"Look at this," June said. "You can poke out the middle of a ragweed stem and make a tube." June blew air through a stem she had hollowed out with a twig.

July tried to break a stem, but the whole plant came out of the ground. "I've got a sword."

Polly tugged on a stalk that towered over her. It came right out of the ground. She broke the stem over her knee to remove the big glob of dirt clinging to the roots. "Take that, you no good pirate!" Polly stabbed at the air.

June yanked another ragweed giant from its hold in the earth. "Today, you die! Release Peter Pan at once!" June demanded.

"Never!" July took the voice of Captain Hook.

"Walk the plank you dirty pirate!"

"Never!"

A whistle blew from up the street. June threw a moldy piece of lumber toward Captain Hook and broke his sword.

"Serves you right, you evil, no good, child snatching pirate."

"Was that our whistle?"

"I think so."

"We better go."

As the girls climbed from the ditch, Polly covered her ear. The east wind was cold and damp. It made her ear ache. She cut through the park on the way home. It was getting dark, so she hurried to her almost leafless cottonwood tree. Without speaking aloud, Polly asked the tree, *How come some people can be happy and other people can be sad about the same thing? And how come people kill mosquitoes with DDT if it kills the birds?*

¶

"Where were you?" Trina strained a pan of noodles into the sink.

"Playing with the twins."

"You left your sister all alone."

"No, I didn't. Hank and Dad were here."

"Hank had to do his paper route and your father went to Gary. Betty Lou was crying when I got home."

Polly bit her lip, "I'm sorry, Betty Lou." She hugged her sister. "Are you okay?"

"Why didn't you take me along?"

"You were in the bathroom and I didn't think you were alone."

"I WAS alone and I could have been kidnapped."

"You wouldn't have been kidnapped."

"Would too."

"By who?"

"By whom, Polly?"

"By whom?"

"Somebody bad."

"Polly, as long as you still have your coat on, bring Ginger in, will you?"

Polly went into the backyard and unclipped the chain that was looped around the clothesline post. "Come on, Ginger, not that way. You're getting all tangled up. Quit pulling. Okay, I'll walk you, but just down the alley a little way." She gave Ginger fresh food and water when she returned.

"Polly, could you open those cans?" Trina pointed to the cans on the countertop. Polly struggled to remove the lids from the tuna fish and mushroom soup cans. Her hands were getting tired. "I can't get this dumb can of peas open."

"Thanks, Polly. I'll get it. This can opener doesn't work very well anymore. When the strike's over we'll have to get a new one."

"Could we use the pretty dishes tonight?"

"No. Well, why not. Let me get them down for you." Trina opened the light-yellow cabinet door above the refrigerator and took out the china. The dishes had come from Holland when Trina's grandmother came to the United States. The plates were ivory-colored and painted with dark pink flowers and vines.

Hank came into the kitchen and threw his canvas newspaper bag over a kitchen chair. Trina put the bowl of tuna-fish casserole on the table. "That's not enough food for everybody. I'm starving."

"It will have to do. The heating bill was more than we expected this month. We have to cut back wherever we can. Take an extra piece of bread."

"When will the strike be over?"

"Soon, I hope. Betty Lou? Supper."

"Where's Daddy?" Betty Lou asked, scooting her chair up to the table.

"Not home yet. Supper's ready, so we're going to eat."

"But we never ..."

"We're not waiting tonight."

After supper and dishes, Polly worked on her arithmetic and then practiced crocheting. Aunt Johanna had taught her how to crochet one day after school and she was trying to make a scarf out of left-over red yarn. "How come it keeps getting skinnier?"

"You must be skipping stiches at the ends." Trina said, "I did that too when I was learning." Trina put the newspaper down and glanced out the window. She came to Polly's side of the table, put her hands over Polly's hands and slowly talked her through the steps. "Now you try it."

"Mom, my ear kind of hurts."

"Did you wear your hat when you were out playing?"

"No."

"It's getting colder, time to wear your hat. I'll put some olive oil in your ear. You can keep it warm with cotton tonight. It should feel better by morning." Trina put her face against the window and peered into the dark. "Betty Lou. Hank. Time to get ready for bed."

"We can't go to bed. Daddy isn't home yet. Do you think he had an accident?" Trina put her arm around Betty Lou.

"I'll stay up with you, Mom," Hank said.

"Okay, for a little while."

Polly was tired. She and Betty Lou went to bed.

♭

Polly woke up with a thumping in her ear. She adjusted her ear on the pillow so the noise would stop. She heard a door slam downstairs. Her dad's voice was louder than usual, but Polly couldn't understand what he was saying. She leaned over the bed to check for boogie men before she put on her furry pink slippers.

Her dad was standing outside the closed bathroom door. "We were celebrating, Trina. Can't a guy have a couple of drinks with his buddies when he's got something to celebrate?"

"You had more than a couple."

Polly touched her dad's sleeve. He startled, stepped backward and stumbled. "Polly, what are you doing up?"

"My ear is thug, thug, thugging."

"Thugging? Come, sit on my lap."

"Daddy, you smell funny."

"I was celebrating the election."

"Are you drunk, Dad?"

"I don't think so. Do I seem drunk?"

"You're talking kind of slow."

Trina came out of the bathroom. "Polly, come on now. Back upstairs." Trina took Polly's hand and guided her up a few steps.

"Is he …?"

"He's okay, Polly. Don't worry."

*

The next morning Trina put fresh olive oil and cotton in Polly's ear. "It hurts only a little," Polly said.

"If it gets worse, you should ask to see the school nurse. Keep your hat on at recess."

In the classroom, Polly kept her hand over her ear so no one could see the cotton. She couldn't hear Miss Puddinga very well, but she didn't ask to sit in the front. At recess, she kept her hat tied under her chin. She was going hand over hand on the monkey bars when Spit DeGroot ran under her, grabbed her and tackled her to the ground. "You want your face washed, Lollypop Polly?"

"Get off me, you big lug!"

"Try and make me!"

Polly's friends went screaming for the teacher. Polly kicked and hit Spit, but he held her down. Although there was only a little snow left on the ground, Spit swiped what he could from around the base of the monkey bars. He rubbed his glove, wet with muddy slushy snow, all over Polly's face. Her hat slipped off and Spit saw the cotton. "Oh, poor Polly can't hear. Does little Polly have an ear ache?" He took another handful of slush and smashed it into Polly's ear. Someone shoved Spit backwards. "You lay a hand on my sister again and you won't hear for a week. You got that?"

"Sticking up for your baby sister?"

"Yes, I am. Now get your drooling mouth out of here."

"Your time is coming, Hank Spooner."

"Oh, yeah? Just try it." Spit took off. Hank held his hand out to Polly. "You all right?"

"Yeah." She would have cried except she wanted to be brave for Hank. "Thanks, Hank." Polly wiped her face and ear with her hat. She couldn't find any of her friends, so she waited in the school's warm entry until recess was over.

Miss Puddinga read from a book called, *The Yearling*, by Marjorie Rawlings. Polly missed some of the words. The cotton had fallen out of her ear and it was thumping again. She felt shivery cold, but her cheeks felt on fire.

She folded her arms on her desktop and put her head down. "Polly?" Miss Puddinga touched her shoulder. "You don't look very well. How are you feeling?" Polly just shook her head. "Come on, Sweetheart. I'll take you to the nurse."

The nurse gave Polly two Saint Joseph's aspirins and she fell asleep until the bell rang. She sat quietly on the bus ride home. She couldn't hear anything but distant talking. When she got home her dad put his hand on her forehead and tucked her under blankets on the living room sofa. Trina came home and decided Polly would have to go to the doctor the next day if she wasn't feeling better.

In the middle of the night Polly woke up. Thump, thump, thump, swoosh. Thump, thump, thump, swoosh. Inside her ear it felt like a balloon was ready to burst.

"Polly, quit making that noise," Betty Lou whispered through the dark.

"I didn't make any noise.

"Yes, you did. You sounded like Ginger crying."

"O-u-c-h," Polly thrashed around. "Can I sleep with you, Betty Lou?"

"Sleep with me? Why?"

"Because my ear hurts."

"Okay, but use your own pillow and don't breathe on me."

Polly cuddled in with her sister. She rocked a little to distract herself. Betty Lou gently patted Polly's shoulder. "You'll feel better pretty soon." She yawned and within minutes was asleep.

Polly slept fitfully. She dreamed she was lying under her cottonwood tree, an eerie fog wrapped around her. Birds were crying and falling from the sky. Men wrapped like mummies were stumbling around in a circle talking to her in words she couldn't understand. She awoke again, lay still and said as softly as she could, "Oh, my beautiful Whispering Cottonwood. Please grant me a wish tonight. I promise Your Majesty, when I am fifty years old, I will do as you wish in return." She saw her cottonwood tree in her mind. She wished and wished and wished.

♭

"Polly, wake up! Yucky."

"What's the matter?"

"Your brains are on your pillow and in your hair." Polly felt the side of her head. Her hair was warm and wet. She looked at the pillow. Red, yellow and green slime was smeared all over it. "I guess your ear blew up."

"No, it couldn't, could it?"

"Sure, it could." Betty Lou pointed to the pillow and shuddered, "It did!"

10. *Just Thinking*

Polly stayed home from school. Her dad called Dr. Summers' office and made an appointment for eleven o'clock. Polly cuddled on the couch and watched 'Captain Kangaroo' and then 'Queen for a Day' but fell asleep before the housewife was crowned. At ten-thirty her dad woke her up and they drove to Lansing, Illinois to see Dr. Summers. Polly lived in Indiana, two miles from the border between Indiana and Illinois. She went to church and school in Illinois. Aunt Johanna lived a few blocks from the state line. Sometimes when they took walks, Polly jumped back and forth between the states and chanted, "Illinois. Indiana. Illinois. Indiana."

As her dad slowed to a stop at the Hammond Avenue intersection, he said, "I'm sorry about the other day."

There had been so many sorry things that had happened during the last couple of days, Polly didn't know what he meant. "For what?" she asked.

"I'm sorry you saw me a little tipsy."

"Oh." Polly didn't know what to say.

"I got carried away and drank too much beer. Your mom was right."

"But everyone else was doing it, right?"

"Doing something wrong is never right just because everyone else is doing it." Her dad paused and said, "I don't know if it's wrong exactly. Your mom thinks drinking any alcohol is bad. Maybe it's not a matter of right or wrong, but I shouldn't drink too much when my family is counting on me." They drove on in silence, passing Burger's Supermarket and Jack and Jill's—Clothes for Children.

"Dad? It made me kind of scared."

"Scared?"

"When you were drunk. What if you had a car accident or fell and broke your leg? What if you couldn't take care of us like after Mom died?"

Polly's dad glanced at her in surprise. He turned back to watch the road and said quietly, "Honey, I'm sorry if I made you worry."

They turned left at the Hal Morris Music Store on Wentworth Avenue and after two blocks turned into the parking lot next to the doctor's office. Dr. Summers wore a long white coat and had a black stethoscope stuck into his pocket. He also wore a shiny chrome disk on a band around his forehead. The office smelled of disinfectant. Polly stepped up onto the exam table.

"The last time I saw you Miss Spooner, if I recall, you came to see me with a dog bite. Is that right?"

"Yes, sir." The summer before last, Polly was sitting with several kids on the steps of Aunt Johanna's porch. A boy came up the steps with his dog on a leash. Polly reached out to pet the little black dog and it snapped at her.

"Let's see how that healed." Dr. Summers tipped his head so the light would fall just right on the shiny chrome disk and be reflected into Polly's mouth. He lifted her lip and looked inside. "Not too bad. I guess it was all right not to stitch it. I wasn't sure, but there is hardly a scar at all." The doctor put a thermometer under Polly's tongue. "So, this time your father tells me you have an earache." He noticed the cotton and tugged. It wouldn't budge. It was stuck in her ear from dried-up goop and he had to moisten it with water to pull it out. "Miss Spooner, does this hurt?" He pulled down gently on her earlobe. She sucked in her breath, her eyes filled with tears and she nodded. He looked into her ear with a pointed flash light. "Oh my," he said. "Polly, your eardrum is ruptured." Dr. Summers took the thermometer.

"It blew up all over my pillow last night."

The doctor chuckled and turned to Polly's dad. "Mr. Spooner, we need to irrigate Polly's ear and I'm sorry to say, give her a big shot of penicillin. She has a bit of a fever now which was probably much higher before her ear drum broke."

Polly's dad held her hand while the doctor and nurse sprayed warm water into her ear with what looked like a pistol. She tried to keep her head still but it hurt so badly she kept turning away. Her dad helped her hold her head still while she dug her forehead into his chest. The shot didn't hurt half as much, but Polly was embarrassed when the nurse pulled her underpants down part way in front of the doctor and her dad.

In the waiting room, Polly wriggled around on the chair to stay off the sore spot made by the needle. Her dad was at the desk. "Would it be possible to pay for this later?" he asked very softly. "I work at the mills."

The secretary seemed to understand what he meant. "I'll speak to the doctor." She came back with a piece of paper. "Yes, Mr. Spooner. Sign here."

Polly's dad turned the wrong way on Ridge Road. "Where are we going, Daddy?"

"I think such a brave girl needs a reward."

"What kind of reward?"

"We'll go to the dime store and you can pick something out."

Polly thought about what to buy, but then she remembered the strike.

"Dad, I don't need a reward."

"Sure, you do."

No, there's not a thing I need."

"But is there anything you want?"

"Just for the strike to be over so you can go back to work."

$\oint$

The next day, when Granddad VanderKamp picked up Trina to go to the cabinet shop, like he did every morning, he dropped off Polly's grandma. Grandma Vander Kamp was going to stay for the day. She set a brown paper sack on the kitchen table, took off her camel-colored winter coat with a real fur collar and came into the living room. Polly was sitting on the couch crocheting her red scarf.

"Vell, dat is nice," Grandma said.

"Thank you, Grandma." Saying 'grandma' was coming more naturally, but Polly was still aware of how much she liked to say it. She also loved her grandma's Dutch accent, but sometimes she was hard to understand.

"Ven your fater called me last night, he said you ver brafe at da doctor's.

"Oh, Grandma, it hurt SO much!"

"How is your ear today?"

"Better. It's not thug, thug, thugging anymore. It just hurts when I burp."

"Better not do dat den," Grandma laughed.

Polly's dad came into the living room smelling like Listerine mouthwash and Old Spice aftershave. "Morning," he said to Grandma.

"Goedemorgen. So, you go to da meeting now?"

"Yes, and I hope it's the last. Negotiations started up again yesterday."

"How long you haf no verk?"

"Six weeks too long."

𝄻

After Polly's dad left, Grandma brought the brown paper bag and two cups of tea into the living room. "Here is a cup for you and von for me." She dug into the bag. "Vat haf vee here?" She pulled out several mismatched socks and laid them on the hassock. She dug deeper into the bag. "Vell, look at this. A coloring book and a box of new crayons."

Polly hugged Grandma Vander Kamp tightly around her neck and said, "Thank you." Before Polly opened the coloring book, she shivered. Somehow, in her mind, stronger than anything, she knew there would be a picture of an ancient, gnarly, magnificent tree right in the middle of the book. Knowing she was under a magic charm, Polly let the book fall open on its own. There was the tree.

While Grandma Vander Kamp busied herself darning the holes in her grandchildren's socks, Polly carefully colored the tree. She drew rhinoceros wrinkles in the bark. She drew in stones of all shapes and sizes. She drew cottonwood seeds drifting in the sky and she drew herself between the mighty roots. "Oh, my beautiful Whispering Cottonwood, please grant me a wish today." Polly started humming 'Buffalo Gals'. When she was finished with the picture and had made her two wishes, one for now and one for later, she whispered, "Your Majesty, when I am fifty years old, I will do as you wish in return."

"Vat did you say, Dear?"

"Nothing, Grandma. Just thinking."

𝄻

At four o'clock in the afternoon, the telephone rang. Polly was in the kitchen to get a drink of water. "I'll get it!" she yelled. Grandma was in Hank's new bedroom changing his sheets. "Really? You do? We are? Okay. Bye." Through the frosty window, Polly saw the school bus stop in front of the house. Hank, followed by Betty Lou, jumped from the bottom step. Ginger knew the sound of the bus and started howling in the utility room.

Hank opened the kitchen door. "You don't look very sick to me," he said pushing past her.

"That's because I'm getting better."

"Right."

"You're a Crabby Appleton."

Grandma came into the kitchen. "Who called, den?"

"Polly whispered in her grandma's ear, "Dad. He'll be a little late, but he has good news. Don't tell, okay?"

"Did the newspapers come yet?" Hank asked.

"Yah. Polly and I folded dem for you. They sit in your carrier on da vashing machine."

"I'm taking off. See you Grandma." Hank swung the newspaper carrier over his shoulder.

As Hank went out the back door, Trina entered. "Hank, Granddad said he'd take you around tonight if you want him to. He's on his way in."

"You are early," Grandma said.

"I was worried about Polly."

Polly was hiding behind the utility room door. She poked her head out. "You don't need to worry about me. I'm much better and I have a surprise, but I can't tell."

"What surprise?" Betty Lou was still trying to pry her red rubber boots off her shoes.

"Dad's coming home late, but only a little. He said not to make any supper."

"What's he up to?"

"I know, but I'm not telling."

Trina warmed a pan of milk on the stove while she and Grandma talked about the family.

"Sylvia is going to haf anodder baby—a tail-ender," Grandma said.

"What's a 'tail-ender'?" Betty Lou asked as she stirred chocolate powder into her milk.

"A new baby dat comes ven da udders are already in school."

"Sure hope it's a girl," Trina said.

"Yah, dat vood be nice."

After an hour, Hank and Granddad drove into the yard. Polly's dad drove right in behind them. He beeped the horn and started shouting. Polly could hear him through the closed window. "The strike's over!" Trina pressed her face to the glass and waved. "It's over!" he shouted again. Trina hugged her mother. Polly hugged Betty Lou. Hank shook Granddad's hand. When Polly's dad burst into the kitchen, he said, "The strike's over," as if he couldn't believe it unless he said it one more time. "Let's go out for hamburgers to celebrate."

"Can we?" Betty Lou asked.

"We sure can. And, another surprise." Polly's dad dug into his coat pocket and fanned out five little pieces of paper.

"What are those?" Hank asked.

Polly already knew, "They're tickets to see 'The Swiss Family Robinson'!"

11. The Hammond Times

Polly finished her finger exercises, practiced Beethoven's "Minuet in G," sang "Peter, Peter Pumpkin Eater" as loudly as she could, and dropped the cover over the piano keys. She was alone in the house. Hank was collecting his paper route money. Trina and Betty Lou were off to the supermarket and the department store. Betty Lou had grown out of her shoes weeks ago and today she was getting new ones because the strike was over. Polly's dad was weatherizing the crawl space under the house.

She checked the work list Trina had put on the kitchen table.

Clean the bathroom

Dust the living room
Sweep the kitchen and utility room
Take the garbage out
Clean your room

Polly sighed. The list was longer than on most Saturday mornings. Usually, Trina and Betty Lou helped with the cleaning. Today, Polly had to do all the chores. If the chores and errands were finished by noon, they could get to Gary early for the best seats at the movie. She took the Comet Cleanser out of the utility room cabinet, stopped at the table to cross off, 'Clean the bathroom', and started her work. "Low bridge, everybody down. Low bridge 'cuz we're coming to a town." Polly scrubbed the ring around the bathtub. "You'll always know your neighbor . . ." Polly dumped cleanser on a pompom brush and swooshed it around in the toilet. "Ick!" She started singing again, "You'll always know your pal, if you're ever navigating on the Erie Canal." She wiped the toothbrush holder with a clean rag like Trina taught her so no germs got spread around, and then realized she should have cleaned the toilet last. Trina said to always work from clean to dirty and wipe anything that might go in the mouth with a clean cloth. Trina knew all about germs because she was a nurse's aide during World War Two.

Polly's dad came in and out of the house, but they were both too busy to talk. Polly crossed off 'Take the garbage out' and went upstairs to her room. "What a disaster," Polly mumbled to herself. She sorted the dirty from the clean clothes, both on the floor. She took the stringy faded pink rugs outside and shook them. She straightened the clutter on her dresser and dusted her knick-knack shelf. She made her bed and noticed her ear explosion left stains on her pillowcase. Polly wasted time trying to comb her stuffed dog's matted fur. She swept the dust bunnies from beneath her bed and said to herself as she turned to check the room, "Good job, Spot."

Just as Polly crossed off her last chore, 'Sweep the kitchen and utility room', Trina, Betty Lou, Hank and her dad filed into the kitchen. Trina quickly warmed up leftovers for lunch. She said they could wash the dishes later—a first, and the Spooners were on their way to Gary at ten minutes past noon.

The lights were low in the Palace Theater. In spite of the dust hanging in long spidery loops from the crystal chandeliers, the light was reflected in the polished brass railings, in the gold painted trim and in the mirrors that multiplied the room over and over and over. Polly held her box of buttery popcorn, saving it in case of a scary part so she wouldn't bite her fingernails. She watched the families come in and settle around them. "Dad?" Polly pointed to a mother who was wearing a colorful flowing gown. "Where are those people from?"

"Don't point, Polly."

She put her hand up to hide her mouth and whispered, "Dad? How come that lady has a red dot on her forehead?"

"I'm pretty sure they're from India. I'm not sure about the dot. I think it's a religious symbol."

"How come the father doesn't have one?"

"I don't know."

Polly thought about a song she learned in Sunday school. 'Red and yellow, black and white, they are precious in his sight. Jesus loves the little children of the world.' Polly never saw people with shades of skin different than her own unless she went to Gary or Chicago.

The lights dimmed. Polly couldn't wait to eat her popcorn and by the time the pirates started chasing the Robinson boys—Fritz and Ernest—she had chewed both her thumb nails ragged. She sat on her hands during the rest of the movie except during the battle when she had to cover her eyes. Even though she wasn't supposed to talk during the movie, she couldn't help it. She whispered to Hank, "That girl, Miss Montrose, is acting like a sissy. I'd never act like that."

Hank jabbed her with his elbow. "Shut up, Paint."

"I loved the part when the boys were racing the ostriches," Betty Lou jabbered on and on, retelling the movie all the way home. Polly tried to hypnotize herself by staring into the snow that was hitting the windshield. June said if you stared at something moving, like a fire or a swinging watch, you would go into a deep trance and see fairies or angels. Polly didn't have any success with the trance and after a while became lost in thought about tree houses, beaches and fraidy cat girls in long dresses.

Polly's dad made waffles for supper. Ginger was allowed into the house and ran around so crazily she knocked one of Trina's ceramic geese off the end table. The Lennon Sisters sang, "The Yellow Rose of Texas" and Polly, once again, escaped the clutches of the boogie men when she ran upstairs to get her pajamas.

♭

It was snowing so hard the next morning Polly couldn't see her cottonwood tree in the park across the street. Trina and Hank were folding the thick Sunday Hammond Times. "I'll never get done in time for church, Mom. I hate this darn paper-route."

"Hank, watch your language. If you don't finish in time for church, it'll be okay." Trina came to the window and looked out with Polly. "I don't know if I'll be able to go either. Maybe I should try to get the car out now and take you around this morning."

The snow hadn't been plowed and Trina got stuck in a drift as she backed into the road. She stamped the snow off her feet in the utility room. "Ach Heden!" she said. "I'm sorry, Hank. You'll have to walk."

"I'll help him," Polly offered.

"Would you, Polly?"

"Sure." She thought trudging through the deep snow would be an adventure. She would pretend to be Admiral Byrd trying to get to the south pole. Trina pinned an old towel and a scarf together for Polly to use as a carrier and then helped her bundle up.

The snow was so deep, Polly and Hank were out of breath by the time they crossed the park. They stopped at the corner of Potomac and Independence Drive. "Listen, Polly. We'll get done faster if we split up. I'll do Hudson Court. You do Potomac. Every house on the street gets a paper except the yellow one and the light blue one with the black shutters. Try to open the storm door and put the papers inside so they don't get buried in the snow."

"But what if I get done first?"

"Wait for me. I'll come around the block on North Delaware and meet you. We'll walk home together."

"Why don't you go on one side of the street and I'll go on the other?"

"It doesn't matter, Paint. Let's just do it this way."

Hank took off. None of the sidewalks had been shoveled. It was early on a Sunday morning and no one was in a hurry. Besides, there wasn't much point in shoveling when it was still snowing so hard. Polly fought her way up one sidewalk and then another. Her legs were tired by the time she was half way up the block and she could barely lift them out of the drifts. Polly came to Mrs. Van Doodle's house. A light was shining through a window. Polly tugged the storm door against piling snow. She laid the newspaper on the threshold and tried to push the door closed. A sudden gust of wind caught the door and blew it into Polly's nose. She stepped backwards and stumbled down the buried steps. Her carrier came apart and all the newspapers tumbled into the snow. She took off her mittens and tried to pin the bag back together. Her fingers were so numb she couldn't work the safety pins. The papers were getting wet. Polly didn't know what to do. Tears of frustration filled her eyes.

Sitting on Mrs. Van Doodle's steps, Polly stuffed as many newspapers as she could inside her coat. She stood up, but fell back down because she couldn't lift her legs against the bulge the papers made. They began falling out the bottom one by one. Polly sensed the light brighten. She looked behind her. Mrs. Van Doodle had opened the front door. As she picked up her newspaper and leaned out to pull the storm door closed, she saw Polly. "Is that you, Polly?"

"Yes, Ma'am."

"Are you okay?"

"No."

It took only seconds for Mrs. Van Doodle to understand the problem. "I'll get my boots on and help you." She came outside with a basket and helped Polly dig the newspapers out of the snow.

When they had recovered every paper she said, "Come in and warm up. I have some hot chocolate on the stove."

"But Hank will be waiting for me."

"Come in, Polly. Warm up for a minute. I'll get dressed and help you."

"You will?"

"Yes. It's dangerous out there."

While she was waiting, Polly looked around. A baby grand piano, with its lid wide open, filled most of the living room. There was a violin on the couch and a flute on the piano bench. Polly quietly went into the living room and slid her thawing fingers along the glossy finish of the keys. She startled, when from behind the lid, Mrs. Van Doodle asked, "How are your lessons going? Would you like to play my piano?" Polly pushed down middle C. She played an arpeggio. It was a lovely sound, very different than her upright piano. "Polly, why don't you come to my house after school on Monday. I get home around four-thirty. I have an idea."

"I'll ask my Mom." Polly had no idea what Mrs. Van Doodle's idea might be.

Mrs. Van Doodle put a plastic bag over the basket of newspapers. She and Polly went along the rest of Potomac Avenue. Mrs. Van Doodle delivered most of the papers because her legs were long enough to step over the drifts. Hank was just coming around the corner when Polly took the last paper out of the basket. "Did you have any trouble, Hank?"

"No, not really, but I'm sure getting cold."

"Come on, children. I'll walk you home." Mrs. Van Doodle took the basket in one hand and put her other arm around Polly's shoulder. When they got home, Hank invited Mrs. Van Doodle in to warm up. She and Trina talked while Polly went to the bathroom to dunk her hands into warm water.

Her dad came in with his bathrobe on and his hair sticking up all over. "What's going on?" he asked.

"I got stuck in the blizzard and I'm thawing myself out." She whispered, "Mrs. Van Doodle's here."

"Why?"

"She helped me out of a catastrophe."

"Why didn't someone wake me up? I could have helped you kids."

"We didn't know how deep the snow would be." Polly went into the kitchen after the feeling in her fingers returned. She waited for a break in the conversation and said, "Thank you for saving me, Mrs. Van Doodle."

"You're welcome. I talked to your mother about an after-school visit. She said it would be fine." Polly wasn't sure if wanted to go to her house after school. *What did she want anyway?*

Mrs. Van Doodle rose to leave. "I wonder if anyone will make it to church this morning? The dominee will have to preach to himself." She chuckled at her own joke.

Dominee? Oh, yeah. Grandma Vander Kamp calls the preacher 'dominee' too.

12. Joined in Heart

On the Saturday after the snowstorm, Polly was just about to go sledding on a mound in the new subdivision, when Mrs. Van Doodle called and talked to Trina. "Polly, Mrs. Van Doodle wonders if you want to come over and practice again."

"Right now?"

"Yes. She's expecting you. You'll have other chances to go sledding. This is important."

"But I went three times already."

"Practice makes perfect."

"It's an easy song, Mom. It sounds pretty good." Polly went to the piano and grabbed her music. "Mom? Can I ask the twins to come to the Christmas program?"

"You can ask, but don't be disappointed if their parents say 'no'. Did you tell Dad yet?"

"No, I want him to be surprised." Polly suddenly became so worried that she held her head in both hands. "But what if he won't come?"

"Oh, Honey," Trina hugged Polly to reassure her. "He will, I promise."

♭

On Mondays, Wednesdays and Fridays for two weeks Polly went to Mrs. Van Doodle's house after school. Finally, it was the Sunday before Christmas. The day dragged on and on. Polly tried to take a nap like she was supposed to, but her stomach kept doing flip-flops. For a while, she talked to her stuffed dog. Eventually, she went downstairs. Her dad was sipping a Hamms Beer and watching a Harlem Globetrotters basketball game on TV. "Can't sleep?" he asked.

"No, I've got the willies."

"What are you so nervous about? It's just a Sunday school Christmas program. You've been in them every year."

Polly eyed the beer. "You won't drink too much beer today, will you Dad?"

"No, Spot. I've cut back to one on Sunday afternoons. Does that seem okay to you?"

"I guess so."

"You want to watch the game with me?"

"Sure."

Finally, it was time to go to the Sunday evening service. The TV was turned off just as the "Wonderful World of Disney" started. The ride to Illinois and church seemed longer than usual. Every traffic light turned red as they approached it. "Welcome to Illinois." Trina always read the sign.

Polly, Hank and Betty Lou went into the church basement as soon as they arrived. It was swarming with children, parents and Sunday school teachers. Children gathered by age into corners and put on their costumes. Polly's class dressed in choir robes; they were supposed to be angels in the heavenly host. All the angels, including the boys, were given candles. The heavenly host was to follow the other children to the front pews of the sanctuary. Mrs. Van Doodle was bustling around getting bossy. She had been really nice at her house. "Polly?" she asked loudly. "Are you ready?"

"Yes, Ma'am." Polly wasn't really that confident, but she didn't want Mrs. Van Doodle to worry about her.

The preacher said with authority, "Children!" An immediate hush filled the room. "Let us pray," he said. "Lord, grant that we have a blessed Christmas program. Fill each child's heart with goodness and light. Amen." Polly knew what that meant. They better be good or you'll hear about it later.

Everyone lined up and climbed the stairs. The procession started. The heavenly host waited patiently until all the other children had entered the sanctuary. Two teenage girls lit the candles held by the angels and then the organ started playing, 'Hark the Herald Angels Sing'. Polly's class entered the church walking in the special way Mrs. Van Doodle had instructed them. Step with one foot, slide the other foot to meet it. Step, slide, step, slide. The line slowed down about half way to the front. The little kids had entered the wrong pew and had to come out again.

Polly's cousin, Boo, was behind her. "Oops. Sorry." Boo was concentrating so hard on his feet he didn't notice the slow down and stepped on Polly's robe. They stood quietly for a minute. Polly sniffed something funny.

"You're on fire, Paint!"

Miss Puddinga, who sat in the pew next to Polly, stood up and whacked Polly's neck and the back of her head. Polly ducked down; she didn't know what was happening. "You're on fire!" Boo repeated. Miss Puddinga got the fire out right away. Polly felt the back of her hair. It was rough and little frizzy pieces broke off into her hand. The procession started again, and she fell back into step. "Be careful, Boo," was all she could think to whisper.

The little kids held up letters that read, A CHILD IS BORN. The older kids read the Christmas story from the Bible and stood around the manger in their nativity outfits. Two of the wisemen got into a pushing fight because one of them couldn't see his parents.

The first graders sang, 'Oh, Little Star of Bethlehem'. The dominee said a few words about 'keeping Christmas in our hearts all year' and the children went back to their seats.

Mrs. Van Doodle walked up to the microphone. "Family and friends. It is my privilege to introduce a very special girl who has worked hard to play and sing a beautiful song to end our Christmas program—Polly Spooner.

That was Polly's cue. She stood up and climbed the three stairs to the enormous piano on the stage. Her heart pounded in her chest and in her ears. Mrs. Van Doodle reached behind the podium and pulled out her flute. Polly sat down. All the lights in the church were turned low. Polly and Mrs. Van Doodle had special lights to see their music. One tall candle stood on the piano. Mrs. Van Doodle played a phrase on her flute and Polly joined her on the piano and began to sing in a shaky voice.

> 'Blest be the tie that binds
> Our hearts in perfect love.
> The fellowship of kindred minds
> Is like to that above.'

Mrs. Van Doodle played her flute between verses and Polly looked around. She could make out Grandma and Granddad Vander Kamp. Behind her grandparents were several sets of Aunt and Uncles. Aunt Jane blew her a kiss. Polly noticed some movement in the balcony. June, July and their parents were standing up and waving. She began to sing the second verse.

> 'Before our Father's throne
> We pour our ardent prayers.
> Our fears, our hopes, our aims are one,
> Our comforts and our cares.'

Polly started the third verse without an instrumental in between.

> 'We share our mutual woes,
> Our mutual burdens bear.
> And often for each other flows
> The sympathizing tear.'

Again, Polly had a chance to look around. She saw Spit De Groot in the second-row drooling. She saw Boo and several of her other cousins. They were making silly faces at her and she almost missed her cue.

> 'When we are called to part
> It gives us inward pain,
> But we shall still be joined in heart
> And hope to meet again.'

The candle on the piano flickered. Polly felt quiet inside. She sang as much like an angel as she could. Her voice wasn't shaky anymore.

> 'The glorious hope revives
> Our courage by the way,
> While each in expectation lives
> And waits to see the day.'

The sound of the flute filled the church. Simple and pure. Polly saw Miss Puddinga and Mr. Miff. There was Aunt Johanna, right up in front, dabbing her eyes with a handkerchief. She saw Hank; he nodded.

Betty Lou waved until a teacher pulled her hand down. And then, quickly scanning the full church, she saw her dad with his arm around her new mom, Trina. A narrow beam of light showed a tear sparkling on his cheek.

> 'From sorrow, toil and pain,
> And sin, we shall be free.
> And perfect love and friendship reign
> Through all eternity.'

Then, Mrs. Van Doodle said into the squealing microphone, "Please join us as we sing the first verse again." The whole church swelled with the singing of happy people. Polly played and sang with all her might.

> 'Blest be the tie that binds
> Our hearts in perfect love.
> The fellowship of kindred minds
> Is like to that above.'

When Polly got home, she asked to take a little walk. The full moon cast long shadows on the deep blue snow. She lay down beneath her cottonwood tree. The stones in the bark sparkled like the stars. "Oh, my beautiful Whispering Cottonwood," Polly always began her wish this way. But she paused and said, "Your Majesty, I have everything I've always wanted. Here is something for you." Polly pulled a tiny misshapen pearl out of her pocket. It was from a shell her mother had given her before she died. She carefully put the pearl between the ridges of her cottonwood's rhinoceros bark. And then, while spinning in circles all around the park, she sang, "Buffalo Gals won't you come out tonight, and dance by the light of the moon."

Rants and Rattlesnake Stories

First Rant

The Dry Bluff Prairie Revivalists should have talked to me before they shaved the ancient red cedars off the edge of the bluffs to make more habitat for timber rattlesnakes. The Bluff Prairie Revivalists from who knows where, not from around here, should have asked the locals about the abundance or lack thereof of rattlesnakes. And those poor endangered dry bluff prairie wildflowers. Have the Revivalists bothered to climb the bluffs in springtime to look around before they made the decision to burn the slopes naked? A decision probably based on some article they read by some expert to see what kind of flowers bloom on the edge of the bluff when the sun soaks the limestone in April and awakens the flowers from their sleep? I can tell a pasqueflower from a dandelion.

Golden eagles? The Revivalists want golden eagles to return? From where, from when? They say golden eagles used to live here and ate little rodents and rattlesnakes. Recently, people claim to have seen golden eagles ravishing dead carcasses. But juvenile bald eagles, which can vary considerably in color and size can be easily mistaken for goldens. A few years ago, my brother and I hiked the Pacific Crest Trail through much of Oregon. We saw a few golden eagles. They have a slightly different contour and plumage than juvenile bald eagles, but what do I know.

Bald eagles are everywhere, though. There is a pair that courts and mates above our house every year, circling in joy on the thermals. Peregrine falcons, though rare, live in nooks and crannies on the bluffs.

Our bluffs look like they've had a bad haircut. Could the Bluff Prairie Revivalists have compromised and left the oldest red cedars, twisted and shaped by the worst of wind and snow? The tenacious cedars, which have hung on to shear rock for decades, become more exotic every year.

I'm not from around here either, so maybe it's none of my business. I was not raised on the bluff. I'm a flatlander from

Indiana, which is why the bluffs and coulees so amaze to me. I raised my children here. My life on the bluff is not an imitation, not a wildlife painting. It is a real life and wild.

Before the chain-saw toting revivalists clear-cut the Mississippi River bluffs near my home in Buffalo County, Wisconsin to encourage "dry-bluff prairie," or "goat prairie" as it's sometimes called, to make room for rattlesnakes, golden eagles and wild flowers, they should have consulted me.

The Transformer

My brother, Chuck, is a forester. He has loved the woods since he was a boy. On Saturday mornings, while my mom did her errands, she would drop Chuck off at the edge of the forest preserve and he would poke around identifying trees and flowers and just chill out. The hubbub in the suburbs on the south-side of Chicago was chaotic.

Shortly after we bought the bluff farm in 1980, Chuck came to visit. My husband, Jim, and Chuck took a hike in the woods to identify the trees, study the health of the woods and to discuss good management of the forest. Our beagle mutt, Raspberry, nose always to the ground, circled in and circled out.

A buzzing sound started not far from where they were easing their way down a steep limestone outcrop.

"What's that noise?" Chuck asked.

"It sounds like a transformer," Jim said. "But where is it? And why would there be a transformer in the woods?"

They slid down the hill toward the buzz. Raspberry started barking wildly, growling at something on the ground. Jim and Chuck stepped closer, then, jumped back. "Is that a rattlesnake?" Jim asked. They decided together is was. "I didn't know we had rattlesnakes around here."

Chuck said, "It's really fat. Must be a timber rattler."

They vamoosed. Out came the "Reader's Digest Animals of North America" as soon as they got home. Sure enough, a timber rattler it was.

We found out from the locals there had been a bounty on rattlesnakes until 1975, five years before we arrived. The snakes were in abundance and were a menace. The snakes would occasionally crawl into town. The bounty had been abolished for fear of decreasing their numbers too much. At least one snake was doing well. Cool, we thought, to live in such a wild place.

Step Forward, Right Now

Noah and Eliza, our two youngest kids, decided to go for a bike ride to the next bluff south. It wasn't an easy ride along a hilly deserted path overgrown with tall grass, goldenrod and Queen Anne's lace. When they got to the edge of the cliff, Noah wanted to take pictures with his new camera. "Eliza, stand over there and turn toward me. I'll get the river behind you." he said. Eliza did as she was told, backing up as far as she dared.

Noah busied himself trying to get the perfect shot. Through the camera lens he saw movement. He lowered the camera and said quietly and sternly to Eliza. "Step forward, right now!" Surprised, she obeyed immediately. Noah pointed. Eliza turned to see the rattles of a snake's tail slide over the cliff not more than two feet behind her. Freaked out, the two skedaddled home.

The next day, I asked Eliza to check if the apples were ripening on the old tree in the pasture. "I'm not going," she said bluntly. This was not her usual attitude. "Why not, Honey?" I asked.

"There are snakes out there in the grass,"

"Make a lot of noise and bring the dog with you."

"No. I'm not going!" And that was that.

Where's the Head?

 y husband, Jim, used to carve amazing sculptures with his chainsaw from wood left behind by loggers from around the county. "Jim," our friend Gary would ask, "I've got a huge piece of walnut; you want it?"

In the front yard, Jim would begin, the form showing itself as he buzzed away. One day, he came into the house, animated and unusually excited. "I just cut a rattlesnake in half." The kids were hungerly gathering for lunch. "Cool. Where is it?" the kids asked, already heading for the door.

Jim warned, "No stop. I don't know where the head is." The kids looked puzzled. "Only the tail-end of the snake fell out of the log. I don't know where the head is."

Yikes. What did that imply? The head of a rattlesnake was who knows where? "Better get the dogs in," I said.

We went outside together. On the ground was half a rattlesnake still wiggling and contorting along the ground. We looked all over for the head. "Dad, do you think it's still in the wood?" Noah asked.

"I guess it must be."

Snakes can writhe for a couple hours after they should be dead. We worried the head could still bite us or the dogs if we stumbled upon it. We stayed away until the back half stopped moving. The dogs stayed inside.

The head was never found.

On the Road Again

"I had to do it," Jim said, one hot August day. He paused, guiltily.

"What did you have to do?" I asked, having no idea where this was going.

"I killed a rattlesnake on the road," he said. "I just thought I should. We've seen so many this year."

"What happened?" I asked.

"I straddled this enormous snake and drove on for about fifty feet. Then, I stopped and just sat there for a while. I looked in the rearview mirror, the snake was still there. It was huge, maybe five feet long and five inches wide. I backed up until I could feel the wheels thump onto the snake. It was pinned. I got the shovel out of the back of the truck and cut its head off. Maybe I shouldn't have."

"I don't know," I said "I really don't know."

Running with Rachel

Running is my exercise of choice, although now it's more like jogging, trotting really. I used to run all over the bluffs until the "not-from-around-here" hunters started buying or renting the land and kicked me off. My oldest daughter, Rachel, was quite the runner. She would likely have gone to the state championship if she hadn't had strep throat at the section finals. Though she did her best, her legs just wouldn't carry her at her usual amazing pace.

We rarely ran together, I was so slow, but one day we did. We turned off the main bluff road onto a tractor path. Within less than one hundred feet, Rachel jumped over something and gasped.

"What?" I asked.

"A snake."

I hadn't even seen it, so absorbed I was with panting and trying to keep up. We looked back. A tiny, very tiny rattlesnake had stopped in its track—stretched out, quiet. "Is it dead?" I wondered.

Rachel threw a pebble at it. The snake moved forward a few inches. "What should we do?" Rachel asked.

"We should probably leave it alone, but one baby snake means more baby snakes and we have plenty already. Let's kill it."

(This attitude is currently politically incorrect. Rattlesnakes have been protected since 1997. A part of me regrets what we were about to do, and did.)

"How should we kill it?" Rachel asked.

"I don't know."

"Maybe we could stone it," she replied.

Afraid to frighten the rattlesnake into coiling and springing at us, we decided we must kill it square away. We went into the ditch at the side of the road and together picked up the big rock. We carried it as close as we dared to the snake. "Okay, on the count of three. One, two three!" It was all we could do to heave the stone, but it landed squarely on the little guy and squished him.

"Maybe that wasn't necessary," I said, guilty of murder. We looked at each other.

Rachel shrugged.

Another Rant

My friend, Donna, loves to hike. I told her I knew how to get to the bluff above the Nelson cemetery from the top. The land had recently been sold to a nature conservancy project and opened to the public for hiking and hunting. I had tried to take my brother, Chuck, up from the bottom and got hopelessly tangled in prickly ash and black-raspberry canes. I couldn't find the old logging trail and we had to climb straight up hanging onto saplings lest we slide right back down again. Donna and I had better luck and found our way from my house crossing through the fields and woods. We rested on the geode studded outcrop watching a train pass through town from high above. The Chippewa River delta stretched for miles. We could see Lake Pepin in the distance. "Let's see if we can get below the bluff," Donna suggested.

"It looks pretty steep," I said.

"From here, but maybe we can climb around." Donna led the way. Sliding on our butts, we circled around and found an outcrop of sandstone, then a ledge along the bottom of the limestone which towered one hundred feet above our heads.

Amazed and excited, we followed the ledge, studying the layers of rock and the shallow caves. Donna filled her pack with samples until it was heavier than she was.

"Better get back," Donna said. "Rod will be wondering what happened to me." We had been gone for over three hours.

We could see the Nelson sewage ponds and knew the cemetery was straight below us. We began to descend. A short distance below the ledge, we noticed large oak trees with rings deliberately cut into the bark—deliberately girdled.

"Who would do this?" I asked, feeling both angry and sad.

A bit further down, we noticed the area had been clear-cut and burned. Stumps of cedar, walnut, hickory, poplar and oak scarred the hill. The treetops and brush had been piled randomly along the bottom edge below the burn.

"This is a mess. What the hell. Another fucking goat prairie. Why can't these people let nature do its own thing? Why kill the most beautiful trees?"

I ranted some more. "I'm sorry, Donna. I don't mean to go off like this. I just don't get it."

Donna didn't respond. She was surprised perhaps at my outburst.

Watch Where You're Weeding

I planted wild roses around the lower side of the house. They were thriving in the subsoil and stone dug out when the house was built. The roses spread by runners under the ground and were difficult and agonizing to weed. I should have been wearing long sleeves and gloves, but it was so hot and the scratches I incurred would quickly heal rubbed with a bit of comfrey root and aloe. Our old dog, Lucy, feeling an obligation to show a little interest in what I was doing, took a walk around the house every now and then. She reluctantly left her latest cooling hole under the red dogwood. Lucy was a quiet, sweet lab/setter mix; she never got excited about much. It surprised me when she startled, fur rising on her back. After a couple short yaps, she backed up and fled. I didn't see anything unusual—maybe a toad, I thought.

I moved a few steps to the left, almost to the lower deck, only a few more feet of this tedious chore and I would be finished, a Leinenkugel's waiting. Both hands were in action now, the last weeds were easy to pull, a couple of pigweeds to the right and a couple of lambs-quarters to the—a rattlesnake! Huge, it was coiled merely two feet from my hand. No rattling, no movement. It just stared at me, its forked tongue darting. I stared back not daring to move, not daring to breath. Slowly, very slowly, I stepped away.

What to do? Leave it be. It was 1997 and illegal to kill a rattlesnake. But it was so close to the house. Six feet, if that, from the patio door. No, I better do something. I circled around the house and pulled the garden hose as close to the snake as I could. I would spray the snake and scare him back into the woods. By the time I was ready to aim and fire, the snake was gone. But where? I sprayed the cold water all over the deck and the flower gardens anyway.

Shaken and wound up, I went into the upper yard to find Jim, who was mowing, to tell him the story. "I can't believe it," I said. "I almost put my hand into the middle of a coiled snake and it didn't do a thing. It just stared at me."

"Do you think it's gone?" Jim asked.

"I hope so. Let's go in for lunch." When we got to the front door stoop, we heard the familiar vibration of a rattling tail. The snake had slithered around the house instead of into the woods and was a foot from the edge of the porch.

"That's it," Jim declared. "Too close. I don't care if it's against the law. I have to kill it." He went to the garage and came back with a spade. Without saying a word and without pausing, he beat the snake to death.

Jim hung the snake over the fence to dry. Our neighbor, a taxidermist, thought better of tanning the skin. "It's against the law, don't ya know, to kill the critters."

Picnic Point

"There's a one eyed, one horned, flying purple people eater and it sure looks strange to me." I sang the song to my nieces and nephews as we hiked to our favorite picnic spot. The nieces and nephews were a bit gullible, coming from the city, and I couldn't help teasing them about the monster that lived in a cave under a rocky shelf where we ate our sandwiches. "The Point" as we called it, was not as far from the house as the big bluffs overlooking the river. It was a cozy spot tucked in among snarly old paper birches and cedars.

After lunch the kids slid down to check out the shallow cave. Where could the monster have gone?

Years later and we're off again, this time with grandchildren, to have a picnic on the point. "Don't go too far ahead," I said. "Let's make sure there aren't any rattlesnakes on the ledge." I was never as careful with my own kids in my younger days. Sure enough, a snake had claimed the ledge for the day. We had our picnic in a grassy meadow closer to home. We tried again and again to have a picnic on The Point, but it was now Mr. Rattlesnake's permanent home and we have not been back to The Point to this day.

How to Catch a Rattlesnake

I put the laundry basket next to the washing machine in the dimly lit utility room. There was a tiny snake tucked in the corner between the floor and the cement-block wall. I held my breath and grabbed the little guy's head. I wasn't afraid of everyday snakes; this one was probably a baby bull snake. I turned, snake in hand, into the light of the basement where my granddaughter was playing with my old Barbie dolls.

A shovel-shape head! I spun around and flung the snake to the floor. Dumb. I had a good grip on it right behind its head, but I was startled. Now what? There was a rattlesnake on the loose in my basement and my granddaughter was sitting on the floor not more than ten feet away. I whisked her into my arms and carried her upstairs. "Grandma, what's wrong?"

"There is a snake in the basement. It's okay." I lied. "You stay up here and I'll see if I can catch it."

Catch a rattlesnake. Yeah. I took a heavy cooking pot from the kitchen cabinet, put on a jacket and a pair of work gloves. I already had on high top hiking boots and blue jeans--that should do. I ripped a piece of thin cardboard from the back of an oversized artist sketch pad and grabbed a flashlight. I was ready. I had to do this.

I carefully stepped into the utility room doorway, flashlight beaming. The little rattlesnake was angry, coiled and ready to zap me with his fangs. "No way, Buddy," I scolded. "You're out-a-here." Judging the circumference of the coiled snake and the circumference of the cooking pot, I guessed, with a limited ability for spatial concepts, the pot would fit over the snake. I reached out as far as I could and dropped the pot straight down. "Gotcha."

With one foot on the pot, just in case, I released a little pressure and gently slid the cardboard under the pot, slipped my hand under the cardboard and flipped the whole business over. "You're out-a-here." I said again and elbowed open the door to the lower deck. I walked down to the edge of the woods. "I'm not going to kill you, but you better not come back here, because next time you're a goner." I flung the pot and all over the side of the hill.

The Final Rant

"I guess I need to crack open my closed mind," I said to my brother and his wife as we puffed our way from the bottom to the top of the bluffs behind town. We had met a cheerful man at the trailhead of the new park. He cleared the trails and denuded some of the steepest side hills to establish dry bluff prairie, and then donated the land to the town. He was enthusiastic and I couldn't help liking the guy even though I have certain rather strong opinions on the topic of dry bluff prairie. This person grew up here, so his understanding of the "natural" state of the bluffs probably trumped mine.

There were problems on the hill, though. The trails were acting as funnels for rain and in spots seriously eroding. New grass had been planted, but with the grinding feet of the hikers it was not doing well. The deciduous trees that had been felled were sprouting from the trunks. Now, instead of one large tree there were as many as ten new suckers. Thorny ash and buckthorn loved the increased sunshine. "It's going to take constant effort to keep this prairie from either being washed away or reclaimed by the brush and trees," I said. "Only one year, and look what's happening."

But there were some new prairie grasses and wildflowers taking hold. The bees buzzed and the butterflies fluttered. The sun soaked into our backs as we climbed.

The view, as always, was astounding. We rested on the "Second Sister" and watched a train, which was longer than the town, pass below us. Two eagles, a group of turkey vultures and a red-tail hawk sailed high on the thermals. We cut across the top of the bluffs, through the fields and forests, to get home.

A few days later, I got on the internet and did a search on the history and benefits of establishing bluff prairie. Buffalo used to roam here and kept a balance between grassland and trees—okay, maybe. The Native Americans periodically burned the bluffs to maintain the grassland. But is that natural? Burning on purpose is not natural. Lightening ignited grass fires which climb the hills are natural.

A video popped up. An unknown Revivalist spoke of the aesthetic value of shaving the bluffs. I argued with her virtual nonsense. Then, Dale and Sandy, Todd, Carl, Chris and Myrna talked about their prairies. They strolled as they looked for new species of grass and flowers. Species they had planted. I know these folks. They are people from around here. They own and love the land. I better settle down and be more compromising. Things change, whether naturally or unnaturally. I miss the bluffs—the way they were. And I still can't help but wish the Revivalists had consulted me.

Not That Tree

I love trees. Pathologically. I can't kill a plant. I've been trying to de-clutter, but plants are living beings. One can't just kill them. I guess in regard to plants, I'm pro-life. My husband, Jim, not so much. He believes in careful planning and if it's not the right balance, elimination is the better choice. If the trees are getting too big or too crowded and they are killing out the diminutive species, well something's got to give.

Shade. I love shade. I love the sun dappling me with warmth and light through a canopy of leaves. The Creeping Charlie loves it too, and moss, and bare dirt upon which the grass long ago died. Cucumbers, peppers, tomatoes, okra. My vegetable garden doesn't much like shade. My yield has been decreasing. The majestic forty feet tall cottonwood cloned from a wee stick shades the latest garden. I've moved the garden four times to a sunnier spot as the trees grew. There aren't many sunny spots left.

Who would have known the tree seeds and saplings and cuttings we planted in what was the cow pasture on the land that is now the yard of our retirement house would have grown so dense and so tall in twenty years?

Jim says we must thin the trees. We're overshadowed by trees. We can't see the sunset anymore. The Lombardy poplars block the view. In the summer, we can't see past the living room window. The paper birch scratches the window in even the slightest breeze. I've done a bit of compromising. "Okay," I say. "You can cut some of the wild plums but leave enough for the birds and a batch of plum jam."

A few years ago, a giant cottonwood/big-tooth aspen cross I planted close to the house fell in a straight-line wind. It bounced off the roof and knocked everything from the cabinet tops. It knocked the pictures off the walls, and it smashed the bushes next to the house. The tree didn't break through the roof, so no serious harm was done. One day while sitting on the stoop, Jim said, "I think I should cut down that cottonwood." He pointed to the twin of the tree that fell on the house.

"No, no, no," I begged. "It won't hit the house if it falls."

"Unless the wind is from the west which it usually is," Jim replied. "Half the tree will fall onto the house."

But for now, it still stands.

Our disagreement over trees started years and years ago. We are high-school sweethearts who grew up on the flat expanse of the suburbs on the Indiana/Illinois border just south of Chicago. Trees aren't in excess there. They were mostly planted by the pioneers for an escape from the sun. There are forest preserves here and there- -a few acres of trees that escaped felling along a creek or on soil that was not so good anyway. Beyond the city limits, one can see to the horizon over miles of corn and soybeans. Trees are special. I climbed a tree or two when I was young but didn't have an affinity for trees until later.

In 1978, we moved our young family to a valley up a creek near Missoula, Montana. We had de-cluttered down to a pick-up truck load of belongings. He drove out first to find a place to live and I followed with the three kids. Jim was waiting when we got off the train. One breath of damp Montana air and I almost cried. It was raining and the smell of pines, firs, and spruce put me in an alpha state. Jim drove us to our cabin in the mountains. My life had become perfect.

The four to six-inch diameter lodge-pole pines were close together. Very close. "But they're so healthy," I said, as Jim gassed up the chain saw.

"If I thin them, they'll grow bigger and be more likely to survive."

"But can't you leave them for a couple of years?"

"No, they should be cut now."

Shortly after the first thinning, the goats, Millie and Susie, who we bought shortly after our arrival, grew big enough to straddle the trees, walk them down and eat the tops. "Okay." I agreed. "Cut the ones the goats ruined and a few more of the weakest."

Then the fire came. We could see the flames shooting from the pines at the top of the valley. "I have to cut the trees around the house," Jim said. "The cedar-shake shingles will go up like kindling."

"Can't you just water the roof and wait? Maybe the fire won't come down the valley," I hoped.

"The evening air is cooling and the fire will change its course. That's what we were warned about." I knew Jim was right. He cut all the trees in a circle around the house.

Clouds moved in. The evening air didn't sink as much as usual. The uphill direction of the blaze held. A light rain came later in the morning and the fire disappeared, as had the cooling shade.

Three years ago, we bought a second farm. The widow from whom we bought the forty acres of cropland and the forty acres of woodland was as ancient as the trees. Pointing to the biggest tree in the yard, she said, "I planted that one when my son was just four years old. I have a picture of him standing next to it. Now look at it."

Yes, now look at it, a seventy-five feet tall Norway spruce. Weeping branches as in a fairy tale. But the branches were touching the house. The insurance company didn't approve, and Jim didn't like the knobs that were left from improper trimming years ago. The chainsaw did its work. Much better. The shock of destroying too much cambium at once stressed the tree. Two years after the cutting, the ancient tree lost its needles, mostly.

I woke up at night and gazed through the same bedroom window through which the widow must have gazed at the tree she had planted, and which now was struggling for its life. "Please don't die," I prayed to the spirit of the spruce. "We tried to do right. Please don't die." As winter turned into spring, new buds formed on the very tips of some branches. Some branches died. The top of the tree grew an abundance of cones. The spruce will survive-- injured and imperfect. It will live to haunt us.

My son manages the woodland on the forty acres now. He cut many trees and built a timber-frame barn, but he selected carefully. His sheep have a haven. The young trees in the woodland have room to gather the light. In the summer, when we walk, we can see the sky and the blackberries bloom, and the wildflowers thrive and all seems right.

My love of trees is a tough love. When I hear the chainsaw buzz, I repeat as a mantra, while my heart sadly beats--choose carefully, use thoughtfully, and be thankful.

Acknowledgements

T hanks most of all to the main character in my life and in our shared stories, my husband of fifty years, Jim. For his reading, his critiquing, his proofing, his sense of humor, and for keeping my ego in balance, I owe him talk-free quiet-time. Thanks to the River Junction Arts Council's group, Writers Helping Writers. A special thanks is given to Peg Bauernfeind and Nicole Borg for their honesty. Thank you to Victoria Moore who gave me the final nudge to submit my work for publication, and to Tom Driscoll of Shipwreckt Books for accepting those submissions with kind words.

"Uriah's Hypothesis" could not have been written without our exuberant friend, Jeri Miller. Jelani Smit's computer "whiz-dom" saved hours of frustration. Thank you to my children, their partners and my grandchildren for being the characters in my life.

Earlier versions of stories and essays appeared in the "Green Blade" and in "The Carp," a quarterly newspaper. Thank you to the editors of those publications.

About the Author

Gloria Smit says, "The truth with a twist is funnier than fiction." That's her writing philosophy. Aspiring to be a humorist, Gloria began crafting *mostly* true five-minute vignettes for open-mic sessions at the Rural American Writer's Center in Plainview, Minnesota. She spins experiences from her life on a Mississippi River bluff as a farmer, a wife, a mother, and a nurse into tales intended to make people laugh. She has also, over the past twenty years, composed more serious work, including novelettes, essays and poems. Gloria lives with her husband, Jim, a dog, two cats and a handful of Icelandic sheep near Nelson, Wisconsin.